Queen's Knight

Book 9 in the Struggle for a Crown Series

By

Griff Hosker

Published by Sword Books Ltd 2022

SWORD
BOOKS

Cover by Design for Writers

Dedication

To my grandchildren, Thomas, Samuel, Isabelle, Michael, and William; you are a joy.

Contents

Queen's Knight... i
List of important characters in the novel 2
Prologue 3
Chapter 1 6
Chapter 2 18
Chapter 3 29
Chapter 4 39
Chapter 5 46
Chapter 6 54
Chapter 7 65
Chapter 8 74
Chapter 9 87
Chapter 10 99
Chapter 11 108
Chapter 12 118
Chapter 13 131
Chapter 14 141
Chapter 15 151
Chapter 16 162
Chapter 17 168
Chapter 18 179
Epilogue 191
Glossary... 192
Maps 195
Historical Notes.. 197
Other books by Griff Hosker... 199

List of important characters in the novel

(Fictional characters are italicized)

Dowager Queen Catherine - widow of King Henry V[th]
Henry VIth King of England
Duke of Bedford- brother of King Henry V[th]
Humphrey, Duke of Gloucester – brother of King Henry V[th]
Eleanor Cobham- the second wife of the Duke of Gloucester
King Charles of France- brother of Queen Catherine
Edmund Beaumont- Count of Mortain
Jean Poton de Xaintrailles-Seneschal of Limousin
Étienne de Vignolles- La Hire- French commander
Sir John de Cressy
Owen Tudor- grandfather of King Henry VIIth

Prologue

Les Pérets June 1431

I am Sir Michael of Weedon and I was saved from death by Sir William Strongstaff and his men. That was a lifetime ago, the year of Agincourt. I had been trained as a warrior by Sir William and one of his men at arms, Rafe. I had been lucky and I had been knighted. More than that I had made such an impression on Sir William that in his will he left me his home, Weedon. As he said his family did not need it. They had huge manors and lands while Weedon was small. As a reward for my services in France I had been given the manor of Les Pérets. It was tiny and lay on the banks of the Seine but it suited me. After I had temporarily finished fighting the French and delivered Jeanne d'Arc to the Burgundians I went to my new manor with my battle-weary men.

Since the uneasy truce between England and France had begun, I had enjoyed that rarity amongst warriors, a time of peace. With my wife, Isabelle, and her family in my new manor of Les Pérets, I was learning to become a farmer. Isabelle's father, Henri who acted as my steward, was patient and he guided me but we both knew I would never be a farmer. A sword in my hand felt more comfortable than a pitchfork but I listened to him for he was a kind man and he viewed me as a son. Jack and Eleanor had been married and, even though I had not yet knighted him he and Eleanor returned to England where he would be the steward at Weedon. Rafe, the man I owed my life to, had been the steward but he was now dead and Jack would be able to take over the duties whilst still having the old warrior as a human crutch. It would prepare my squire for the time when he became a lord of a manor. He had still to be knighted. Edgar and some of my archers had returned to England where he would be the steward of my manor at Iden. close to Rye. For my part, Isabelle and I were happy at Les Pérets for her parents were there and we lived a harmonious existence. Henri and Maud had something they had lost, a home, and although they missed their daughter who now lived in England the birth of our son. Jean, made up for it. Of course, I always pronounced it, and still do, John but it sounds the same.

Although I was a warrior and I had been trained by the best I had not missed the two years without war. I was no farmer but I enjoyed the life of the manor, the hunting, the seasons and their order and the people who called me lord. I still trained but I had no squire and most of my men had either returned to England with Edgar and Jack or left me to seek work as swords for hire. I had three archers who had stayed with

3

me: Nicholas Warbag, Robbie Red Fletch and Dick of Tarporley. There were just two of my men at arms: Thomas of Chester and Geoffrey of Yarpole who had chosen to stay in France. They continued to spar more than I did for often I was with Henri as he tried to explain how to tend the orchards and the fields. While my archers acted as gamekeepers, the two men at arms functioned as squires and, when I needed them, labourers. It was a good life and we were content.

The day in June, when the rider brought the news from Rouen that Jeanne d'Arc had been burned at the stake was a sad one for me. The men who brought the news were excited as were most of the villagers who saw her as a witch. I was not happy because I had seen beneath the mask. She was no witch and those lies had been spread by England and Burgundy alike to make her death acceptable, demanded even. I had come to know her when I had escorted her to Burgundy. She was little more than a child and while she may have been deluded about her visions the fact remained that she believed them. A child should not be burned for what she believed was true. It saddened both me and my men. Isabelle also understood as I had told her about the maid. The other reason I was sad was more practical. I knew that the burning would inflame the French and that we would have to endure more fighting. That meant my peaceful life would be changed. While the Maid had been alive then the French had been less belligerent, hoping for mercy from the Norman court.

It was not mean to be. I was invited to the coronation in Paris of the child King Henry as King of France but I did not go. I knew that it would further alienate me from the Duke of Bedford but the king's uncles were no friends of mine and I would settle down to become a lord of the manor and make my home at Les Pérets a peaceful and happy place. I chose a new life and I hoped that I would be allowed to fade into anonymity.

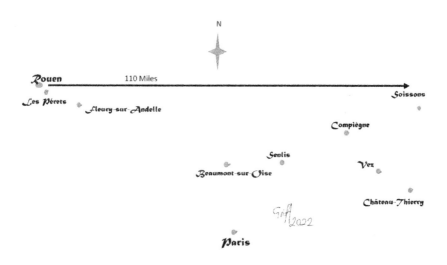

Chapter 1

My life changed when Sir John Talbot was exchanged for the French leader Étienne de Vignolles. Following his release he returned to England and after a meeting with the Duke of Gloucester and the council that ruled England he was sent back to fight in Normandy under the command of the Earl of Somerset. Sir John was a good leader. Many said he was the best since Sir William Strongstaff. I was too loyal to Sir William to agree with that statement but I did regard him as a good leader. His mistake at Patay, which had resulted in the fall from grace of Sir John Fastolf was something that gave me reservations but when he returned to Normandy in the late summer, I was summoned to meet with him in Rouen and I went with heavy heart for I knew it meant that I would be leaving my home.

Isabelle knew that I had to go to meet with him for I held lands in Normandy and that meant I could be called upon to defend the land. The return of English armies meant the resumption of hostilities. She was learning to be mistress of my hall and the lively three-year-old Jean was not making life easier for her. I was more than grateful for the presence of the two grandparents who were able to keep my son amused. I also acted as a sort of troubadour for him but as soon as I was summoned, I knew that our lives would change. She lay nestled in my arms and I felt salt tears on my bare chest. Tears had not been uncommon in both pregnancies but I knew the cause of this one was not one of mood.

"It may not mean war, my love. I served with Sir John before and he may just wish my opinion."

I felt the laugh against my chest, "And you do not believe that for an instant. You know that you will be called upon to fight and it is in your nature to take up your sword. I am grateful for the few years of peace but in my heart, I always knew that you would have to return to the world of war." She was silent and I said nothing for she was right. For one so young she was astute. Her family's hardships had helped her to grow faster. "I wish that you had taken Iden and left Edgar White Streak here." She almost blurted the words out and I knew that she would regret uttering them.

"I could and I still can but that would leave Edgar to go to war again and your parents would not see Jean. Would they wish that?"

"No, but I do not wish to lose my husband."

"And you may not. There will be time for tears when I have met with Sir John. Until then this is idle speculation. Let us enjoy each other while we may."

She was soon asleep. I had noticed when she was carrying John that she slept more and she was following the same pattern with the new unborn babe. I could not sleep. I had served Sir William and he had told me of his regret that he had been forced to leave his family as often as he had to serve the king. I suppose I had not understood that for I had no family. Sir William was my family and as I always followed him to war, I did not have to suffer parting. I had sunk roots into the land of Les Pérets. I was still Sir Michael of Weedon but I felt more like Seigneur of Les Pérets. I finally drifted off with the image of the great warrior and defender of kings, William Strongstaff, filling my dreams.

I took my two men at arms with me on the short ride four-mile ride to Rouen. That they had chosen to stay with me had given me comfort but as we rode their words told me that they had yearned to be back in the saddle once more. Geoffrey voiced his fears first, "Sir John is a good leader, my lord. It will be good to take the fight back to the French. It did not sit well with me that despite our capture of the Maid, we were bested by the French. We are better soldiers."

Thomas nodded, "Aye but not all our leaders are of the same quality. When you were guarding the young king we saw then, my lord, that not all the men sent to lead us against the French knew what they were doing."

After the death of King Henry, I had been chosen to guard both his queen and his son. I had been happy to do so but the king's brothers had other ideas and the control of the young king had been taken by the Duke of Gloucester and the council of regents to mould him into their man. I prayed he would turn out well but it was out of my hands.

Geoffrey waved a hand at the river to our left, "The French have made inroads south of the river and to the east." I cocked a questioning eye at him. He shrugged, "When Tom and I drink in the inn by the river we speak with the bargemen and the soldiers who pass through. The Burgundians are not having the best of it and the Duke of Bedford," he lowered his voice, "is not the man his brother was."

I reined in Storm, "Whatever you do I beg you not to even think those thoughts and do not utter them. If I have learned anything about the royal family it is that they have thin skins. They brook no criticism. King Henry was different. God took him and it was the greatest disaster to strike England. Had he lived then France would be at peace and the two lands would be as one. Now keep your ears open. I will be closeted, I do not doubt, with Sir John but you two speak with the men who came from England. They will have a clear picture of what England wishes. We have lived in Normandy too long to gauge the mood of the land of our birth." I dug my heels in my courser. I did not need a warhorse for the ride but he needed the exercise and I enjoyed riding the black beauty.

"Does not Jack write from Weedon, my lord?"

"Aye, Geoffrey, but it is news for Lady Isabelle's family. I would not expect him to commit words about the politics of the land to a letter."

"Will you not need a squire, my lord?"

"No, Thomas. If we are to go to war, I will have a servant to help me to arm and to watch the horses but I have no time to train one to ride to war and, if I am honest, I do not wish to. You two and I will be the three lances from Les Pérets."

That made them both grin from ear to ear, "Who would have thought, that when I left Yarpole, I would be elevated to be a lance."

I smiled at Geoffrey's obvious pleasure at such a tiny title. The three of us were all fortunate. Me more than they for I had been knighted. Being a lance meant that they would be paid and paid well for fighting. They would have to pay for their own mounts and armour, neither of which was cheap but I had paid them for the last years and they had not wasted their money. Although we did not wear armour for this ride, we three had the best plate armour that money could buy and the hats we now wore, when we rode to war, would be replaced with fine sallets.

We entered the gates of the city and made our way to the castle of the Conqueror. My livery was known and, as we had been sent for by Sir John, we were expected. We passed through the outer ward to the inner ward and the mighty keep. Ostlers took our horses I nodded to the men at arms and archers who were chatting by the bakery. They were waiting, no doubt, for a fresh batch of bread to be baked. I said to Thomas and Geoffrey, "Go and join them. Enjoy the bread and discover what you can."

"Aye, Sir Michael," and they headed in the direction of the smell of fresh bread.

A squire left the keep and headed towards me, "Sir Michael?"

"Yes?"

"If you would come with me, Sir John awaits."

Inside the tower, it was a maelstrom of movement. Pages, squires, and scribes raced through the corridors. Sir John had arrived and there would be orders sent to muster the army. He was not an idle man and already taking the reins that had been allowed to slacken during his incarceration. The Earl of Somerset would be the titular leader but we all knew who would be the one forcing the pace. He was poring over a map and when he looked up and saw me, he beamed, "Sir Michael! I feared you had done like so many others have done and returned to England to enjoy the fees from your Norman manor! I am pleased that I was wrong."

I am not sure if he meant an insult but the words implied one.

"No, my lord, I still live by the river."

"Good! And how many lances can you bring?"

I feigned ignorance, "Lances, my lord? For what?"

"Why, Sir Michael, to retake the parts of France we lost to that witch."

I did not like the title accorded to the unfortunate young woman but I kept my face neutral. My views would not be popular. "Aah, then it will be three lances."

He frowned and was clearly unhappy, "Three? That is far too few."

"Les Pérets, my lord is a small manor. I have more men but they are in England." I knew that if I wrote to Edgar and to Jack that they would send men but I wanted Sir John to ask me to do so. It was much to ask of my people and I felt that it would take every man we had to hold on to the parts of Normandy and Aquitaine we still held. The Maid had been an unstoppable force and she was now ever more revered dead than she ever had been alive. Her fiery death appeared to have inflamed the French. I had heard of riots in English held towns further north and east.

"Then send for them. I wish you to have eight lances."

That meant eight men at arms and twenty-four archers. "That will take time, my lord and," I waved an arm around me, "from the activity I see here I am guessing that we leave sooner rather than later."

He nodded, "I would have my force in the saddle and the field by the start of the harvest."

"A chevauchée, my lord?"

"You have a sharp mind. We cannot gather enough men to take the war to the French yet but they still harass the people around Compiègne. For that is where you captured the Maid and they wish to wreak vengeance on the town. If that bastion falls then the towns around it may well begin to think about shifting their loyalty. The French are trying to starve out the people there. We managed to resupply the garrison a month since but it cost us twenty men and those sent with the supplies are now besieged too. We have to do something to make the French break off the siege. I need mounted men at arms and archers. You have a reputation as did your mentor the great Strongstaff and I will need men such as you." He lowered his voice. "You appear to be untainted by defeat and your name will attract others."

I had not thought of it like that. When I looked inward at myself, and that was as seldom as possible, I still saw the young raw knight. I supposed having been chosen to protect the young king I should have had a higher opinion of myself but I did not.

I nodded, "A month then my lord?"

Shaking his head he said, "A fortnight and a short fortnight at that. We leave fourteen days from today. You had best ride back to your manor and start work."

"And the contract?"

"The *Chambres des Comptes* is financing the men. Sixpence a day for your mounted archers and a shilling a day for your lances. Horses will be provided and there will be recompense for any of your own mounts that are lost. Your pay, as Captain, Sir Michael, will be twenty pounds per annum. You have a squire?"

I shook my head.

"Then there will be a payment of a shilling a day for your servants. They must be mounted."

"Of course, if I could have the use of a scribe, my lord, I can send a message to my men in England."

He smiled broadly, "A warrior who wastes not a moment. Of course," he waved over an older man with a tonsured head, he had been a priest, "Philip."

The man looked up from his work and, after laying down his quill shuffled over to us. He had the hunched look of a man who has spent his life bent over parchments and the ink stained fingers confirmed it. "My lord?"

"Sir Michael has some letters he needs to write. I would have you write them and then return to the copying out of the muster."

The scribe sighed, wearily, "Aye, my lord." As Sir John turned to head off to his next meeting the scribe said, "If you would sit, my lord."

I joined him at his table and he cleared a space and chose a small piece of parchment. I could see that he was unhappy, "You like not this work Philip?"

"Scribbling out a muster that will be forgotten before the year is out, is not the sort of work I like. I was hired to copy out some of the great books that have come recently from the east. They take longer to write but they will last long after the kings and queens who now rule are dead. Their children's children and their children will read them."

"And that gives you satisfaction?" He nodded, "But you will be dead."

10

"So long as another reads the words that I write then I live. Men will admire my script and wonder at the scribe who toiled on the work." I had not thought of it in those terms. "And now, my lord, your letters?"

There was tiredness in his voice and I felt guilty. I made the letters as brief as I could so that Philip could return to his true vocation and even as I did, I knew that until we left for the northeast he would have to do the work he hated. In the letters I did not ask Jack and Edgar to come, in fact, I told them to stay but asked that any who wished to go to war with me should take ship and come to Les Pérets. Philip's hand was exquisite. It seemed a shame to waste such skill on my letters. When they were dry, I handed him a silver coin and then folded them before sealing them.

"Thank you, Philip and I hope that you can return to your work soon."

"So do I, my lord. I am old and I pray to the Good Lord for the time to finish each tome. I would not die in the middle of a book. My colleagues are skilled but their hands are not mine. It would offend me to have a reader frown at a strange letter. Now, if you would excuse me."

He returned to his writing and I left, clutching my letters. Geoffrey and Thomas headed towards me as they saw me emerge from the keep. They led our horses. "Come we will walk to the river. We have letters to send to England and we go to war."

Thomas nodded, "I know, my lord. We spoke to some of those alongside whom we had fought and they told us."

"You two will be two of the lances I need." They nodded, "You know that means you need archers?"

Geoffrey grinned, "And we are going to the right place. When Sir John returned then hopeful archers in England took ship, seeking a place. There will be men to hire by the river and if we seek a ship to return to England then that will be a good place to start."

My men were always optimists. Perhaps this chevauchée might turn out better than my sinking heart expected.

The river, at Rouen, was far from the sea and, even more than a port at the coast was ruled by the tides. We reached the ships at a propitious time. Men were preparing the ships for a return downriver in two hours' time. We sought a ship returning not only to England but, more importantly, Rye or Winchelsea. Although the latter was not as good a port as it had been and Rye was also silting up, they were both close to Iden and I knew that if the letters reached there then Edgar would ensure that Jack received his as quickly as possible. *'The Maid of Rye'* fit the bill perfectly. She was not the largest cog that had tied up but I knew that, with winter approaching, she would be heading for her home port. Her captain, John Husband, was more than happy to deliver the letters. He knew the manor at Iden and was almost reluctant to take payment.

"Take the coins, Captain, for I believe that a man is worth the hire and you can also help us out by telling any archers and billmen that you see that I seek men to follow me."

He smiled, "You are young Sir Michael but you have a reputation. The man who caught the Maid is a leader who can be followed." He pointed at an inn, *'The Red Vine'*, and said, "I brought a dozen men over when I landed in the early hours. They may well still be asleep in that inn." He smiled, "It was a rough crossing. Harry Longbow runs it. He is an English archer who lost his fingers when he was caught by the French after Patay. He can help you."

After thanking the captain we headed for the inn. We had killed two birds with one stone and although I would have asked the seaman for his recommendations an unsolicited one was even more valuable. It was not yet noon when we walked in but the place was heaving for they served food. Even though I was not wearing armour, my fine clothes and spurs marked me as a knight and the owner, easily recognised by his maimed right hand cleared a space for us.

"My lord, this is an honour."

His words implied familiarity yet I did not know him. "You know who I am?"

"Aye, Sir Michael. I served with Sir John Fastolf. I was with you at the siege and your men spoke highly of you." He nodded to Thomas and Geoffrey, "These two I also know and you are all welcome." He poured three beakers of ale from a jug, "Have a drink on me for old times, my lord."

I raised my beaker and said, "To old comrades; those who still live and those who died."

It was the right thing to say and as most of those in the inn had English connections the toast was taken up by all.

"You come here for food, my lord?"

I shook my head, "No, men. Sir John Talbot has asked me to serve King Henry and I need lances and archers."

"Then providence has sent you to the right place." He swept an arm around the inn. "Men arriving from England congregate here and there are new archers freshly arrived." He waved an arm at two of his serving men, "Hob and Much, clear a table for Sir Michael." He beamed at me, "If you would sit then I will rouse the archers and I dare say there are men here who would join you. Your name and that of William Strongstaff will be enough to ensure that you have the best."

I was flattered, gratified and more than a little relieved. I might be able to fulfil my contract with Sir John and, hopefully, I would have men upon whom I could rely. By the middle of the afternoon, we had hired fifteen archers and found four more lances. I would only need an extra one from England but archers would be needed. I was about to leave when four billmen came to speak with me. The man who was their spokesman was Cedric of Barnsley, "My lord, I know you sought lances and we, as billmen cannot do what you wish but we are good warriors and we would serve you if we could."

I liked the look of the three men with him for they were all fit young warriors. Each had a mail hauberk and a good helmet as well as a falchion and billhook. "What brought you to France? Is there not work in England for men such as you?"

Cedric looked a little downcast, "I will be truthful with you, Sir Michael for you have a reputation of being a good knight who is honourable. We four fell foul of Henry Percy, the son of Harry Hotspur. We served William Neville in Durham and our lord sent us to protect a farm from Percy raiders. We did so too well and killed one of their knights. The Earl of Northumberland called it murder and had us declared outlaws. We fled England. We are not murderers, my lord."

"And why did William Neville not speak up for you?"

Cedric looked angry for the first time, "Because, my lord, he is a weak fool. He is not strong enough to defend his own lands from the ravages of the Percy family. We were abandoned."

I felt sorry for them and decided to make an offer which I was not sure that they would accept, "I can offer you a place at my manor, Les Pérets. When I lead my men away, I would have you watch my family. I cannot promise either treasure or action but you would be employed and my manor is a fine one."

He briefly glanced at the other three. They all nodded and he said, "We will accept, my lord, and I thank you for your integrity."

In truth, it was one of the best decisions I ever made.

We were about to leave when we heard a commotion from outside. Two men were sprawling in the street. I recognised neither and that meant they were not Englishmen seeking work but I was a knight and a lord has a responsibility to keep law and order. "Thomas, have them separated."

My men obeyed instantly and the two men were pulled apart. Both had been bloodied by the encounter and as I looked at them, I saw that they had been warriors. Both wore a jack and the buskins of men who have tramped to war. They had fought hard and they panted although neither looked as though they were ready to back down. I decided to use my authority from Sir John.

"Hold! I am Sir Michael and I serve Sir John Talbot who commands the army of Normandy. This is not seemly. What is the cause of this disagreement?"

The slightly smaller of the two, who appeared to have had the better of the encounter, spat out a gob of blood and said, "I am sorry, my lord, I was about to seek employment with you when this man, whom I thought to be a friend for we have fought in the wars for the Maid, called me a traitor and threw the first punch. He said he would not let me serve the English."

"Is this true?"

The man I had addressed stood defiantly, "Of course it is. I hate you English and you have had the Maid murdered. My quest is now to have you driven from my land!"

Thomas said, "Arrest him lord and take him to Sir John. He speaks sedition!"

I smiled, "If every man who spoke thus was arrested and gaoled there would be no room in our donjons. What is your name?"

He looked suspiciously at me and then decided, as my tone was reasonable, to answer me, "Jacques le Couteau."

"Then Jacques, I give you until dusk to quit Rouen. If you are still here after that time, you will be arrested and taken to the castle."

"I will leave, for the air around stinks with the rancid smell of Englishmen."

Thomas took one step forward and punched his fists, "One more word from you and you will eat nothing but soup for the rest of your life."

"Enough! For your insolence, you have an hour now, I would run lest I let my men ride you down like a dog." There was enough of a threat in my voice for him to turn and first walk quickly and then, after watching Geoffrey and Thomas mount their horses, run. My two men at arms laughed.

I turned to the other man, "And you, what do you wish?"

He shrugged, "I am a soldier and I served the Maid. She is now burned and I seek to use my sword." I looked down at the empty scabbard. "We fell upon hard times." Shaking his head he said, "Jacques was not a good man and I drank the same as he. My brother, Henri, would be ashamed of me if he knew."

There was something about the man that had been familiar, the shape of his nose, his hair colouring and the name Henri made me think of Isabelle's father. When he had walked his land he had spoken of a younger brother who had run away to join the army. I asked him, "What is your name?"

"Charles."

"And is your brother Henri of Garonne?"

He looked amazed and I saw Thomas and Geoffrey exchange looks. "Aye, my lord but how do you know?"

I smiled, "Henri of Garonne is my steward and I married his daughter Isabelle."

He dropped to his knees, "Can such things be? I am sorry, my lord, that you find me thus. My brother and I fell out when I left to go to war. I have spent the last years regretting my decision. Jacques and I went to the farm he used to have first but he was not there."

"I think you and your brother will have much catching up to do. Come, ride on the back of my horse."

He shook his head and went to the water trough, "First, I will clean up a little. Maud would not wish to see me like this."

As we rode the few miles to Les Pérets, I wondered about the intervention of Fate. That French soldiers were in Rouen seeking work was not surprising. Professional soldiers had a pragmatic view about their paymasters. The Normans and the English were paying and so even loyal Frenchmen might seek work with them. I just wondered at the one called Jacques. He would not serve the English so why had he been in Rouen?

We returned home a much larger party than had left. When she saw the numbers then Isabelle hurried inside to ask her mother to help her arrange beds for the new men. Henri came out to see how many he would have to accommodate and did not see the man on my horse behind me. "We will find beds for them all, my lord. I am not sure if Maud has enough bed linen but warriors have to suffer some hardships, eh, my lord?"

I nodded and, as Charles slipped from my saddle, said, "Aye, Henri and here is one that has suffered long enough."

There was shock, surprise and delight in equal measure on the face of Henri. The two men threw their arms around one another and hugged. "Maud!" Maud rushed to the door at the sound of her husband's voice. to the door and when she recognised her brother-in-law her hand went to her mouth and she shouted for Isabelle.

I dismounted and waved to my men to take the horses and the new men away. Henri and his family needed space. Isabelle came with Jean in her arms and I put my hand about her waist. She said quietly, "I was a young girl when he left but I recognise him. It upset my father when his youngest brother left us. he felt guilty that he had not protected him from himself."

"He is here now and he need not go to war. He can stay at the farm."

"Thank you, Michael, you are the kindest man I know."

As Charles and Maud hugged, Henri looked at me gratefully, "I am sorry about that unseemly behaviour, my lord."

Shaking my head I said, "The Bible teaches us about prodigal sons." Charles and Maud separated. She had her arm around his waist as though preventing him from flight. "Charles, you are welcome to stay here and you need not go to war but it is your choice."

Maud said, "Come, brother, let us get you cleaned up before you enter Sir Michael's fine hall."

I spoke with my three archers and Henri to explain to them what was needed. Henri, despite the obvious need to speak to his brother, was all business and he listened and offered suggestions as we spoke.

Nicholas Warbag smiled when I said I was not sure if enough archers would be sent from England, "My lord, you have fetched fifteen, there are three of us. That makes eighteen. We have four archers here on the manor. We three have not wasted our time and we have young men who whilst not as skilled nor as strong as we three have potential and will give a good account of themselves. We will only need four or five from England and I am sure that Edgar will secure at least that number."

I was relieved.

Thomas added a word of caution, "What we do not have enough of, yet is horses. The twenty odd men we hired today are without mounts. We have a few spares but…"

Henri nodded, "Will there be funds available to buy them, my lord."

"Of course, Henri. Sir John had promised that he will pay for horses."

"Then I will secure them. There are men I met before I lost my lands. They know horses and I will procure them. I will leave on the morrow and be away for a week, no more."

"Five days would be better, Henri, that is all the time that I can allow."

I allowed Maud and Henri as much time as they liked to be reunited with Charles and Isabelle and I spoke, as we ate of the strange events that had conspired to bring him back to us. "He can help your father, Isabelle, and I confess that I am happy to be able to leave warriors to watch you. Cedric and the others are a beginning but Charles is family and that is even better." My words made Isabelle start. It was as though the arrival of her uncle meant that she had forgotten my impending

16

departure. My son was at the table and she said nothing but her eyes told me of her fears.

It was, inevitably, when we lay together, that night, that Isabelle poured out her misgivings, "Is this to be our future, my love? Will you be spending all your time on campaign? I could not bear that."

"I will be truthful, it is likely that as Lord of Les Pérets I will be called upon to defend Normandy."

"Yet where you go is many miles from the borders of Normandy."

"And I shall speak with Sir John about that. This first foray is an emergency. I have no intention of being a knight who fights far from home."

That contented her and soon she was asleep. I hoped that Sir John would be understanding about my request. I now realised the problems with having such a fine reputation. You were overused whilst if like William Neville, you were a poor leader, you were allowed to stay at home. I had even more sympathy now for Sir William Strongstaff who had endured this life for a long time.

Charles was put to work by Henri. I told Henri that his brother and my billmen would become the ones who would guard the manor. Henri nodded but said that on my farm there would be no idle hands and the new men would not be allowed to simply watch others work. I liked the idea.

The letters from England reached me just a week after I had returned to my home. Henri fetched the horses on the same day that one of Sir John's pages rode into the manor clutching the two letters. One bore a crude seal; that would be Edgar's whilst the one from Jack had the Weedon seal. "These letters arrived today and Sir John thought these might be important, my lord and he sent them immediately."

"Thank you."

"He also asked if you would be ready for the muster."

I nodded. That was the real reason for the page, "I will be at Rouen Castle at the appointed time."

He left and I slit open the two missives. They were from my brothers in arms and both promised that they would do all that they could. I saw then that both men had sent the letters the day they had received mine. I wished that they had found the men first and then written. This way I did not know who would be arriving. I blamed myself. Jack had been my squire and I had neglected his training. Edgar was a simple archer and would never have encountered the task I had set him. It could not be helped.

Chapter 2

It was the captain I had sent with the message who ensured that my men reached me two days before the appointed time. He felt a loyalty to his hometown and waited for a tide for the men sent by Jack. The ship was seen heading up the river and I was sent for. Hairy Bailey knew I was waiting for men and he recognised the ship. Thanks to the winds that did not cooperate I arrived at the quay the same time as the cog was tying up. Four archers stepped from the cog, Will Green Hose, Harry Bodkin Blade, Mark the Bowyer and John the Fletcher. Two men at arms followed, David of Denbigh and Richard Richardson. Even more welcome were the horses they led from the ship.

"Master Jack was disappointed that we sent so few men, my lord but some of those who left here to return to England now have families and…" David looked around at the busy quay.

I knew he had more to say, "Speak David, if you do not know me now then it is a sad day."

"Some think that the war is lost. The power of the Maid lives on, my lord."

I nodded. Unlike many of the soldiers who had fought her my men had come to know her and did not fear her as a witch but as a symbol, a talisman who was as powerful in death as she had been in life. "I understand and this will be enough. Sir John may be disappointed that there are not as many archers as he might have liked but that cannot be helped. Come we have but a day or so to organise ourselves before we ride to Compiègne.

Richard's eyes widened, "It still holds out?"

"Aye, the fact that the Maid was captured trying to take it makes it a prize for the French. We do not reinforce it but keep the French too busy to assault."

As we rode to Les Pérets I told them their pay and gave them a rough idea of how I saw the campaign developing. I spoke to the two who had been men at arms but were now elevated to lances, "Your pay means that you can hire a squire or a servant if you wish. For my part, I have taken on four Normans who have experience of war. They each have a jack or brigandine and weapons. I do not expect them to have to fight but if they need to then they can."

"What have Geoffrey and Thomas done?"

"There were youths from the manor who were keen to go to war. They have squires." I turned in the saddle to the archers, "Nicholas Warbag will captain the archers."

Will Green Hose asked, "And when Sir John commands, then who will lead the archers?"

"I know not. This has been arranged hastily. We need to be prepared to live off the land. I am just pleased that our bowyer and fletcher chose to come."

Both Mark and John were skilled craftsmen and could have made a good living in England plying their trade. The fact that they had come was comforting but I noticed that their boots were now well made and their horses were good hackneys. They had been paid well for their services and unlike many old warriors had used their coins wisely. Once we reached my manor, I knew I could leave my men to reacquaint themselves. I went to speak to my father-in-law, Henri. We always found it easier to talk outside and we walked through the field that had just been sown with winter barley.

"I know not how long we will be away, Henri, and you shall be in sole command of the manor. I know that the farming side will not be a problem but there are other matters you shall need to deal with and I wanted to give you the opportunity to ask me questions." He nodded. "The minor infractions in the manor must be heard by my court. In my absence, I appoint you and Father Michel to make the judgements. I have every confidence in both of you for you are good men."

"Thank you, my lord. I confess that having seen injustice, it makes me even more determined to see that justice is done."

"The takes will need to be collected. Father Michel will know what to do."

"Maud has a mind that understands numbers. She will ensure that we pay what is fair."

I smiled at the memory of Lady Eleanor. Sir William had told me that she was the real force behind his successful manors. I was a rich man thanks to her efforts.

That done we returned to the hall and I sat with my men, old and new and explained to them how we would work. That done all I needed was to speak to the men who would watch our horses and cook for us. I was taking not only Storm but another horse, Shadow. I would need two for a chevauchée meant we had to be well mounted both for attack and for flight. There were risks in such raids.

That evening as Isabelle lay in my arms, I sensed that she was more content. "Thank you for hiring the billmen, husband. That was thoughtful. We all feel safe here but that is because of the curtain of steel you and your men lay around us."

I knew that she and her family had suffered when they had lived from hand to mouth and they had been easy targets for predators. I had

19

considered building a castle but I had not for the simple reason that such a building would be more likely to attract an attack. We were a small manor and close enough to Rouen to be safe from everything except a band of brigands and my four billmen would be a good deterrent.

The next day we left the manor to the cheers of the villagers. Some of their menfolk were coming with us as armed servants and we made a colourful display in our new, bright, tabards. I had spent some of the annual fee I would receive to make my men, all of them, look as one. When we rode then our enemies would learn to recognise us. I knew it was a double-edged sword for whilst they might fear our prowess it would also identify us as worthy enemies. I hoped that by behaving like men and not animals then, should the worst happen and we lost, we would be treated well. Charles now wore my livery as did Cedric and the others. They bore weapons and had metal-studded brigandines. Henri's brother now looked like the warrior he had been and the five of them looked determined to protect my manor and my family.

We reached Rouen by terce and joined the others who were gathered in the outer ward of the castle. It looked to me as though there were more than a hundred lances. I knew that Sir John commanded at least forty lances and his name would have attracted others. It meant we were a sizeable force of more than five hundred men when those who would help us were added. Raiding in winter meant that the towns and villages we attacked would be stripped of their food for we would take much feeding. That would feed us and weaken the French but I wondered at the wisdom of such action as it could only serve to make the French resent us even more. I kept my thoughts to myself. My men were in good heart and it would not do to dishearten them. This was where I missed Jack and Edgar White Streak. One old and one young, they had provided me with two men in whom I could confide. I realised that they had been replaced by Isabelle and she would not be there either. I would be alone. Perhaps that was the reason for my downcast expression.

Sir John frowned at my face and my silence, "Come, Sir Michael, you should be smiling. We go to bring hope to the people of Compiègne and when Lord Somerset joins us in the Spring then we may well be able to do more than just raid. We can take the war to our foes."

"Lord Somerset will not be with us? We are not just the vanguard?"

The smile left Sir John's face, "I fear he has to await more men from England and they will not be here until after the winter storms."

We wasted not a moment and Sir John led the brightly coloured column from the castle to resounding cheers from the people of Rouen on the streets. They had burned the Maid and to them, we were Normandy's only hope. They would be safe behind their mighty walls and any hardships would be endured by us. It was the French who would starve and not them. I wondered if that was the real reason for the sudden resumption of hostilities. Had Sir John been deliberately exchanged to re-ignite the fires of war? We had just ninety miles to travel to the east. We were all well mounted and it took just two days to reach Verberie a few miles south of Compiègne where we would stay. The village had no castle but was a good location for us as the forest that surrounded the village would afford both shelter and food while the plentiful lakes and waters ensured that we would have grazing for our animals. I do not think that the villagers were happy to see us although our presence meant that they would not, at least, be raided.

While we spent the next days building the shelters we would use, Sir John rode the land with his mesne to see where we might be best used. I know that men in England who are not used to such war wonder at its nature. Battles were rare. Sir William had told me that. War in France was about controlling the land with a mailed gauntlet. By holding key towns such as Compiègne and the routes they guarded then it prevented an enemy from moving large numbers of men. Sir John would be assessing the dangers from the castles that lay within a day's ride of Compiègne and from that list would select the places we would raid. There would be no question of taking a castle. It was too expensive in terms of men and resources. Instead, we would starve the castles so that they could not mount an attack on us.

When he returned, I was invited to a council of war held in the abandoned manor house he had taken over. Soissons had been identified as the key to the enemy's plans. The town held bad memories for the archers as before Agincourt an English garrison of archers had been massacred by the French there. When the Maid had recaptured it four years earlier there had been great celebrations. The Seigneur and the populace were keen to retake Compiègne. It was just twenty miles from the besieged town and to avoid hurting the people of Compiègne we would have to select our targets very carefully.

"Ten miles to the east of Soissons lies the village of Braine. There is no castle there but there is a small palisade behind which the villagers bring in the animals each night. They do not slaughter all their animals in autumn but spread out the butchery during October, November and December. The village provides food for the castle at Soissons. We leave on the morrow to attack the village and take their food."

Sir John de Cressy was one of Sir John Talbot's friends and he led eighteen lances. He asked the obvious question that was on all our minds, "My lord, the French know we are here and they will have

21

watchers. They may ambush us before we can reach the village. It is thirty-five miles away."

Sir John smiled, "I know but the journey we take will be more like forty miles for first we head south. My plan is simple. I intend the enemy to think that we head for Senlis and Meaux. The knowledge that we head for Soissons is for this room only as I know that there are spies who not only watch from without but are planted within. Sir Michael, you and your men will leave an hour before the main body and you will head through the forest to protect our left flank and to intercept any who try to ride east to warn Soissons and Braine. You are small enough to escape too much attention and yet I know that your men will be able to keep us safe."

I nodded, "Yes, my lord."

"We will turn the main body and head east north of Senlis. We will meet Sir Michael at the donjon at Vez. It has been abandoned since Soissons fell. I intend to reach the village at night and attack between Laudes and Prime. I think that we can take the village easily enough but getting back may prove tricky." He looked at his friend, Sir John de Cressy, "You, my friend, have many Frenchmen in your company and it is you who will protect our flank on the return to Verberie."

Sir John de Cressy seemed quite happy with the plan. The fact that some of his men were French might help them deceive any who came to stop our return. A hesitation might well give the advantage back to us. If the French knew what we were about then they could easily outnumber us. We had to hit and run.

"Sir Michael, you had better go and give your men their instructions. Do not mention Braine."

I knew I could trust my men but I dared not disobey Sir John. I did not know if he would have men watching me. He was close to the Duke of Bedford and he could make my life at Les Pérets difficult. "They shall not know our destination, my lord until we reach Vez, by which time the world will know where we are headed."

He gave an enigmatic smile, "Perhaps, perhaps not."

I made up the plan as I headed back to our camp. Smiling I said, "Tomorrow we leave before Prime. We are to head into the forest to the east of us and ensure that there are no Frenchmen watching our camp. Sir John is worried that he and his scouts were seen and may have piqued the interest of the French. Nicholas, we will be reliant upon you and your archers. You will need to ride with strung bows."

He nodded knowing the implications. Keeping a bow strung shortened the life of the bowstring, "Do not fear my lord, we have plenty and when we return to Rouen, we can make good the losses from the armoury." The smile told me that he had already acquired plenty before we left.

"Good. We take no servants but have food and drink with you on your horses. If we discover enemies, we may have to spend a night in the open."

Thomas of Chester shook his head, "It is good that we do it now and not in the depths of winter. I am getting too old to sleep in a hovel beneath a cloak." That brought nods of agreement. The shelters we had built in the village were more substantial than hovels. We had crude doors and beds within each dwelling. Most of my archers slept with four men to a shelter and they would be warm. A hovel was for emergencies.

The servants we had were good men. All were Normans and had fought for England at some time in the past. Too old now to go to war they were still keen to do their part. The Normans had conquered England and had always been the enemies of the French. They spoke a similar language but their heritage was different. The French came from the Franks and the Normans from the Norse. They fussed over us knowing that their sole task would be to watch our camp and to guard it. Guillaume was assigned to me and he made sure that I had a plentiful bowl of food and that my bed would be as soft as possible.

"You make sure that you get a good sleep, my lord. Fret not about waking. I shall have you awake with a hot breakfast well before you are due to leave." He had been a soldier and knew the importance of such things.

"Thank you, Guillaume."

Thomas came over and asked, quietly, "Why does Sir John use our men, my lord? He had both Normans and French available."

"Partly that he trusts us but, and this is probably the most important reason, we are English and although our men speak French it is clear that they are not French. He does not wish for any confusion. When our archers release their arrows, it will be at men who wish us harm. Sir John's conscience will be clear."

I did not sleep well; I rarely did on campaign. It had been different when I had been with Sir William. Somehow you never believed that you would lose or that men might die. We never did lose under him but men did die. I suppose I now felt the weight of responsibility on my shoulders.

Guillaume shook me awake but, to be truthful, the smell of ham frying on the open fire had already begun to wake me. I made water, ate and then asked Guillaume to saddle Storm. Shadow would have his chance but on this first raid, I wanted my best horse between my legs.

23

The rest of the men rose and moved purposefully about our camp. They were waiting with their horses before me. I mounted and waved Nicholas and our archers to the left. We followed. The idea was for us to move east a mile north of the road to Vez. It was not a large road but if the French had men watching for us, they would be close to the road. By having two lines four hundred paces apart I hoped that we would find any watchers. I led the men at arms.

Despite the fact that I knew where the archers were and could even hear their mounts as they moved through the forest, I could not see them clearly for they wore oiled cloaks and their livery was hidden. Even when the sun rose, they would be hard to spot. It followed, therefore, that it would be hard to see the French for they would be hiding. Our hope was to catch them in their camps and pray that they were late risers. The sun was just making its appearance when I heard the twang of a bowstring and the cry of a man struck by an arrow. I had a spear in my hand but my helmet hung from my cantle. I spurred Storm as I waved my spear for my men at arms to flank me. There were more shouts and cries as well as the sound of horses now galloping. They would not be my archers. My men could not release from the back of a horse and, in pairs, they would have dismounted for one to loose and the other to hold the horse.

"There, my lord!" Geoffrey of Yarpole's voice and pointed spear showed me the two men on horses who were crossing our front and heading for the road.

As I had spurred Storm already, he was moving quickly and was a better horse than the rouncys we pursued. We began to draw close to them but as Storm was the best of our horses it was I who was the closest. I saw that the enemy wore no mail and were clearly just spearmen who had been allocated the task of forest sentries. I shouted to them in French, "Halt or you shall die!"

One turned and his hand flicked out. He had thrown something. I saw the dart as it came towards Storm's head and I barely managed to jerk his head to the side. They would not come quietly and I urged my horse on. The throwing of the dart had almost worked but it had also slowed down the rider and I pulled my hand back to thrust at him when was within a horse's length of me. In a perfect world, I would have wounded him and had a prisoner but I could not take the chance. When I rammed the spear at his back, I knew it would be a mortal blow. I aimed to the left of his spine and he fell from the horse almost unhorsing an eager Geoffrey of Yarpole. Suddenly we were on the road and the last man dug his heels in to make his horse move faster. It was a mistake for in the gloom of early morning in a forest whose trees had

24

lost branches in recent storms the rider did not see the branch that tripped his horse. The crack as his head hit the bole of the tree was enough to tell me that he would be dead. Thomas recovered the horse and David of Denbigh fetched the horse from the first man I had slain. We reined in and waited for my archers.

"There was a camp, my lord. They had made a cold camp but they were rising. We might have taken prisoners but they saw us and they loosed arrows at us." Nicholas shook his head, "Piss poor archers, my lord. They are dead and e have their horses, bowstrings, bows and arrows." My men wasted nothing.

Nodding I said, "You and your archers continue to ride through the forest although I doubt that there will be more watchers. The camp was close to ours and yet far enough to escape casual scrutiny. The French might worry when they do not receive word from them but by then it will be too late."

Thomas asked, "Do you tell us now where we go, my lord?"

I nodded, "Sir John made me swear to keep it secret. He fears spies." I shrugged, "I trust all of you but..."

They understood such things, "Aye, my lord, an oath is an oath."

"We ride to a village close to Soissons and raid it. We will head for the donjon at Vez and await Sir John there. His precaution and its result will please him."

There were clearings along the road and we were cautious as we passed through them. Some would have belonged to those who used to make a living from the forest, foragers, charcoal burners and the like but the wars in this part of the world had made their existence a parlous one and now the forest was returned to animals, birds, and trees. I saw lightness ahead and knew that we must be approaching the village of Vez. I suppose that at one time it had been more important for the stone donjon there had to have been built to protect something. I was relaxing a little knowing that Sir John and the main column would take some time to reach us. When John the Fletcher appeared from the trees to our left all thoughts of relaxation left me.

He pointed as he spoke, "My lord, Nicholas sent me. There are men in the tower in Vez. They watch the road."

My mind worked quickly. Sir John had told me that it had been abandoned but watchers meant it had not. Nicholas had not said the tower was manned. 'There are men in the tower' implied a few men but they could still alert Soissons. "Thomas, take the men at arms and ride through the forest. Cut off the donjon from the east. No one gets through."

25

"Aye, my lord." He gave me a questioning look; he wished to know the rest of my plan.

"Just go." I turned to John the Fletcher, "Ride back to Nicholas. I want the archers dismounted and their horses tethered. I will ride in and the archers can cover me. If there is any danger to me, I want arrows to protect me."

"You ride alone, my lord?"

"And do you think they will fear one knight? They will be curious, aye, and they may even seek to restrain me but so long as their attention is on me then they will not send for help." He looked dubious, "Go." Left alone I dismounted and tightened my girths. I stroked Storm and spoke to him, "Someone knew we were coming. I am guessing a spy in Rouen and that gives me hope. While we are not in Rouen, they cannot spy on us. Come, old friend, let us trip the trap."

I mounted and headed towards the tower. My lance was fastened to the saddle and my helmet hung from my cantle. I rode in a relaxed manner for I did not wish the watchers to be alarmed. If I needed a weapon then my sword would be the one I would use. The greatest danger lay in a crossbow bolt but my defence against such an attack would be my archers who would recognise the danger. As the trees thinned so I saw the handful of houses that made up Vez and the two-storied tower. Even from a distance of four hundred paces, I could see that the mortar was crumbling and stones had fallen on the ancient building. It had not been refortified, just occupied. I saw the movement from the top of the tower and was then aware that the village appeared deserted. The smoke that rose told me it was not but the villagers were hiding. That suggested either collusion or fear. Seeing a water trough by the base of the tower I headed for it. I kept my movements casual but I was watching for danger. The entrance to the tower was six feet from the ground up a small set of stairs. That suggested a third storey to the building that was partly below ground. I reined in and keeping myself between the wall of the tower and Storm, I let my horse drink. I took my ale skin and I drank. The only way that a bolt could be sent at me would be if a crossbowman leaned over the parapet. If he did so one of two things would happen, either my archers would slay him or the bolt would simply fall from the weapon my archers called the infernal machine of the devil! I heard the door to the tower open and I hung my ale skin from my saddle. I turned but kept my right hand resting lightly on the hilt of my sword.

There were three men emerging from the tower. One was a knight and a second was his squire. The third was the real threat for it was a crossbowman and his weapon was aimed at my chest. Even my breastplate would not stop the strike from such a close range.

The knight spoke as he descended the steps, "What is an English knight doing here in the heart of France? What is your name and your purpose?"

I knew that my archers would be getting closer to the tower knowing that all the attention was on me. I played for time, "I heard this donjon had been abandoned. I was wrong."

"And that is why you came here, to occupy it all by yourself?" He looked around and studied the road, "Where are your men? Your squire?"

"My squire is in England and I came here for I am riding to Rheims; I hear it has a fine cathedral."

He laughed, "And you are a warrior and not a student of architecture." He suddenly seemed to see my livery and his eyes narrowed, "You are Sir Michael of Weedon and that means Sir John Talbot is close at hand! Kill him! Roland, ride!"

Everything seemed to happen at once. I drew my sword as an arrow slammed into the crossbowman who had raised his weapon. As the knight leapt down the stairs to get at me a second arrow pinned the squire to the wall and I heard hooves from behind the tower. Roland must have been a rider waiting to take a message. As I blocked the blow from the knight I heard a cry from the top of the tower as my archers took another defender down. His body crashed to the ground just paces from us. The knight was more distracted than I was and I was able to draw my rondel dagger and stab it at his armpit while my sword blocked his. He was good and he drove his sword came down to deflect the dagger and to push me away. At the same time, he manoeuvred himself so that his back was protected by the tower and my body before him prevented any more arrows.

"You cannot win, my lord. Surrender for I have archers aplenty and they can disable you in a heartbeat."

He pulled his own dagger and launched a flurry of blows on me, forcing me back, "You fool! You cannot win. When Roland reaches Soissons, he will return here and it is you who will be my prisoner."

Sir William had suggested me as the guardian for King Henry as he recognised that I knew how to use a sword. Some of the other weapons, a poleaxe or a war hammer, that knights used were not as effective in my hands but a sword was my weapon of choice. I chose to end the fight. I lunged with my dagger at his face for, like me, he wore no helmet and then. As his head was forced back I spun on my right leg to swing my sword into the place where his faulds met his breastplate.

27

Such a juncture was always weaker than the rest and my sword managed to find the leather fastening. Severed, the terces of the faulds began to fall and more importantly the blade tore through his gambeson and into flesh. I saw his eyes widen in surprise and pain. I sliced my sword back and aggravated the wound. Suddenly three archers appeared behind me and their arrows were aimed at the knight.

I stepped back and smiled, "You have done all that honour demands. Now surrender. I do not seek ransom just your sword."

Nodding he handed me his weapon, "You have skill, Sir Michael. I am impressed for I have earned gold at tournaments all over France."

"And I am not a tournament knight…"

"Sir Guy, Sir Guy d'Albreche."

"Sir Guy. I was trained by the protector of kings and when I fight it is to win and not to hear the applause of a baying crowd." I turned to Nicholas, "Secure the tower and fetch your horses."

"Aye, my lord."

"John the Fletcher, see to Sir Guy's wound and help unpin his squire from the wall." His squire's arm had been pinned to the wooden lintel along the side of the door and I saw that the youth could not manage to remove it himself. I sheathed my sword and then turned, "Those in the village, show yourselves for I do not like folk hidden when we mean them no harm. If you remain within your homes then I will assume you wish us harm and act accordingly."

Although my men were not cut from the same cloth, I knew that many English archers had behaved badly when passing through small villages. The doors opened and led by their men, the villagers emerged sheepishly. Just then there was the sound of hooves as Thomas led my men at arms into the village. All eyes swivelled and I saw Sir Guy's shoulders slump as he saw his man, with a bloody coxcomb with them. Roland had been taken and word would not reach Soissons.

Chapter 3

Sir John Talbot rode in at the head of the main column in the middle of the afternoon. He was in an ebullient mood until I told of the knight we had captured. Our news of the two ambushes upset his plans.

"You have done well, Sir Michael, but now we have to consider if Braine is the right choice of target."

That he was seeking my opinion was clear but I was not sure I wanted to put my head above the parapet. It was then that I realised that if I said nothing he would act anyway and he was determined to raid. "I see no reason why we should change our plans, my lord. They obviously do not know we are heading for Braine and it might be they think we are going to Soissons. All their precautions appear to be on the road to Soissons. We would have to keep men watching the Soissons Road and it would mean that we could not tarry long." I pointed to the tower, "Perhaps we could use their own tower as a surprise. If they did discover that we were at Braine then by the time they had reacted we could be on the road to Compiègne and if they were close then archers on the top of the donjon would be able to hold them up."

I saw him debate and then he said, "Come, you too, Sir John."

With Sir John de Cressy and their squires, we entered the dilapidated tower. The knight and his men had merely used it for sleeping and no attempt had been made to improve it. When we reached the top, we saw that it had a clear view for half a mile or so to the east and the west along the road. The trees were to the north and south.

Sir John Talbot nodded, "You are right, Sir Michael and you have a good eye for defence. We will do as you suggest. Sir John, have ten of your archers remain here to watch the villagers and ensure that they do not send word to Soissons as well as to watch for our return." As we made our way down the stairs he said, "You and your men will be the rearguard. Let others set off ambushes and traps. You and your lances have earned your share of whatever treasure we find already." He stopped as we neared what would have been the main hall had the castle remained occupied, "What did you say to the knight? Did you ask for ransom?"

I shook my head, "He surrendered and I did not ask for ransom."

"You are a curious young knight, Sir Michael."

I shrugged, "Sir William left me enough money and lands so that I do not need to seek more and I want no resentful family seeking revenge for my taking their fortune."

"Then we will keep him here as our guest until we return. He knows of our numbers and dispositions."

Riding at the rear was no great hardship although we all grew stiff necks as our heads turned at every sound behind us. Being at the rear meant that our horses had to search for grazing at each stop and the water was already soiled by the ones before us. They were minor considerations and as we had but one day to endure it, we would survive. We were the last to arrive at the muster point. Sir John was an immaculate planner and the men who would surround Braine were already heading to camp at the far side of the animal rich settlement. There was a wooden palisade around the village but we knew that once dawn came the animals would be released to graze on the pastures beyond the wooden walls. We would attack then.

My men had gained not only horses in the two skirmishes but also food. We ate better than most that night as we all endured a cold camp. Our bread was a day fresher than the rest and the cheese and ham needed no fire. I enjoyed the wine from the knight's wine skin. Sir Guy had been remarkably sanguine about his capture. That his squire was merely wounded and had not died was a relief to him as it was his nephew. He was a local man and knew that there was a rhythm to this war. The Maid had seen the fortunes sway in favour of the French whilst our capture of her had put us in the ascendancy. He was patient and would wait for the pendulum to swing back. I was glad that I had not been forced to kill him. I was a killer; Sir William had seen that in me but I only killed when it was necessary and that was normally in the heat of battle.

"You are quiet, my lord."

"Aye, Thomas. I like not these raids on villagers. I know that if we are to win the war then we have to protect the towns and castles we have captured but it does not sit well with me."

Thomas nodded, "Yet without them, we would have no employment. I am not a farmer, my lord. I stayed with you in Normandy and I have followed a peaceful path yet I am a soldier and a soldier needs to fight. These last days have made me feel alive."

As I lay down for a few hours of sleep I thought about his words. I was a soldier too and yet if I had not been asked to fight again, I would have been content to stay at Les Pérets with Isabelle. Had marriage and fatherhood changed me? I would not have enjoyed the farming but the responsibility of caring for villagers was something I did enjoy. Like Sir William I had been born with nothing and I appreciated everything that I had.

The villagers of Braine were not expecting us, that was clear. As we galloped towards the men when they drove their animals out to graze the shock was clear to see. Not an arrow needed to be sent nor a lance plunged into a defender. They simply surrendered for surprise was complete. Knowing that, despite our precautions it was likely by the end of the day word would have reached Soissons, we worked quickly taking every draught animal and wagon that we could to fill with the food intended for Soissons. Forty archers were assigned to the herd and the flock that would be driven back to Vez and then Verberie. They would, perforce, be slower than we. Sir Richard Tarporley and his men at arms led them. Once again, we would be the rearguard and Sir John had taken all that there was to take by early afternoon and we left the emptied village. All the treasure and coins were now in our possession. Not everything was in Sir John's hands. Our men were veterans and they knew where to seek coins hidden in pots and below ground. They and the wine they had taken meant all the men were beaming as they left. Of course, that might change but as we headed west there was an optimistic air amongst the men. We had achieved all that we had hoped and lost not a man in the process.

This time we were in greater danger at the rear. Sir John de Cressy guarded the wagons in the middle of our column while Sir John Talbot led us, we and the lances of Sir Geoffrey d'Issy were the rearguard. My actions at Vez ensured that the older knight listened to my words. I had my archers spread out on both sides of the column and to the rear. They would bring us warning of danger. They did not ride with strung bows. Instead, they would ride to us if they heard pursuit. We made fifteen miles and reached the tiny village of Longpont before we halted to rest and to eat. We had caught up with the animals and it was a noisier camp than we might have wished. The stink of defecating animals also made the air unpleasantly pungent. We had to keep one-third of the men on watch both to ensure the animals were safe and to see that no villagers left to raise the alarm.

We rose before dawn and the animals set off once more. It was only ten miles to Vez but the animals would take until noon had passed to reach it. We rose and ate a hot breakfast courtesy of the village who, like the folk of Braine, would go hungry for a day or so.

I kept us two hundred paces behind the men of Sir Geoffrey d'Issy. I had been taught that strategy when I had served with Sir William. The few moment's grace could often save lives. My archers, riding behind us, were our eyes and ears. The woods followed us all the way to Vez but they were not continuous and that allowed us to have a better view of the land behind when we came to occasional clearings. We were in French territory and that meant the people we passed were unfriendly. They were not belligerent and even allowed us to use their water but they were enemies and we were wary. They would tell those who pursued us of our numbers and formation. That we would be pursued was obvious. The men of Braine would have told Soissons but that news would have been unlikely to reach the French garrison until the middle of the night. We had taken all the horses from Braine.

We were just three miles or so from the donjon with the tower when Nicholas Warbag alerted me to pursuit. He said it was a large number of horsemen. Nodding I said. "Thomas, ride ahead and tell Sir Geoffrey. He can inform the rest of the column."

"Aye, my lord."

Nicholas waited for my orders and I viewed the land around us. We had just passed through a clearing and so I pointed west, "We will push on and ambush their vanguard at the next clearing." The clearings were, by and large, where the local people lived. The French would be slightly more relaxed as they passed through. I sought any advantage that I could.

Sir Geoffrey had waited for us to catch up with him. He had ten lances and forty archers. Between us, we were a sizeable force. He looked expectantly at me. Pointing ahead I said, "We will have the archers dismount at the next clearing and we will wait in the clearing. The archers can thin their numbers and we can bloody their nose. We need to make them cautious and allow the slow-moving animals to reach the safety of Vez. We should ride hard and they may think that we fear them. I want them to see our men at arms but not the archers."

None of the archers had strung their bows and they would need time to do so. We found the next clearing just half a mile from where we had been alerted. A small track crossed the road and there was an old deserted and dilapidated farmhouse at the small crossroads. The war that had gone on for generations had taken its toll on such isolated communities.

I shouted, as we entered the clearing, "Archers dismount and string your bows. I want you on both sides of the road. Lances, in the centre. Await my command."

No one argued with me. Sir Geoffrey respected me and knew that Sir John had assigned me my position for a good reason; I was good at what I did. The archers tethered their horses close to their positions. We did not need to hide. The attention of the French would be on the handful of lances that faced them. I had Sir Geoffrey next to me and there were eight of us in the front rank. The archers had just managed to string their bows when the flash of colour and sunlight glinting from spearheads in the distance told us that the French were coming. The archers would wait to see their target to choose their arrows. I doubted that it would be plated men who would be in the fore and so the men would not need bodkins. I held my lance so that it rested on the ground. There would be time to raise and couch it. if the French chose to halt and await reinforcements then it would not be needed.

The horsemen we saw were light cavalry. The French had learned from the Bretons and emulated them. There were forty of them. Wearing mail shirts beneath jupons they were fast but lightly armed. They were riding with their small shields over their left arms and in their right each of them held a short spear. The knight who led them had a red livery with five gold stars and he was followed by his squire. He saw us and made his fateful decision. He ordered his men to charge us, telling me that he had not recognised the danger from the trees.

I pointed my lance, "Charge!" I wanted the French distracted and I saw the French knight wave his spear and order his men to close up and to face us. The distraction had worked and when we were just one hundred paces apart I shouted, "Nicholas!"

The arrows flew. The half on the side where the French had shields were less effective than those on the spear side. Two men were unhorsed and I saw others wounded. I watched the light horsemen looking around for the danger and that compounded their error. They were not looking at us as we slammed into them. Even as my lance took a horseman in the shoulder, I saw the banners of the main body approaching. Before I could even order us to withdraw the French knight, his horse wounded, by Sir Geoffrey, ordered them to fall back.

"Hold!" I raised my lance and then pointed west. We turned and headed towards Vez. The archers did not bother unstringing their bows but ran to their horses and mounted them so quickly that we were all riding west at the same time. Horns behind us told me that whoever led this column was remedying his mistake and putting better-armed soldiers to the fore. It was too late. We had delayed them long enough, I believed, for Sir John to have secured the animals and formed a defensive line close by the donjon. To my great relief I saw logs across the road as we approached. We were waved to the side where a gap had been left for us. Sir John had dismounted his lances and his archers stood ready to rain death. One flight of arrows was enough to discourage them and, leaving five men on the ground the rest withdrew beyond the range of our deadly bowmen. I dismounted and handed my reins to David of Denbigh to take to the rear with his horse. I joined Sir John Talbot.

He was speaking to an archer at the top of the tower and cupping his hands to amplify his voice he looked down to me and shouted, "How many?"

I make it more than four hundred mounted men, my lord. Most appear to be men at arms. There are crossbowmen dismounting too."

He raised his hand in acknowledgement and after descending joined us. He looked happy with both our news and the situation. He said to his friend, Sir John de Cressy, Sir Geoffrey and to me, for we were the closest, "I think we have given them a problem. It will be dark soon and they will not relish a night attack."

I ventured, "And I am guessing that they will have raised the local levy as they passed. They will be on foot but by the morning there could be another two hundred men there and peasants and farmers will know how to use the woods. They will wait."

"Sir John, have your men rest. They will begin to drive the animals west at terces."

Sir Geoffrey shook his head, "And they will know then that we are moving."

"Aye, but the majority of us will still be here at the barricade and if they are foolish enough to attack then they will pay a heavy price. We will leave here at noon. Our horses will be well-rested and we can ride them hard." We all nodded. "And tomorrow, my lords, it will be me and my men who will bear the brunt of the attack. We shall be the rearguard. I will not ask another to do that which I will not. We will bring our horses close to the barricade so that when I give the command we abandon the walls, mount and head to Verbier."

We kept one man in four on watch but the French fires were enough illumination for us to see them and with snares set in the woods, we were unmolested. When the animals complained about being moved and made a noise that alerted the French we heard their horns sound and we stood to. We could hear them as they mounted their horses but when the first riders reached the barricades and were struck by arrows, they pulled back. While we, knowing our own plan, went back to bed, the French kept watch, waiting for us to mount our horses and flee.

I was on the early watch and I relieved Sir John Talbot himself who had insisted upon taking on a duty. He chuckled as he headed for his bed, "They have been speaking and we heard them say that we will not trick them this time. They and their horses will be tired come noon."

I wandered the lines after he had gone. I knew some of the men but others were new to me. I made myself known to them. It ensured that they would stay awake for I asked them their names. I had a good memory for such things and knew that a man felt better about his duty if he thought his superior knew his name. I returned to the log barricade and found that Will Green Hose had joined me. "Were you supposed to be on duty, Will?"

34

He shook his head, "I did the first shift but I had to make water and you know how it is, Sir Michael, when you wake, sleep is almost impossible."

Will was one of the older archers and had served with Sir William. Perhaps it was to do with age. I had no problem returning to sleep normally although the weight of leadership had made my sleep thus far lighter. I saw that he had not strung his bow, "Do you not wish to string your bow, Will?"

He shook his head, "They will not come and even if they do night is not the time for arrow work." He patted his short sword. "We are all as skilled with a sword as most of those who we will face, my lord. Give me daylight and a clear line of sight and I will rain death on all that I can see." He smiled, "I hit the long mark each time we practise."

I knew that every archer, even the older ones, would have taken part in the Sunday practice back in their manors. The area chosen would have a series of marks, some would be shorter than others. The longest would be more than three hundred paces long. The narrow target was hard to hit and the best archers took pride in striking the wood at the top of the three hundred pace mark. I had seen men do that who were not even looking at the mark, such was their skill. Once they had hit the target they could keep drawing and hitting almost the same spot each time. Edgar White Streak told me that in battle that was not always advisable. If the enemy warriors were moving then it was good but loosing against crossbows or other archers would be a waste of an arrow.

I watched the shadows moving as the French conferred and studied us. My movement along the line would have alerted them and made them think that we were up to something. Sir John had been clever. Instead of being predictable, he was not doing what the French expected. They would not have done as we had and they were confused. We watched the sky lighten behind the French and heard the commands as they rippled down the French lines. They had wisely dismounted but not we heard the creak of leather as they mounted and the winding of crossbows as they loaded their weapons. We would be in the dark for longer than they would be and they were anticipating our flight. They had been reinforced by the levy and we knew that they outnumbered us. It made sense for us to flee and just before dawn would be the best time. Sir John added to the confusion by ordering, just before the sun climbed above the horizon, the horns sounded. It was just ordering the men to breakfast but the French did not know that and from my position at the fore, I heard the order to prepare to charge. A couple of captured animals had been slaughtered and the smell of their meat cooking confused the French. I saw the knights who were in the centre, now illuminated by the sun, in conference. I recognised the knight with the red livery and golden crowns. There were others close with him wearing a similar livery. The way he waved his arms and shouted commands told me that he was a senior lord.

I was relieved by Sir Geoffrey who came to get me dabbing the meat juices from his lips, "It is fine pork we eat this morning. Sir John ensured that there is plenty left for your watch, Sir Michael."

I nodded, "They are still confused but I would have the archers string their bows. They may tire of just watching and try to take matters into their own hands."

The pork had been fried on iron skillets. As we approached, I saw the men assigned to cook it turn the meat, guaranteeing that it would be hot and juicy. The last of the stale bread was also being fried in the pork juices. I found myself salivating as I approached. The piece proffered to me was from the belly and the fat was just as I liked it, crispy and salty. I had eaten half of it when we heard the horn from the barricade. Clutching the meat in our hands we raced back. By the time we reached the barricade I had crammed the last of it in my mouth and wiped my hands on my tabard. The archers were loosing their arrows already and I saw that Sir Geoffrey had donned his helmet. Mind was at the camp and I would have to rely upon my coif and arming cap. Slipping the mail mittens over my hands I drew my sword and joined my men.

Thomas of Chester pointed as I climbed up the barricade to the step that had been made, "They have made pavise, my lord, and are advancing their crossbows behind them." The Genoese had first used the huge wooden shields called a pavise and they were effective. They allowed crossbowmen to move forward without being struck by arrows.

I nodded and then looked down the barricade. The archers were not discomfited by the move. A crossbow might be ready to release once the pavise was lowered but our archers anticipated such a move and would have an arrow winging its way even as the pavise was lowered. Of course, not every arrow would hit flesh. Many of the crossbowmen now wore mail and some plate. My archers would not waste bodkins until they knew at what they were aiming but even a war arrow could damage a crossbow or ricochet off plate and strike another. The cracks from the crossbows told us when a bolt had been sent. Sensible men ducked behind the logs but I heard the odd cry from down the line as some men were too slow. A bolt striking a helmet could still hurt. I risked another look over the top and saw that a dozen or so crossbowmen had been felled. Some were being helped back to their lines while at least six were dead.

Behind them, I saw that the horsemen had dismounted and were forming a line. They were backed by the levy. Sir John had arrived and seen the same scene as I had done, "Be ready to repel an attack."

There were spears and lances laid by the logs and, sheathing my sword I picked one up and held it in two hands. We continued to duck when bolts were sent but our archers had thinned their ranks enough for them to be sporadic. I heard a command to switch to bodkins. The lances that advanced were encased in plate. War arrows would be wasted. Once the advancing line reached the crossbows and pavise then the bolts were no longer a threat and we could all raise our bodies higher over the barricade. The log barricade could be scaled but not while holding a weapon in two hands. I saw that the front rank carried either pikes or halberds. They would not be climbing for they held two handed weapons. It was the ones behind who carried maces, hammers, axes, and swords who would do that.

The problem men have when fighting an enemy who is above them is that they have to look up and even if they wore a visor they would have to lift it to enable the warriors to see above them. It gave defenders a chance. If we had brought darts with us then we could have guaranteed victory but we had not. The shielded men kept a steady pace as they approached. I saw the knight with red livery with the gold stars. Four men wore a similar livery but theirs had fewer stars. They appeared to be making for our part of the barricade. I knew that was understandable. We had bloodied the knight's nose and now he was bringing his familia to seek revenge. There were eager men at arms who ran at us and tried to use speed to leap up the crude barricade. The barricade was only four logs high but the crude platform we had gave us the advantage of height. The man with the halberd who was the first to reach the logs flailed it above his head to clear a space so that he could use the hook of the halberd to either pull down the barrier or to pull himself up. I waited until the head had passed and then rammed the spearhead into his upper arm. He was a tough man and did not drop the weapon but stepped back. My archers had now selected bodkins and as the plated men at arms and knights drew nearer to us, they were able to send their arrows through the plates of armour and into flesh. It thinned out the numbers. The red liveried men were cautious and full of purpose. They held shields for protection from our arrows and they came at us in a wedge with another five men. I saw their intention. Two had halberds and they would do as the first man had done and pull down the barricade.

Thomas of Chester put down his sword and knelt to pick up a huge stone. He went to the edge and hurled it down. It cracked and smashed into the red shield with the four stars upon it making the man reel and fall back. As he did so I spied my chance and I threw the spear into his right shoulder. It was not the knight but one of those who followed him. It drove through the plate and into flesh. I saw the blood spurt. The one with the five stars shouted, "Get my brother back to the healers." Even as Will Green Hose sent an arrow at him, he flicked his shield up. The arrow went through it forcing him back. The soldier in me wanted to order my archers to kill this leader and to end the attack but the man raised by Sir William had a merciful streak in him. I had hurt his brother, probably killed him and I let him retreat.

I drew my sword. I would not use a shield but, instead, used my mailed left hand as a weapon. The halberd's blade that bit into the top of the log was a danger. The halberdier called to others to help him to pull it. I leaned across and grabbed the hook with my mailed left hand. I could not stop them from pulling but I could slow down their efforts. I raised my sword and hacked down at the wood that was not protected by metal, the langet. My edge was keen and it sliced through the wood easily. The men fell and two arrows slammed into them. I grabbed the halberd and freed it from the wood. I sheathed my sword and held the langet of the halberd so that I could use it as a close-quarter weapon. It proved effective immediately as I hacked down at the helmet of the man who had begun to scale the timber. It dented it and the man fell back. I could see now that while the archers had thinned the ranks of those attacking it was only a matter of time before the barrier was either scaled or knocked down. Sir John showed his skill by choosing the perfect moment to order the horn to sound.

"Back!" I made sure that all my men and archers left the barricade and then ran.

It was as though the presence of so many of us had given the barricade structure for the barricade tumbled and fell along with the French who were pushing. They sprawled helplessly on the ground and tried to rise. Had we not been racing for our horses then we could have made a great slaughter. As it was, we had mounted and the vanguard headed down the road before they rose to run after us. A man in plate armour cannot run very quickly and I knew that the pursuit from the men of Soissons had ended. Our first chevauchée had been spectacularly successful. As we reached Verbier and saw the animals being penned we knew we had enough food and that we would not need to attempt such a large raid again. We could hit and run using our mounted archers to hit at a distance and to disrupt the life of this part of France.

Chapter 4

It was in the middle of January and the ground was hard when Sir John sent for the leaders of his lances. We had spent a couple of months riding wherever we wished raiding villages and taking animals. We lost not a man and the greatest danger we had was the supply of arrows. When the snow came at the end of December, we used the week to make new ones. The rest helped both men and horses. We had taken fodder on our last raid before Christmas as well as some animals. It meant we ate well as the New Year approached. When the snow stopped and the ground was covered in a white blanket we hunkered down in our camp. The woods provided the kindling for our fires and we were hardy men. With the wine we had taken we dined like lords although it was in the open air. I ate with my men and shared the same conditions as they. The result was that I saw little of Sir John and the knights closest to him as they planned our next moves. In the absence of my real family, the brothers in arms alongside whom I fought were a good substitute. The younger ones were like my children while the older ones were like Isabelle's father, Henri, and we acted like a family, albeit one made totally of men. They told tales and sang songs. They shared memories of battles past and warriors now dead. I saw the younger ones taking in their words. Many of the songs and stories were about Sir William. He had made mighty footprints and I was daunted at the prospect of following in them. So when Sir John de Cressy fetched me for the meeting with Sir John Talbot, I was ready for with Christmas gone I was anxious to get the job we had come here for, done.

Our charismatic leader was in an ebullient mood, "We have done well since we came here and we are all richer." We had not taken ransom but some of the villages and smaller towns had offered us money to stop us raiding. They could not eat their coins and as the money was intended for Spring taxes, they would worry about that when the time came. "I had not planned it this way but I think that we can relieve the siege of Compiègne."

We all looked at each other. Raiding was one thing. We could hit and run but attacking siege lines was an altogether different prospect. The French camps were like hamlets surrounding Compiègne. The walls were not being assaulted but the people starved. Our raids had slowed the food reaching the besiegers but the people of Compiègne were suffering more. I understood Sir John's hope but feared it would cost us men.

He smiled at the doubt on our faces, "I am not so foolish as to think that this will be easy but on my last raid, I passed close to the French lines. They keep a watch but they have become complacent. We were with two hundred paces before we were seen."

I immediately saw what Sir John had. Archers could loose from that range and unsuspecting men in the French camps could be easily slain.

"We use our archers to approach one section of the camps while the lances wait mounted. When ten flights of arrows have descended then we follow up with horses. My intention is to destroy one part of the French lines and then ride along the rest to sweep them away. The ground is hard that will suit our horses and we shall have complete surprise." He smiled, "Only a fool would attack in the middle of winter, eh?"

He had thought it out well and the detailed orders he gave us all showed that he had been thinking about this for some time. I suppose we all knew that we would be relieving the siege at some stage but we had enjoyed such success raiding and building up our supplies that we had lost sight of the ultimate aim of the chevauchée.

"We ride after Laudes and I plan on attacking as the sun rises to the east. We will attack from the southwest and should enjoy winter morning darkness. Heed the commands from my horn. If nothing else our attack on Braine showed us how to work together and to listen to my orders. Tomorrow will be even more crucial and may mean that we can travel home come the next summer." He smiled, "By then Lord Somerset will have assembled the army with which we can retake France."

My men were keen for action and with a new supply of arrows and horses that had rested for almost two weeks we were confident. The servants would not be coming with us but they had enjoyed the enforced sojourn of a snowbound Christmas. They would prepare our home for our return.

Our archers did not ride with us but went ahead. They would have to walk the last half a mile and get into position. Sir John had his own captain, Ralph of Cheshire commanding them and he would be the one to order the arrows to fall. Our small conroi of lances walked our horses towards the siege lines. The fires lit to keep the besiegers warm were a clear marker for us. The ground was hard but there was enough snow left to deaden the sound of our horses. Sir John had planned cleverly. Most armies did not fight in winter. Our camp, being so close to the French lines gave us a unique opportunity to break the unwritten rules. I knew that the French siege lines would have been ready for an attack when we had arrived in late autumn but our raids, especially the one on Braine, would have led them to believe that they were safe. The French warriors would be huddled in their blankets and praying that the people of Compiègne would surrender soon.

Sir John had to have scouted out the ground recently for, even though the snow made a blanket of the land he knew exactly where to stop. He held up his hand and dismounted to adjust his girths. Most of us emulated him for a slipping saddle could be fatal. When he clambered back into his saddle he donned his helmet, unslung his shield and held his lance. I did not bother with a helmet but I hung my shield from my shoulder with the long strap. It was an old fashioned habit; I knew the Conqueror's horsemen had done the same with their long shields but Sir William had used the technique and I saw no reason to change it. The advantage was that my left hand was free to guide my horse more accurately. He waited and seemed to be listening. I heard the noise he sought at the same time as he. It was the sound of bowstrings thrumming and arrows soaring through the air. He did not sound a horn, that would be needed later, but instead, he pointed his lance and we began to trot in a long double line towards the campfires.

The cries and shouts told us that the French had been struck by the shower of missiles. Sir John, like the rest of us, knew just how long it would take for ten arrows to be sent and as we began to gallop, I reckoned that we would strike the disorganized camp just moments after the last arrow had plunged to earth. The fires illuminated the camp and I saw that a swathe through the middle had been cut by the archers. There was a patch of their lines one hundred and forty paces wide and all that we could see were bodies of the dead and wounded while the odd survivor tried to help wounded comrades. Our hooves thundered and they abandoned their merciful task and ran towards the other camps which, while not yet attacked, were confused by the cries and the thundering hooves that came out of the dark night. When a man wakes in the night he is disorientated. We struck the next camp as men left their tents and hovels to seek the enemy. The man at arms I lanced had managed to don his mail hauberk and grab a sword but his weak swash did not make my lance deviate and he died quickly as the lance struck his body and I flicked aside as I passed. We could not help but trample on some of the besiegers. The sun was a thin line of light to the east and the fires were still the main form of illumination. As we passed through the second group of tents Sir John, who was just ten men from me, turned to his squire who sounded the horn twice. That was the command for the archers to mount and follow us and for us to reform our lines.

I reined in Storm and patted his neck. He was not even sweating yet for the magnificent animal had been made for war. "Good boy."

41

I found that I was next to Sir Geoffrey and Sir John de Cressy. Sir Geoffrey raised his visor. "We caught them unawares, eh?"

I shook my head, "But now they are awake and we will have to face armed and visored men. This will not be as easy."

The horn sounded three times, the signal to charge and we began to trot towards the French who were now forming their own defence in a long double line. Sir John intended to take us due east towards the rising sun and to sweep up the French. They might have outnumbered us when we had begun our ride but they were spread around the town in a circle and each group we charged were themselves outnumbered. Unless they rallied all their men and brought them together to face us then all would be lost. That Sir John had scouted well became clear when we saw the flags and standards of their leaders. Our first attack had been upon the camp closest to theirs and with that destroyed their leaders and their bodyguards were hastily donning mail, plate and arming themselves. I saw a line of spears and lances ahead. They had taken their lances and other long weapons to ram them into the ground before them. The snow had been churned up by their feet and the wood of their lances had a little purchase. I knew it would not be enough. The problem for us would be to get through the wooden wall. Our horses wore mail and plate about their heads and chests and for that I was grateful. It would take a lucky strike to find horseflesh. Had they used poleaxes I would have been more worried. An axe head could take a leg and unhorse a rider.

We kept a steady pace as we neared the French. Sir John was not riding too fast to the embedded lances and spears for he wanted us to hit at the same time. The sun had now risen and was shining, albeit through clouds, at us. The occasional shaft of sunlight peering through flickered off polished plate and mail. We had parity of numbers with the men on foot. Ralph of Cheshire and our archers would be running behind us ready to add their arrows to the attack but we would have clashed with the spears and lances by the time they arrived. Sir John Talbot was in the centre of our line and we were to the left of him. He was a leader after my own heart. He led from the front. It was his lance that made the first contact and his horse that bore the brunt of the first French lances and spears. The metal heads clattered and clashed off his horse's armour. I was not watching him but the sound was a warning that soon I would be the one negotiating the herisson of spears. I did not wait for them to strike me. Standing in my saddle I leaned forward to thrust over the waiting weapons at the face of the man at arms holding his long lance in two hands. The head of the spear struck Storm a heartbeat before my lance slid into his face. His weapon fell from lifeless hands as his body slid to the ground to become a barrier, not for us but his comrades. Sir John de Cressy must have enjoyed similar success for the integrity of the line was broken. Some of the spears and lances that had faced us were shattered and our metalled mounts shouldered aside men who had managed to don some mail and plate. Horses' hooves trampled those who slipped and fell on the claggy surface on which they tried to stand. The French did not break, they were simply destroyed by horsemen who had caught them unawares. It was the rest of the French who broke. With the sun now risen the other camps had heard the noise of battle and now with dawn upon them, they saw a line of armoured horsemen holding bloody spears galloping towards them. There was no order to the French. We had broken them and there was no Maid or la Hire to rally them. The lack of flags and standards was enough to tell them that their lords and leaders had been defeated and they took to their heels and ran. Those that could tried to grab horses but most were just happy to escape with their lives. By the time we had rounded the town and reached the north their camps were abandoned and there was a stream of men heading east. Had we had more men or some light cavalry then they could have been pursued and then destroyed. However, Sir John had achieved all that he wished to achieve. The siege was over and the town we had captured some years earlier was now secure in English hands once more. I wondered if he would allow us to return to our homes.

He did not although it was an act of nature that prevented us from simply travelling back to Rouen. After clearing the French camps, an act that brought great profit to all the men who did so, we were sent in four columns of lances to scour the land and ensure that all those who had fled had left the territory controlled by us. It took two weeks. That long week was a period of benign weather but then it was as though nature decided to punish us. Ice first descended, actually freezing to death one sentry on the walls of Compiègne and then a wall of snow fell for three days before the freeze returned. We then fought a war, not against the French but nature itself and the battle was to get enough firewood to keep fires burning and to, slaughter, each day, enough of the captured animals from Braine to keep us alive.

Each company became responsible for its own survival and I was lucky that I had so many older heads to help the younger ones cope. We had been sent back to Verbier to guard the animals and so we were in the temporary structures we had erected in autumn. That we had built well saved us for my men had hewn trees to make log shelters and packed the spaces with mud. The freeze made them as solid as stone. The proximity of the forest gave us enough wood for our fires and my skilled archers ensured that we had enough fresh meat as they hunted the older, weaker deer who were succumbing to the cold. The battle drew us together and each night we gathered around fires that, with the death of the frozen sentry in mind, were kept constantly fed. We told tales and we spoke of plans for the future. I was with, in the main, bachelors and it was as we sat beneath whatever skins and furs we could find, that I heard of their wish to become fathers. This was a change from the army I had followed at Agincourt. Then all thoughts of family and future were forgotten as men fought for a courageous king in whom we all passionately believed. Now we knew that this was a war we could not win. Sir John Talbot was a hope that we might not lose but even when the army had tramped around the Pays de Caux, trying to escape the mighty French army, we had not thought of defeat. Now we did.

"And you, Sir Michael, what are your plans?"

We had grown so close that Mark the Bowyer's question, which might have seemed impertinent to some lords, appeared perfectly reasonable to me. I smiled, "I have a son but Lady Isabelle will hopefully bear me a second." I laughed, "I hope for more. I will be content with another two children."

"Aye, lord, but in Normandy? You have two manors in England that are both bigger and more profitable."

Mark had returned to England with Edgar White Streak and he spoke with authority.

"Les Pérets may not have the income of the others but Lady Isabelle's parents live there and, to be truthful, Mark, I like its situation. I am not so ambitious that I seek more and more wealth. I have enough to pay men like you," I swept my hand around the campfire, "and my wife does not crave richly decorated clothes and fancy knick-knacks like many ladies. I have known what it is to have nothing and I was pulled back from the brink of an eternal sleep by Sir William and Rafe. I value each moment of every day now."

Nicholas nodded as he threw another piece of wood on the fire. There must have been some resin in it for it sizzled and sputtered as he did so. "Aye, this would be a good time to return to England for we could do so with the knowledge that we had left with a great victory. It was no Agincourt and we fought men who were unprepared but we won and after the devastation wrought by the Maid that is enough for me." He lowered his voice, "Perhaps she was sent by God and we should heed the warning."

The time we had spent escorting Jeanne d'Arc had made my men understand her better than most Englishmen and Normans who seemed to regard her as some sort of witch. I knew that she had been many things but a witch was not one of them for she had believed in what she said. I did not know if God had spoken to her. That seemed blasphemous but she believed it and if it was a delusion then it had been one which had defeated us.

Chapter 5

It was the start of April before we were able to return home. The icy weather had lasted until the end of February and then Sir John seemed keen to impress his authority on the French. We were sent to raid deeper into French held lands. It was almost as though he was daring the French to challenge him. We heard that they now had two leaders, Jean Poton de Xaintrailles, Seneschal of Limousin, and the man who had been exchanged for Sir John Talbot and Étienne de Vignolles who were gathering armies to fight us. Étienne de Vignolles was known as, La Hire, the Wrath of God and had been at Agincourt. Both men were not to be underestimated. The fact that de Xaintrailles had been exchanged for Sir John showed how much the French king regarded him. There was also a rumour that our allies, the Burgundians, were becoming disenchanted with the alliance. I knew that if they deserted us then we would struggle to defeat the French and if they joined the French then we would most definitely lose.

Sir John showed no signs of wishing to leave this part of France but when Lord Somerset arrived at the end of the first week of April with fresh soldiers, I sought an audience with him. I was forced to wait for more than an hour for he was in conference with Lord Somerset but, eventually, he emerged and we walked the walls of Compiègne to enjoy the spring sunshine, "So, Sir Michael, now that Lord Somerset is here, we can finally take this war to the French. Good news, eh?"

I shook my head, "No, my lord, it is not. My men and I have fulfilled our obligation. We did as we were asked and, I hope, we have satisfied you."

"Yes, and more. I confess that I am disappointed in your words. I had hoped to have you as a lieutenant who would ride at my side when we face La Hire and de Xaintrailles. You have lived up to my expectations and more."

"Thank you, for those kind words but I would return to my family and my men are of the same opinion."

He leaned on the parapet of the stone walls of Compiègne and peered east. He said nothing for a while and then nodded, "I am loath to lose you. What say I give you and your men a furlough for three months. Let us see what effect that time has upon you. I am gambling that you and your men, the dogs of war, will find that you need to go to war and will return, refreshed and ready to retake France."

Three months was not enough but I would take it and hope that Sir John forgot about us. "Thank you, my lord."

He smiled and wagged a finger at me, "I shall send a rider for you, three months from now and I will expect you to respond immediately." His eyes told me that he would not forget.

The arrival of fresh troops meant that, as we rode west, to our home, it was through a land that had been agitated by their passing. Friend and foe alike guarded food, water and shelters. It was not a long journey but an uncomfortable one and we were all keen to reach Les Pérets and its comforting welcome. The last afternoon we hurried to reach the comfort and warmth of our riverside home.

We found a burning hall and the men of the manor working under the supervision of Charles and Cedric to salvage what they could. The fire had taken half of the hall but the other half smoked and sizzled as buckets of river water were used to douse it. The villagers looked to have won the battle but the hall would need to be rebuilt. I dismounted and walked towards them but I was terrified that I would hear news that might destroy me. My fear must have been clearly marked on my face for as Charles strode towards me, his face was dark, he said, "My lord, your wife and son are safe and are with the Archbishop in Rouen."

I felt the relief surge through my body but knowing that my family were safe made me want to know what had happened. "Is Maud with them? Where is Henri, your parents?"

His voice almost broke as he said, "They are dead, my lord."

Cedric said, "As are John and Walter, my lord." They were two of my billmen.

Thomas of Chester took Storm's reins, "You three speak, my lord and we will see to the horses and help the villagers."

Charles said, "All is not lost, Thomas, the hall was destroyed but the barns, kitchens and outbuildings survive. There will be a roof over your heads this night." Thomas nodded and Charles added, "We have a table and chairs we recovered. The tale is one that needs to be told while you are sitting. I am not yet sure if I can tell it."

As we headed to the table with the wine and beakers upon it Cedric said, "Then I will tell it, Charles and Sir Michael can decide if I am fit to serve him still."

I walked in a daze for I was stunned. I had returned to a home that was a home no more. Henri and Maud are both dead and, from the newly turned graves, others too.

Charles poured and handed me the wine while Cedric spoke. "It was a week since that Lady Isabelle decided to ride into Rouen for she wished to buy some material to make into new bedding. Henri asked Charles to buy some nails from the smith and to buy hoops for the new barrels we would need. He gave Charles the chest with the gold and asked Robert and me to act as guards. We left before dawn for we had much to do." He shook his head and sighed, "Things did not go smoothly, my lord and the hoops were not ready."

He hesitated and Charles said, "It is my fault, lord, I said that rather than make two journeys we should wait for the hoops to be finished. We did not leave Rouen until it was almost dark."

I saw that Charles was distressed and Cedric put his hand upon Isabelle's uncle's arm, "Peace. None could have known. The building was fired just before we reached it and we heard the horses as the men who did this fled at our approach. Perhaps they thought we brought more men. The villagers joined us as we fought the flames and found the bodies. Henri had been slain outside the door. Maud and two of the servant girls were burned in the hall and even Father Michel had been slain as he tried to protect the church. Four men and youths from the village were also slain."

"John and Walter?"

"Walter had been on duty, I think, for his throat was cut. John had been gutted by an axe but he lived long enough to tell us what had happened. The villagers confirmed it. The raiders, there were twenty of them, came upriver and slipped ashore from a barge just before dawn. From what I gathered from their words they must have come not long after we left. John was in the kitchen helping to prepare food and Walter must have been killed by an assassin. It was Henri who saw the men and raised the alarm but by then it was too late. The foxes were in the henhouse. John managed to kill one and Henri another but the men who came were soldiers."

I knew that I was still in shock but none of this made sense. "But who did this and why? It makes no sense."

Cedric said, quietly, "John said that the man who fought with Charles was with them." I knew then that my men had been right. I should have had the man arrested. "They were led by a knight with a red livery and five gold stars. One of the villagers said he heard him addressed as Sir Maximilian."

It was the knight from the battle in the woods. I should have killed him along with his brother. My mercy had brought this upon us.

"I will go to my wife and child." I could see that both men were distraught and I knew from their words, blamed themselves. "The two of you have nothing to be ashamed of. My wife and son are safe and that is thanks to you. If anyone is to blame it is I. Jacques should have been gaoled and I had the opportunity to slay Sir Maximilian and did not."

Charles asked, "What will you do, my lord?"

I shook my head, "I do not know yet. After I have spoken with Lady Isabelle, I will have a better idea."

"Do you need an escort, my lord?"

"No, but I will spend the night in Rouen." I swept a hand around the remains of my hall, "What is left for me here?"

I was angry as I rode an already weary Storm towards Rouen. I could have ridden Shadow, which was now my only spare horse, the rest having been stolen but I wanted the comfort of my best horse. I was angry because I had been far from my home when it was attacked. Had I been there then Henri, Maud, Father Michel, and the others would be alive for none would dare attack whilst I was in residence. The war that Sir John Talbot fought was a pointless war we could never win, I saw that now. It was not a long ride but I debated, during the ride about what to do. Much would depend upon my wife but I knew that I could not leave Sir Maximilian alive. It was not simply a matter of revenge, it was of a more practical nature. He had come for vengeance of his own and the deaths of two old men and a woman would not satisfy it. I guessed that I must have slain someone close to him during the chase along with his brother, wounded at the battle of Vez. I was still alive and so long as I was then the worm of vengeance would eat at him. I knew as I reined in outside the archbishop's palace, that I would need to put on a face for my wife. She could not see the anger that burned within me. She would be grieving for her lost family.

The archbishop had his own guards and I was relieved to see that they were alert. The sergeant at arms said, "I am sorry for your loss, my lord. It was a wicked thing that happened."

I nodded but I knew that Sir John had emptied the garrison of its best warriors and horses when we had set off on our raid. The ones who had been left were the old, the drunks and the ones unfit to fight. Sir Maximilian had known that he could raid with impunity. That he had not taken the gold hidden beneath the floorboards was pure luck.

"Aye, and had we had a full garrison here..."

"We heard they came and left by barge, my lord. The winds for the journey upstream were propitious."

I knew that I needed more information about Sir Maximilian before I could even contemplate ridding the world of him. I put that thought from my mind as I was taken to the rooms the archbishop had allocated. I was gratified that there was a sentry on that door too. Isabelle would need reassurance. The guard opened the door and stood back. Isabelle saw me standing in the doorway and ran to me. She was now well into the pregnancy and heavy with child. I saw that Jean was asleep. She said not a word but sobbed silently into my shoulder and I stroked her hair. This was not a time for words but soft touches. She stopped and I led her to the bed where we sat while our son made the soft gurgling sounds of a child content and asleep.

Isabelle nestled her head in my arm and looked up at me, "Why did death sweep his hand to take away my family?"

I kissed her forehead, "Death is cruel and strikes where least you expect it but you have a family: there is Jean and there is me. You have Eleanor in England and an uncle you thought dead. My heart breaks as does yours for Maud and Henri for they were as close to me as my own parents but we cannot bring them back."

She began to sob again, "But the fire, the blood…"

"Put those from your mind. Know that they were good people who were killed and will be with God." We both made the sign of the cross.

Her sobs subsided and after she had control of herself she said, firmly, "I will not go back to Les Pérets. It was our home but even if you rebuilt it then I would still be haunted by the memory of what went on. I cannot return there."

"And you need not. There is Weedon and Iden. Both are good manors. Eleanor lives at Weedon and I bear its name."

She looked up and her face, though wet from tears was bright with hope, "Then let us take ship now and go there. We shall quit this land of Normandy where there is death around every corner and so much hate that it permeates the ground."

I could not dash her hopes nor could I simply leave France for with Sir Maximilian still walking the earth there was always a chance that he would seek vengeance. I either had to kill him or bring him to justice. "I have work to do at the manor but I can send you and most of my men back to Weedon while I see to the stewardship of the manor. We owe the people that much." I was being economic with the truth and implying that I would be hard on her heels; I would not.

She stared into my eyes looking for the lie. "We should all travel together."

Shaking my head I said, "The archbishop has been kind but it may take a month or more. The sooner you and Jean travel then the happier I will be."

I was not sure she was convinced but she nodded, "They need headstones. We buried them but the graves should be marked. One day our son, or his son, may well wish to return to visit their grandfather and grandmother."

"Then decide the words and I will pay Philippe of Rouen to carve stones in the same stone they used at Caen." Philippe of Rouen was the finest Norman mason and his work would not be cheap but Henri and Maud deserved the best.

"I am content. You will stay the night? I would lie in your arms again and Jean needs to see your face." She gave a soft smile, "Just hold me for the babe will be born within the next month or so."

I held her tightly. It was now even more imperative to take her to safety. "Then our new child will be born in England."

I left the next morning and was at Les Pérets as the house was rising. Men had not been idle and the damage was already being repaired. It was almost as though the men were trying to scour the scar from the land. They were at breakfast in the barn when I arrived and every eye swivelled to me. I had decided, during my trouble night of intermittent sleep that I would be as honest as I could be with my men. However, as with my wife, I could not let them know my innermost thoughts. I had spoken to the archbishop who knew much and he told me that Sir Maximilian lived at Château-Thierry as a guest of the Seigneur of Soissons.

His words had been cautionary, "Sir Michael, I understand your loss but the castle is a secure one and Sir Maximilian, although he has committed a most heinous crime is safe under the protection of the Seigneur. We all know that he and his men perpetrated this atrocity but there is little direct proof as the ones who reported his presence are not men of substance."

"But their birth should have nothing to do with their evidence."

The old man smiled, "That should be true but we live in a world, Sir Michael where my word and that of a duke or a king carries greater weight than that of a noble, even one as highly thought of as you. And we both know that a knight's word is considered to be more truthful than a simple farmer."

Those words still rang in my ears. I had hoped that I could bring Sir Maximilian to justice through legal means. That would not happen now. I looked at the expectant faces around the table. The one I knew the least was Charles, Henri's brother and yet he would be the one who, like me, yearned for vengeance.

Thomas of Chester said, "How is Lady Isabelle, my lord?"

Honesty would be the best policy in regard to my wife, "She will not return here to Les Pérets. I intend to send her back to Weedon as soon as I can manage to secure a berth for her," I paused, "and those of you who wish to return to England."

Their faces told me that they all wished to do so. Charles' face wrinkled in a frown, "And what of the manor, Sir Michael? Is that and

51

its people to be abandoned?" There was thinly veiled criticism in his voice.

I turned to look at him, "I will speak openly for all those around this table, Charles, have shed blood with me and for me. We are brothers in arms and there are no secrets. You and I have yet to fight together yet we have shared a common loss. You have lost your brother and I have lost a good friend and the steward to my land. When I have done what must be done then I will return with my wife to Weedon for I would be where my family resides. I will seek a steward for my manor. I had thought to ask you. What say you?"

He looked stunned, "I would be honoured but you barely know me."

"We are family and that is enough." I turned my gaze to the others, "Are there any of you who would wish to be a steward for me here as Edgar White Streak is at Iden?"

Nicholas Warbag laughed, "The sooner we quit this troubled land the better, my lord. Seeing what has happened here makes me even more determined to do as Edgar has done and start a family and put down roots in good English soil."

I saw my other men all nod, "So Charles, what do you say?"

"I will agree, Sir Michael, but I need to know what happens to Sir Maximilian? Does his crime escape justice?"

"No, for when my men and wife had left Normandy I shall travel to Château-Thierry and apprehend this killer of women and return him here for English justice."

The barn erupted as every man tried to speak at once. The odd word I heard was an objection to being left behind. I held up my hands for silence and eventually, the rage subsided. "What I have to do is personal. I do not want this French knight to follow us to England and to hurt us. Although it is unlikely that he will the possibility means that I must quash it. I cannot ask any man to follow me and so I will go alone."

Nicholas Warbag said, "You need archers with you, my lord and I know I speak for all my companions when I say that we would be honoured to do so."

"And archers would be perfect save for one thing, Nicholas." Every archer looked quizzically at me, "We have to travel through France in disguise for Château-Thierry is deep in French territory. Even a disguised archer cannot hide his longbow. If I took even one archer then word would spread of Englishmen travelling east. Sir Maximilian would hear of it and the quest would end before it began. I do not intend to leave any more friends in France."

Thomas of Chester said, "Aye, but you can take men at arms!"

My lances all banged the table until I shook my head, "The number who travel must be few. If I am to travel with any then it would be three companions at the most."

Hands were raised but before I could speak Charles said, quietly, "Sir Michael, your French is perfect. You could pass through France, disguised, of course, but most of your men would stand out as soon as they spoke and mutes would be viewed suspiciously. I can see that you will need me, not least because I served with the French army around Soissons and I can find ways to get there, unseen."

He was right of course and it made perfect sense to me. I nodded. "You can be one of my companions."

Thomas of Chester said, "Sir Michael, Charles' words make sense but there are just four of us who served with you in England. Take us four, Geoffrey, Richard, David and me."

"Four is the number and I know that Richard and David have roots already in England." The two men at arms looked at each other. They had confided in me that when they had been in England both had been courting young women and having obeyed the call to arms, I had made would when they returned to England they would wed. "You and Geoffrey have been with me here the longest and your French is the best. You shall come with me."

Thus it was decided.

Nicholas War Bag was resigned but he asked, "And do you tell Lady Isabelle of your plan, my lord?"

The silence was as thick as a winter fog. I sighed and shook my head, "No, and none of you, on the journey to Weedon, shall tell her. We have a week to find a ship and for you to settle any affairs you have here at Les Pérets. As far as my wife is concerned, I need to travel east to speak to Sir John Talbot and to tell him of my decision to leave France. That she will understand."

They nodded and Thomas of Chester grinned, "And that, my lord, shows your cunning for we can travel east openly as far as the English campo and merely adopt a disguise when we make the journey to Château-Thierry."

He was right but he was giving me more credit than I deserved, that thought had not even entered my head. "Thomas, you, Geoffrey and Charles will select the horses you will need. I will take Shadow. Storm is too well known although I will ride Storm to Compiègne to add to the illusion. We will need a sumpter too. I will work out the rest of the plan when my wife is safely at sea." I lowered my voice. "All of you are trusted. Not a word should escape for if it does then there are four of us who shall not return from our quest."

Chapter 6

During the week, although I spent as much time with all my men as I could I spoke the most with the three who would be riding with me. We refined the plan. It was Thomas who suggested that when we left Sir John Talbot, we pretended to be swords for hire heading for Italy and wars that seemed to fill the troubled land. Each night I rode back to Rouen to spend time with my family and to let the archbishop and the castellan know of my plans. That was important as I knew that there would be spies in the city who would report even such minor details to their lords and masters. It would be only after I left Sir John that I would disappear. While Isabelle was slightly suspicious, she understood that I would have to tell my liege lord that I was leaving Normandy and ask his permission for Charles to be steward. That was the part of the plan she liked for she saw that there could be continuity between her father and his brother and she knew that the graves would be tended. She understood that the dead had to be remembered.

As part of the plan, I searched for surcoats, not plain ones for that would have aroused suspicion but faded old ones, all different, with liveries that were hard to make out. There were some in the manor and I found others for sale in Rouen market. Old soldiers sold whatever they could to buy food and wine. The warrior hall had been largely untouched by the raiders and the old armour and weapons were still there. They had been left in the roof space. We found four old mail hauberks and old-fashioned helmets. We had to appear as soldiers who were down on their luck. Of course, we could not present ourselves to Sir John wearing such war gear and so four of my archers would ride with us to his camp and they would bring our plate back to Rouen and thence to England.

By the sixth day, all was in place. My family and most of my men, not to mention our horses, would leave the next day on the two cogs I had hired to take them to Tilbury and thence to Weedon. I stayed, along with my men in Rouen. I was accommodated with my family and my men in inns. Once again it was part of the deception and the illusion. They would all talk of the return to England and my enemies would have the news confirmed. The archbishop threw me a feast. It was a small one but Charles was invited. The archbishop had approved of my choice of steward. And this was a way for the two of them to get to know each other.

After the meal was finished and Isabelle had taken my weary son to bed the three of us spoke. "I am sure that Sir John and the Duke of Bedford will approve of the choice of steward but you realise that this will involve a commitment from you to defend Normandy?" He spoke to Charles, who nodded.

"I do and you should know that while I fought for the Maid, now that she is dead, I will honour the man who gave my family a home. I will defend it with my life."

I patted the back of his hand, "Let us hope it does not come to that. I just hope that Rouen is better defended."

Charles nodded grimly. He had not wasted the week and had spoken to the men of the village at length, "Do not worry, Sir Michael, the men of Les Pérets have told me that they feel guilty that Sir Maximilian was able to do what he did. They will make the manor and the village stronger. I will make them into warriors."

That night Isabelle lay in my arms, "You will follow us as soon as you can, my husband?"

"Of course. I shall speak with Sir John and then spend a few days with Charles to ensure he is happy with his task and then I shall return to England. I will be no more than a month."

"A month!"

I heard the alarm in her voice, "Peace, peace, I have to hire another ship. It may well just be a fortnight but if I say a fortnight then you will worry and fret when I do not arrive. A month is longer than I shall need. It will pass soon enough for you will have much to tell Eleanor and the two of you will need to work out an arrangement for the hall. She is the mistress at the moment but you will be the lady of the manor."

She had not thought of that and we spent a short time speaking of the house before she fell asleep. I hated the deception but I could not have a pregnant woman worrying about me.

The ship left on the morning tide that was at its height before dawn truly broke.

I returned to Les Pérets and it seemed emptier somehow and more desolate. Less than a quarter had been destroyed but as it was the main living quarters it seemed to hurt more. There were no guards left. My billmen were with my family on the ship. The manor would be watched over by the villagers. We eight warriors, with four sumpters, left Les Pérets on that chilly Spring morning, and I was not sure that we would return. I had been riding through France for many years but having a Frenchman with us made it, somehow, easier. My French was good but perhaps too good as people knew I was English. I had no regional accent. Charles knew the right words to speak and the right places to stay. The journey east was very easy. My archers knew that they had the easier task and when we reached Sir John their work would largely be over. They took it upon themselves to be our sentries and to ride at the front as well as at the rear so that the four who would perform the quest were cocooned. The four of us who would have the task of, somehow, securing Sir Maximilian did not waste the precious time bought for us by the vigilance of our archers. We spent the whole time working on our story and planning how we might achieve our ends.

Charles' knowledge was proving invaluable and he pointed out pitfalls we had not considered, "I think, Sir Michael, that this will not be easy. The castle is a strong one and the men who guard it will be wary. I am not sure that can affect an entry to the castle."

I had been able to think about this for longer and I had an answer to the objections from Charles, "We do not try to enter the castle. He must leave the castle sometime. Perhaps he hunts or he might have a dalliance with a young lady. Who knows he may have to visit some elevated lord to be given commands? We watch and we work quickly. When we see him either alone or with a few men around him we take him. We need to be neither subtle nor gentle. Once we have him then we make our escape."

Thomas shook his head, "I am sorry, my lord, but we do need to be subtle. When we take him, it will be clear who has done this and they will know that we will head for Rouen. No matter how clever we are we cannot escape that."

He was right and, as we approached Compiègne I set my mind to the problem of finding a way of escaping with our lives.

There was an armed camp outside the town but it was half-deserted. Lord Somerset had men probing the French positions. Neither he nor Sir John Talbot were in camp. While my men made a small camp, far from the centre, I sought news from other knights alongside whom we had fought. I found Sir Geoffrey in the town at his quarters. Men knew both me and the knight and were happy to direct me.

"You are back sooner than we expected. Sir John will be pleased."

I was non-committal and merely nodded, "How goes it?"

He poured me a beaker of wine, "It is strange. The French seem reluctant to fight. I do not think that they fear us but their leaders are more cautious. They squat behind the walls of their castles and walled cities and seem to dare us to take them. Of course, we will not. Attacking walls merely wastes men."

That was not quite true. We had failed badly at Orléans but the Maid had succeeded. I suppose it depended on how desperately you wanted it. She had wanted the monumental victory and even though she had been wounded she had succeeded and we had lost many good men.

He poured me a beaker of wine and continued, "We do much as we did when you were here and take animals and crops. They have learned from Braine and now they have patrols of their own so that there are clashes on the roads. There, they are the equal of us, for our men cannot loose arrows from the back of a horse. No one wins."

If I had harboured any doubts about my decision to return to England then the conversation with Sir Geoffrey dispelled them. The war would grind on interminably and suit only those who sought to become more powerful. More importantly, it also gave me a glimpse of how I might take Sir Maximilian.

I waited until Sir John had returned and spoken to Lord Somerset. As he walked back to his quarters, close to those of Sir Geoffrey, I accosted him and his squire. He looked genuinely pleased to see me, "Sir Michael, this is a joyous meeting. You are back and refreshed."

I shook my head, "The very opposite, Sir John. I come to tell you that I will be leaving France."

His face darkened, "Come, this is not the place for such words, Robert, have food fetched."

We entered the house. It had belonged to a rich French sympathiser and when the town had first fallen to the English he had fled. Sir John benefitted from the sumptuous quarters. We discarded our cloaks and sat before the fire. He poured me wine and then gestured for me to speak. I told him what I had discovered when I reached my home, I told him who had committed the atrocity and that my wife and men were already heading for England.

"I felt I owed you the courtesy of hearing the words from my lips and not from a letter."

"You are a noble, honourable and courteous knight and I am sorry for your loss. It should not have happened. If we cannot guard the homes of the men who fight to secure the French crown for King Henry then it is a poor show. Will you not reconsider? Your wife and family will be safe in England. You can still fight and have your revenge through your sword."

I knew that Sir John had a wife in England. I did not know the relationship but I had married for love and I had a greater attachment to my family than to a crown. Sir John appeared to value service for a boy-king as being more worthy than a family.

"My lord, my family is more important." I hesitated, "Who is it, my lord, that prosecutes this war?"

My question seemed to confuse him, "Prosecute? Why Lord Somerset and I, of course."

"And the Duke of Bedford, is he not the Governor of Normandy and yet he does not go to war but sits in his home, Castle of Joyeux Repos, reading, I hear, manuscripts taken from Paris?"

His eyes narrowed, "Sir Michael, this does you no credit and borders on the treasonous. I will forgive it just this once as I can see that you are upset but do not impugn our leader."

I knew that the duke and Sir John were good friends but I had started down this path and I had to follow it, "And his brother, the Duke of Gloucester, stays in England shaping the young King Henry to his mind." He was about to speak when I continued, "You know, my lord that, King Henry's father appointed me to be his bodyguard and mentor. When the king died the two dukes removed me."

"So you are bitter and resentful?" He thought he knew me from my words and had the answer. He was wrong.

"No, I merely point out that Good King Henry that was taken from us too soon knew that his son needed a guardian who would shield him from political interference. Sir William Strongstaff had done much the same for him. I mean no disrespect but I am giving you my honest reasons why I cannot stay."

He gave me a wry smile, "I did not know Sir William well but from what I have heard he would be proud of his protégé. Like the old knight, you are not afraid to show your colours. I understand your words and whilst I would have you stay here with the army I cannot while you harbour such potentially seditious thoughts. Perhaps it is better for all concerned if you return to England."

Robert entered with the food. "Ah, food. Robert, have my clerk calculate how much pay is due to Sir Michael for his service thus far and bring it to me."

"My lord, he is at supper."

Sir John's voice became hard, "Do I command here or Ralph's stomach? Do it."

When he had gone and we had begun to eat he said, "Better this way where we part as friends and all debts paid than either of us harbour either regrets or grudges, eh?"

As we ate and spoke it emerged that he was not particularly interested in my decision to appoint Charles as a steward. Sir John Talbot was a soldier, first and foremost. Sir John Fastolf, who had fought with us was an equally good soldier but Fastolf enjoyed life more than he enjoyed being a soldier. I now saw that Sir John Fastolf had the better balance and as I made my way back to my camp carrying the small chest with the coins I had been paid I reflected that had I continued to be the guardian of the king, things would be different. Perhaps he would have been a better king. He seemed overly influenced by the Duke of Gloucester. I had been taken from him before I could mould him. Sir William had moulded our best king in his formative years and made a warrior king, King Henry VIth would never be a warrior king, at best he might be a politically astute one. On the other hand, if I had not come to France, I would not have met Isabelle. Perhaps it had been meant to be.

My men had picked out a campsite far from any who knew us and I gave Nicholas the chest, "Take this with you when you return west and await me at Les Pérets."

My archers will still to be convinced that this was a good plan, "My lord, if there are French patrols on the road then you will need us."

"And I need four men at arms wearing plate and helmets, with one of them riding Storm to head back west to convince our enemies that I am leaving France." I waved a hand, "There are ears and eyes all over this camp. Already Sir John's squire and his clerk are telling all who will hear that I am leaving the army and leaving France. It is news and as such will become gossip spread not only through the camp but also the countryside. Our enemies will hear. I need to disappear and this is the best way. If anything it is you four who are in the greatest danger for our enemies my choose to take you when they think it is me."

My archers were far from being stupid men and they saw the logic in my arguments.

Before we turned in, we checked our equipment. We had to carry some things that we would not normally take, such as lengths of rope, extra daggers, hatchets and spare cloaks. We would be living rough and would need to make shelters as well as having to carry something with which to restrain our prisoners… if we were lucky. Thomas and Geoffrey also had two small bags of leather filled with sand. They were a way to incapacitate a man without killing him. We had thought through what we needed to do and now we were eager to start for the sooner we did then the sooner this would be over. My plans were made and, before dawn, we left the camp. We would share the road until we neared Verbier and then the four of us who were now dressed in old mail and plain surcoats, would vanish into the woods while the four plated archers would head west. They would not stay at the same places we had stayed while travelling east and, indeed, we had chosen places that I had never visited. Nicholas would play Sir Michael and to those who had never met me, he would appear as the genuine knight. He looked close enough to me to pass a quick inspection. Men saw what they expected to see.

We parted at a small crossroads where a track crossed the main road. There was not a soul around and we did not make a great commotion. We simply slipped away from the plated archers. I led my three companions along the track to the east while Nicholas and the others chattered their way down the road. They would continue to be noisy until they reached Clermont and they would not risk Verberie. We had thirty odd miles to travel and none of it would be on roads that passed through towns and villages. Charles led us to a place he called *la forêt de Barbillon*.

"This is where the lords of the castle hunt. It is not the season for hunting and we should not be disturbed. If any chance upon us we say that we had a lamed horse and sought shelter." Charles knew the land and he knew the people. As such he was invaluable.

We headed deep into the trees until we found a small watercourse and a tiny clearing that accommodated us well. It was soon dark and we shed our mail. We needed to reconnoitre the town and castle and to do so needed anonymity. When we rose, before dawn, I left Geoffrey to guard the camp and with just rondel daggers and bodkin blades tucked in our boots we headed through the woods. Leaving Thomas to keep a watch from the woods Charles and I joined the road into town. As was usual there were people on the road heading for the market and we slipped behind a cart and before a large wagon carrying timber. We nodded to those around us and then Charles and I began a rehearsed conversation.

"I pray that we shall find work here, my friend, for my stomach has begun to think my throat has been cut."

My words would be kept to a minimum, "Aye, me too."

"Remember we take whatever is offered. We are beggars now and cannot be choosers."

That our words were heard were clear when the carter leading the horse behind snorted, "The only men that find work these days are warriors and you two look like your warrior days are in the past. Emptying night soil and piss pots may be all that you can get." He laughed.

Charles said, "Thank you, friend, and know even the coppers we might be paid for such work would be welcome."

As Sir William had taught me, every piece of information you could gather was useful. Someone was raising an army and, after the raid on my manor, I guessed that it would be Sir Maximilian. He had not taken all my treasure but he had taken enough to have money to hire more men. That he had lost men was clear from the villagers who had burned the bodies. The line of people slowed as they entered the gate in the town wall. It was not for scrutiny just that the gate appeared narrow. It would accommodate the wagon but only just and the carter would need to manoeuvre it slowly to get through. There appeared to be little security and the two sentries who sat on upturned barrels were just chatting and supping from a wineskin. They were there, it seemed like a token deterrent to wrongdoers. They were old, overweight, and unfit. As sentries, they were as much use as a mangy toothless dog. They could bark and that was about all. It showed that the castellan and Sir Maximilian did not feel threatened here just thirty or forty miles from Sir John Talbot. The warrior in me made me inspect the walls as I passed beneath the gatehouse. They were sturdy rather than daunting and the gatehouse itself was too small in my opinion. As we headed through the narrow streets towards the market, I saw that the castle was a different matter. It dominated the town and I knew, from Charles' words, that it lay next to the river and the bridge across it. An attacker would have to reduce the town walls and then fight his way to a castle whose walls, even from this distance, appeared high and well made. It was too much of a risk to go close to the castle and so we headed for the market.

Charles managed to get us a little work helping stallholders set up their wares. The pay was but four copper coins and would not even buy a cup of wine but we gratefully knuckled our heads and it proved a clever move for the owner of the tavern called us over.

"Do you have strong backs?"

Charles nodded, "And empty stomachs."

The innkeeper laughed, "Aye, I can see that." Without our mail and gambeson beneath the faded tunics, we looked thinner than we were. We had not shaved nor groomed our hair and the soil smeared on our faces helped with the illusion. "Jean, my son will go with you. There are two firkins of ale to be delivered to the castle." He chuckled, "Some fool made a mess in their alehouse and their beer is vinegar. Deliver it and there will be a meal waiting here for you. If you do that work well then I may find other employment." His eyes narrowed, "But it will just be for the day. There will be no bed for you at the end of it."

We both nodded vigorously and Charles said, "We thank you, sir, and look forward to the food."

Jean was little more than fourteen and the chance to order around two older men was not to be wasted. He took great delight in barking out orders. The barrels were not light and I could see why we had been needed. The market was a busy one and the tavern keeper would not wish to miss the money he could accrue from those attending the market. His investment of a hot meal was a wise one. We could have rolled the barrels but that way there was always a chance that they might break and so we hefted them on our shoulders. The weight forced our heads to the side but we had the advantage that carrying them thus meant that the cowls of our cloaks were forced over our faces and were

61

hidden. The barrels made an inspection of the castle difficult but as we would not have that problem when we left, I was unworried. We reached the main gate and Jean told the sergeant at arms who we were. Here the scrutiny was more obvious than at the main gate and the man checked the wax tablet with the orders of the day.

It was as we waited, our muscles complaining from the weight that I heard the imperious voice bellow, "Get those men out of my way!"

"Yes, Sir Maximilian. You three with the barrels move to the side."

Jean pushed the two of us out of the way as the knight and half a dozen men rode out of the castle and through the town. The six hounds they had were alaunts and were each held by a hound master. They were going hunting. The barrels meant we could not see their progress for Jean hurried us through the gate but we could hear the squeals and cries of complaint as the horsemen barged their way through the town.

The kitchen was not in the inner ward. We were ordered to take the barrels not there but to the keep. We could not enter the keep with them over our shoulders and I was relieved when we placed them on the ground and told to roll them towards the cellar. Luckily for us, there were servants there to take them below ground and the young Jean, his work done, led us from the keep. It gave me the opportunity to inspect the castle. The keep had an entrance that was at the top of a short wooden staircase. It meant a ram would not work if an attacker tried to take it. The door to the cellar would be the best way for an attacker to gain entry but it would mean an extra floor to negotiate and, no doubt, a twisting staircase that was easy to defend. The inner bailey had high walls and a fighting platform. With towers on the gatehouse and at the corners, it would be hard to take. As we crossed the outer bailey, I saw that the wall there was lower and if taken then would become a death trap. The outer gate had murder holes and a portcullis. As we followed Jean back to the market square, I decided that it would not be a place for Sir John and Lord Somerset to attempt to storm.

The food we were given was a simple stew that consisted largely of beans and greens although from the taste there had been some meat in the pot. We had none of it but it was filling and had we been as hungry as we said we would have been grateful. We mopped every bit of the stew with the rye bread we had been given. I smiled to myself as I did so. Had Sir Geoffrey or one of the other knights who followed Sir John been in my position they would have given themselves away by showing their distaste at having to eat such bread. Knights and lords were served bread made of the finest white flour. I was of humbler origins and could eat anything.

The tavern keeper, also called Jean, seemed happy with us and we were employed washing pots all day. We had no break and were not able to scout out the town but, as the market began to empty, he paid us a silver coin each and allowed us to eat another bowl of the stew. As the market was emptying so his tavern filled with the stall holders and the local people. We were told to eat our food outside close to the water trough. As we ate ,we heard a commotion and, looking up, saw Sir Maximilian and his column of men return. We used the cowls of our cloaks to hide our faces but both of us peered up as they rode by. The alaunts had bloody snouts. There were two horses draped with the carcasses of deer. They had been hunting. One of the riders said something and the men on the right looked down. I feared at first, they were looking at us but then I saw that they had spied one of the servant girls from the tavern who was collecting wooden platters from the outside table. The man who shouted at her was Jacques, the man Charles had fought. His lascivious comments brought Jean outside and he helped the girl bring in the platters. The horsemen passed and we finished our food. We took the platters back inside.

Jean said, "You are good workers. If you return in three days when we have our next market there will be more work for you."

Charles beamed, "Thank you, sir."

Jean said, "I fear you will not be allowed to sleep within the walls. Since Sir Maximilian arrived as the guest of the Seigneur, then all vagrants are thrashed and thrown from the town at dusk." He shook his head and nodded towards the castle, "They are animals. Did you hear what that one said to my Marie?" He did not wait for an answer but continued, "I will be glad when he goes off to war again. Peace will return to our home when he does whatever it is that brings him pleasure."

"If we are still here then we will happily work for you. The food was most welcome. However, we may try our luck further east, we shall see."

Getting out of the town was as easy as it had been getting in. We waited until we were out of the hearing of the sentries before we spoke. "You saw Jacques?"

I nodded, "And I saw the deer. I hope Thomas and Geoffrey are safe."

I could see that he had not thought of that, "But surely they would have brought them back if they had been discovered."

"Perhaps, but I shall be happier when we see them."

To my great relief, when we neared the place, we had left him, Thomas stepped from behind a tree. In his hand, he held his sword. "We were lucky this day, Sir Michael, come let us get to our new camp."

Chapter 7

Thomas led us to a different part of the wood. We heard our horses neigh as we approached. We had chosen good horses for this task and while they would not give themselves away to an enemy the scent of their masters meant they welcomed us. Thomas waited until we were seated on the logs that he and Geoffrey must have found before he spoke, "I saw Sir Maximilian and his men as they left the town and I watched them as they headed towards the wood. There must be a trail that leads from the town. I ran as fast as I could and Geoffrey and I dismantled the camp and then rode the horses north. We waited beyond the woods. There is a farm that backs onto the wood and a stream. We walked the horses down the stream and hid beneath some willows."

Geoffrey took up the tale, "I returned to the woods. I knew that they did not seek us but hunted for I heard the sound of baying hounds. I kept my post until I heard the sounds fading and then made my way to the scene of the hunt; it was close to where we had camped. I found the offal they had left and as the sounds receded, I went to fetch Thomas. I do not think that they knew any had camped there. We decided that we should find a better camp away from the place that they had hunted. This is not as comfortable for it is smaller and there is no water nearby but now that we have found the stream, we can take the horses there."

"You have done well and I think we can risk a fire. The town is locked up at night and while we have eaten hot food this day you have not." As the two of them lit a fire and prepared food Charles and I spoke of what we had learned.

"Will you return on the next market day?"

"I doubt it, Thomas. We will learn little more than we know already and we risk being seen."

"Then we just wait, my lord?"

Shaking my head I said, "No, Geoffrey, we watch but Thomas has told us where Sir Maximilian enters the woods and we watch there. If he enters to hunt once he may do so again."

"My lord, he was with many men."

"You have hunted, Geoffrey, and know that men can become isolated. We take our chance and try to spirit him away."

Charles nodded, "If Jacques is the measure of the men, he has hired then they are little more than brigands. Sir Michael is right."

"But the dogs?"

"Aye, Geoffrey, if they bring the dogs then we have to put off our plan."

65

We sat in silence as the fire warmed up. Geoffrey finished putting food in the pot and poured us wine into our costrels, "I fear, my lord, that it may be a month rather than a fortnight that we wait for all conditions have to be perfect."

He was right and the meal was a depressing affair. Things did not improve the next day and the day after for it rained; not constantly but it was damp and wet longer than it was dry. There was little likelihood of hunting and that meant that our prey would stay indoors. Poor Marie had best watch out. We watched, nonetheless and I suppose that was the only benefit of the rain. It enabled us to find the best place from which to watch. We found a tree that afforded us protection from view and yet allowed us to watch the gate and the track leading into the wood. On the third day, the rain ceased. I had watched our camp the day before and it was Thomas' turn. The three of us took our places. The cloaks we had used the previous two days were now drying in the camp and we wore our mail beneath our surcoats. The reason was not for defence but practical. We had worn them when it had rained to keep them dry and now, we did not want to put them on damp ground.

We were there early enough to see people entering and leaving. None tried to enter the wood although two men led a laden sumpter along the track that led around the town wall. It was when I saw the old man with the cadge that I spied hope. The cadge held just three hawks, a buzzard, a saker, and a merlin. Sir Maximilian did not adhere to the rules about hawks, that much was clear; however, the important fact was that he was just accompanied by what looked like his squire and Jacques, along with the cadger and the young huntsman. As two were on foot and the cadge would necessitate the use of paths we did not have to move and I signalled Geoffrey to fetch Thomas. We had a chance to take the knight but it would take all four of us.

They had barely reached the trail to the woods when Sir Maximilian reined in and turned in his saddle. He addressed his squire, "Gilles, you have forgotten the wineskins, fetch them." The squire was no longer a young man and I doubted that he would ever attain his spurs. He scowled but nodded and wheeled his horse around. The birds, now stationary must have sensed the proximity of the woods for they began to make noises to bate. Sir Maximilian said, "You two, take the birds hence. I cannot think with the flapping they make."

The codger knuckled his head, "Aye, my lord, come along my beauties." The man's words, which were tender told me that cared for his charges. The huntsman with him was a young man and he followed the cadge.

There was a chance we could take the two of them and I seriously contemplated it but the two men on the tower at the corner of the castles were watching them and they held crossbows. We might be able to take them but pursuit would be imminent. This was not the time for foolishness, it was the time for patience.

Now that the flapping birds had gone and the two horses edged closer to the woods to graze on the lusher grass that grew beyond the trail the two men were close enough for us to be able to both observe and hear them. Both wore leather jerkins and had good boots. The knight, of course, had a good sword but Jacques also carried a longer sword than I would have expected. With hats upon their heads, daggers in their belts and gauntlets on their hands they were set for hunting. Jacques had done well out of his encounter with the knight. Like Charles, the fight outside the inn had changed his life. In Jacques' case, it had taken him to Sir Maximilian who must have seen something in the man he could use.

Sir Maximilian looked around and said, "You are sure where they went?"

"Aye, my lord, like I said they have gone to Weedon. The man I spoke to told me that there is no castle and it was the former home of Sir William Strongstaff. He was a rich knight who served kings. We found little at Les Pérets but Weedon will be a different matter. It is said he buried huge chests of gold."

"And Sir Michael will head there?"

Jacques sounded less confident, "The word I had was that he had told Talbot he was leaving the army and heading back to Rouen."

"Then he may stay at Les Pérets to rebuild the damage we did."

"I doubt it, lord. I spoke to some in the village and they said that the knight was devoted to his wife. He will return to England."

The Frenchman rubber his hands, "Then I shall not only have vengeance but become a rich man in the process. As soon as our men return from their raid we shall leave. I have friends in Le Havre. They know the English coast and will land us close enough to Weedon to sneak through the countryside at night and strike whilst they sleep."

Jacques laughed and it was not a pleasant sound, "Aye, the English do not live in a land riven by war and they will not be watchful. We can be in and out before they know what we do."

"Aye, and this time we leave not a man nor woman alive. This is war. This is for France. Who knows, Le Hire may make me a captain for my services. Striking in the heart of England at the home of the man who was responsible for the deaths of so many Frenchmen cannot go unrewarded."

The knight was deluding himself but I worried now that the spies I had feared were greater in number than I could possibly have imagined. I knew that the people they spoke to in Les Pérets were not spies but would have been merely polite. It also told me that Jacques was a dangerous man and not without courage for he had gone back to the place he had raided. He must have gone in disguise.

The squire noisily trotted up, "I have them, my lord, and a messenger had just reached the castle. Our men will return on the morrow. They were successful."

"Good! Codger, come!"

I signalled to Charles and we moved away from the path so that we were sufficiently far enough away to be hidden and yet to be able to follow. By moving either side of the path we could follow them no matter which trail they took. Our wet watch had done one thing for us, it had shown us the paths and trails in the woods and we each had a mental map of the land through which we would travel. The bells on the hoods of the hunting birds jingled and, along with the clopping of the hooves made it easy for us to follow the hunters. They took the main trail which we were familiar with. Thomas and Geoffrey ghosted up behind me and followed as we stalked the murderer of Isabelle's family. Neither man said a word but I saw that they had brought with them some lengths of rope.

I knew where Sir Maximilian was headed long before we reached it. They were going to the place we had first camped and where they had hunted the first time. Perhaps the knight or his squire had seen something that they could hunt with birds. Whatever the reason it suited me for we knew the place. Sure enough, when we reached the clearing the codger placed his cadge on the ground. He rubbed his shoulders and I could see that he was old even by the standards of codgers.

Sir Maximilian stepped from his horse and took the wineskin and costrel from his squire. As the three horses were tethered, he stared into the sky and after replacing the costrel and wineskin on the cantle of the saddle took out his hawking gauntlet. He pointed to the north, "We will try there. That is where we saw the pigeons. Codger, remove the hoods and I will take Arthur."

He held out his hand, now covered with a thick gauntlet and the buzzard was brought to him. He took a tiny morsel of food from the young huntsman and fed the bird. It would not take away the appetite but was a way of guaranteeing its return. "Pierre, stay here with the other birds. You will hold us up."

The codger seemed relieved, "Aye, my old bones are weary already. Good luck, Sir Maximilian."

"Lead on huntsman."

The young huntsman nodded and headed down a track that led from the clearing. It followed the watercourse. Jacques and Gilles followed Sir Maximilian. I waited until the noise of the four men had disappeared. I took a chance and stepped into the clearing. The old man, who had sat on one of the logs that lay there looked surprised but said not a word. Charles, Thomas, and Geoffrey joined me. I had not drawn my weapon and the three of them also left theirs in their scabbards.

"Welcome friends. We did not expect to see any here this day. None are permitted in this wood without the permission of the castellan." He shrugged, "Not that it concerns me. I carry the cadge and will be paid but a few copper coins for the privilege. It will barely pay for my wine."

I slipped my hand into my purse and brought out two silver coins. The man's eyes widened. I smiled, "And will these ensure your silence?"

"A third would do so for I am a man with a terrible thirst. My wife said my love of wine would kill me but as she died five years ago then who is to say?" I slipped a third coin into his hand. "And now I am silent but before I become a Trappist, tell me, lord, what is it that you do here?"

"Lord?"

"You are English and I can see the marks on your boots from your spurs. You are a knight and a rich one too for you have a full purse."

I liked the man who was unafraid of us and decided to be honest with him, "Sir Maximilian killed my wife's family and I come to take him and bring him to justice."

The codger made the sign of the cross, "Aye, well I can see understand your motives then for he is not a pleasant man. The young women of the town fear him more than the devil. Jacques and Gilles are also men whose mothers should have crossed their legs but Paul, the huntsman, is a good boy. His father was killed in the wars. Be gentle with him, eh, my lord?"

I smiled, "Of course. Thomas, Geoffrey, take the saddles from the horses and hide them. I do not want any to escape. Charles, stand by the trail they will use."

"Yes, my lord."

We all looked up into the sky to the north as the buzzard, that had been circling, suddenly plummeted towards the earth.

The codger sliced some meat from a long, cured, sausage and said, "It will not be long, my lord for Arthur is a deadly hunter. Perhaps if you would bind my hands?" He shrugged, "You may succeed but, in case you fail…"

"Thomas."

"Aye, my lord." As Thomas bound the hands he said, "You are a game one, old man."

"I have seen sixty summers and outlived my wife, children and all else who mean anything to me. Why should I fear death which may be but a sleep away? Each day I wake is as though God has set me another challenge. How to survive in this world?"

Sometimes you have to trust your judgement and I did not think that the old man would betray us. We headed down the trail knowing that the hunters would have to return that way. The odds were now in our favour for from the codger's words the youth would not fight us but I did not wish us to be overconfident. We found a place where thick bushes encroached upon the path and crowned the top of a small rise that would make the men a little out of breath and make them look to their feet. The narrow trail would force the hunters into a single file and hide us. I waved Thomas and Geoffrey to wait in the woods on the other side of the bushes while Charles and I, with swords drawn, squatted on either side of the trail.

Charles counselled, quietly, "Sir Michael, you are a noble knight and harbour honourable thoughts. Put them from your mind when we deal with these men. Only the youth is innocent. The others have blood on their hands and from we have heard plan more."

"Do not worry, Charles, I intend to stay alive and to return to Weedon but it is in my blood to try to be merciful if I can."

Silence filled the woods and that told me that the animals and birds knew that men were abroad. In the distance, I heard voices and knew that they were coming towards us. Their words were indistinct at first and then I made out Sir Maximilian's voice, "A fair start but I would have the saker hunt next . There are ducks and they will make a tasty meal. You, huntsmen, do not drop those pigeons and ensure that Arthur is comfortable."

The slight jingling of the bell told me that the hawk had been hooded.

"Yes, my lord."

Sir Maximilian would not be the first up the trail. That would either be his squire or Jacques. They would cut aside any brambles and vines that encroached. That was confirmed when I heard the swish of a blade as it hacked through the undergrowth. The footsteps grew louder as did the breathing. I nodded to Charles. We could see each other but the bushes and the undergrowth hid us both. When we heard the blade slash at the bush that was just a pace away from us, we both stood up. It was Jacques and Charles gave him no chance at all. He swung his sword at his former comrade's neck and gave him the swiftest of deaths. The squire, Gilles, was quick to step into the breach and draw his sword. He did it so quickly and was swinging it towards Charles' unprotected head that I little option other than to swing my own sword. Gilles tried to block my blow but all he did was to turn my sword and it sliced down onto his head. The edge grated off the bone of his skull and he fell to the ground. If he was not dead already then he soon would be. It was here that the slope came to our aid. As the squire's body fell it began to tumble and Sir Maximilian, who was drawing his own sword could not keep his feet. He crashed back down the trail. Thomas stepped out and smacked him on his unprotected head with his leather bag of sand. Geoffrey's sword was at the chest of the huntsman in a flash and he said, "Do not be a hero."

The youth nodded. His terrified eyes stared at the two dead men. "Charles, help me to pick up Sir Maximilian. Thomas and Geoffrey fetch out horses and be swift. You, Paul, is it?" He nodded, "Walk before us back to the camp."

He did so and we followed. Sir Maximilian was heavy and I was glad that we did not have far to carry him. When we reached the camp, we draped his body over one of the horses that had no saddle and Charles tied him firmly. I said, "Paul, untie…, what is your name?"

The codger smiled, "Jean."

"Jean. Then you can finish off Sir Maximilian's wine."

When that was done Jean drank deeply. I knew that the coins I had given him would be spent on wine. I took Sir Maximilian's purse from his body and threw it to them. "Divide this now and I will dispose of the purse along the trail."

The youth hesitated. Jean said, "He was not a good master and we will not be paid for this day's work. Trust this man for he is a knight and if I am any judge an honourable one."

They obeyed and after sharing the coins had half-finished the wine by the time Thomas and the horses arrived. "Geoffrey, take these two men to the old camp we made and leave them there."

"And then?"

"And then rejoin us." I looked at Jean, "It will tire you but give us chance to escape. Head back to the castle and tell them that you were attacked in the woods and that you fled, fearing for your lives. You do not know my name and I do not mind if you tell them that I am a knight." I smiled, "I would hope that the purse I gave you would make your walk slow."

Jean nodded, "I am an old man." He looked at Paul, "Perhaps, Paul, today is the day that you learn to be a codger for with the contents of

the purse I have enough coins to last me whatever time God grants me."
He looked up at me, "Farewell, my lord. You have given me a tale I can
tell around the fire. Who knows it may even bring me the odd beaker of
wine? Of course, I may embellish it a little but that is the prerogative of
all old men."

I clasped his arm, "And you take care, Jean, do not drink yourself to
death. The world needs men like you."

When they had gone, I said, "Thomas, you stay here and when
Geoffrey returns follow us on the trail west. They will be after us by
dusk and I wish to be at least twenty miles from here when they do. Our
horses are well rested and we have two spares."

As we mounted and Charles took the reins of Sir Maximilian's horse
he said, "We should kill him now, my lord. This is asking for trouble."

"I cannot. I trust to God that what I do is right."

When I found a trail that headed south off the main track, I told
Charles to wait for me and rode a hundred paces down it. I discarded
the purse. It might not fool them but if they were any good at tracking,
they would follow my tracks. To add to the illusion I walked Shadow
backwards, setting those who would hunt us, a puzzle.

Geoffrey and Thomas caught up with us at the forest of Belleau and
we headed west along hunter's trails until it grew dark. We stopped. I
had worried about the condition of Sir Maximilian for he had not
moved or made a sound until we were almost at the forest of Belleau
and I wondered if he had been sapped too hard. He first began to moan
and then to shout. Charles whirled on him, "Make another sound,
murderer, and I will slit your throat." There was enough venom in
Charles' voice to convince the knight.

We were forced to make camp when it became too dark to safely
navigate the trail. We needed daylight for the sun and the right trail. We
had to risk a fire for we needed to keep watch on the French knight.
Charles was in charge of the Frenchman and when he was taken from
the back of his horse, I saw that Sir Maximilian was moving stiffly. The
matted blood on his head told me that it had not been a gentle blow.
Charles had searched the knight when he was unconscious but we took
no chances and Geoffrey kept a sword pricked at the Frenchman's
throat while Charles tied his hands and then hobbled his feet. He could
move and he could sit but not run.

"How do I eat?"

Charles laughed, "Who says we are going to feed you? We can give
you water to keep you alive but if you are a little thinner when we reach
Rouen it will just make the hanging a little more interesting unless you
can hire some hangers on."

Charles wanted him dead. He would have blood for the murder of his brother and his sister-in-law.

"We will feed you but my friend here is quite right. You are only alive so that you can be tried for the crimes you committed at Les Pérets."

He made the mistake of laughing as he said, "And would that the pretty wench you married had been there. I would have enjoyed mounting her too."

Charles hit him so hard that I ran to him fearing that he had killed him. He lay still but breathed. "We want him alive, Charles."

"Did you not hear him admit what he did to Maud and what he would have done to Isabelle? Is it ice that runs in your veins?"

I nodded, "Until he hangs in Rouen then aye, it is as ice and I will be as cold as I can for I want him punished."

I knew then that I would have to watch Charles as carefully as Sir Maximilian.

Chapter 8

The French knight was not unconscious as long this time. When he woke it was a baleful stare and he glared and glowered at Charles as Geoffrey gave him water. "Thomas, you take the first watch. Wake Geoffrey and then you, Geoffrey, wake me. I will give you the dawn watch, Charles." That was deliberate. I did not want the prisoner harmed and Charles was still angry.

We were tired and we were hungry. The hobbled horses grazed on the grass, still damp from the recent rains and we ate a cold supper of sliced, salted meat and wine. We had no time to fill a pot and wait for the water to boil. The fire was there for warmth and light. We needed to be able to watch the wily Frenchman. The Frenchman refused food but drank the wine Geoffrey proffered. He wiped his mouth with the back of his tied hands. For a prisoner he seemed to be overly confident, "You cannot escape you know. My men will follow. They are loyal to me and they know where you will go. This evasion in the woods merely serves to slow you down and to allow them to get ahead of you. They will watch Les Pérets and Rouen."

It was my turn to smile, "And who says we are heading for Rouen? The Duke of Bedford resides in Paris and he will happily have you hanged for he hates men such as you."

The French knight narrowed his eyes. I could see that he had not thought of that possibility. He must have realised that our small numbers aided us. A large group of men attracted more attention. We made fewer ripples. We could go southwest to Paris, west to Rouen or even if we were devious enough south and then west to Bordeaux. The safest bet for the pursuers was to follow our trail.

Charles said, "And, of course, we have the option of slitting your throat long before we reach any of those places. Your head could still be displayed for all to see but Sir Michael is right, a public trial and execution would be a more fitting end for a criminal like you."

"I am a patriot and I fight for France."

Shaking my head I said, "No, you are not. You are an opportunist who seeks to make money from this conflict. What you did at Les Pérets was not for France. It was a vindictive act. A real warrior fights other warriors. You have no honour and are nothing."

I realised that I had angered him for he tried to rise. Geoffrey firmly restrained him. The Frenchman was cocky, "Give me a sword and we will have a trial by combat here and now. Let God decide who has honour."

"No, Sir Maximilian. I did not capture you to see your life ended here in this damp forest and besides the fall and the blow have weakened you. I would win."

"You are so sure, Englishman?"

Thomas stood and stretched, "This is Sir Michael of Weedon, Frenchman, and he was selected to be the bodyguard of young King Henry. He was deemed to be the best of the best. I saw you fight at Braine and I know that Sir Michael would win every day of the week and twice on Sundays." He turned to me, "I will make water, my lord and then I will be alert. When I return you can all turn in, if you wish for I have heard enough of this cockerel's banter."

"Thank you, Thomas, and for those words."

"I speak the truth, Sir Michael, that is all."

While he was away, we made up our beds. We had the saddles in a sort of low wall around us and we had packed the gaps with earth so that there would be no ground-level gaps. It was little enough but it would keep the draughts from us. We had spare cloaks and one would make our beds. Geoffrey made a bed up for Sir Maximilian. We used the cloaks of his dead companions for his bed and he was between Thomas and Geoffrey. The log at his back would afford him some shelter.

"Before we lie you down, Sir Maximilian, do you need to make water?"

He snorted, "I am not a babe that needs to be asked and I need no assistance to lie down." We watched in amusement as the arrogant man attempted to lie down. He managed it but there was no dignity in the fall. Geoffrey kindly laid a cloak over him. I waited until Thomas returned and tossed a piece of dead wood he had found on the fire. He nodded as he took his seat on the log, close to the feet of the French knight. He was taking no chances.

I lay down and pulled my cloak up over my head. We had more than a hundred miles to go. I suppose we could make it in two days of hard riding but that would necessitate using roads and roads meant our passage would be marked. Our pursuers would simply ask if riders with a bound man had passed along the road. They would soon find us. Paris seemed an increasingly safer choice. It was a forty-mile ride and would throw our pursuers off the scent. The Frenchman was right, his men would know where we were going. The question was, would they be anxious to recover their leader? From what I had seen, he was not a popular man. Perhaps they would be glad to be rid of him. Then I realised that I was thinking of the men I led. That would be how they would react but Sir Maximilian had hired men like Jacques. They were

75

ruthless men who respected a ruthless leader. He was their livelihood and they would do all that they could to recover him and the lifestyle they enjoyed. Without him, they would need another paymaster.

I know not what woke me up but something did and I was alert in an instant. I saw that, somehow, Sir Maximilian had managed to free his bonds and Geoffrey was lying on the ground. Even as I began to rise, I saw that the French knight had managed to get hold of Geoffrey's short sword and was swinging it down onto the sleeping head of Charles. I had no choice in the matter. I hurled the dagger with which I had slept. I threw it underhand and I had no idea if it would strike or not. If I did nothing then Charles would be dead. I was lucky and the ballock dagger struck his hand, forcing the sword to the side. It still struck Charles but it was a glancing blow to the side of the head. I did not know if the wound was mortal and I had no time to find out. Weaponless I jumped up and did the only thing I could think of. Even as he back swung at me, I launched myself at him. He snarled and spat in my face. My hands went to his eyes and mouth. I drove the forefinger of my right hand into his eyes and he screamed. I knew that it would wake Thomas and he was my only hope. My right thumb pulled up at the side of his mouth and he punched me in the side of my head with his left hand. It made my ears ring and I saw stars but I pushed even harder into his eye. He roared again and hurled me to the side. The blow to my head disorientated me and I lost my grip but I knew I had blinded him. As I lay on the ground he shouted in triumph, "Three of you and I won. Die!"

Just then a sword appeared through his chest, He had been stabbed in the back and Thomas' voice said, "There are four of us and you are the one who will die, snake!"

"No!" I tried to rise but knew it was too late. All my plans to take him back to stand trial ended as his bloody body slipped to the ground. Worse, both Charles and Geoffrey were hurt. It had all been for nothing.

"Sorry, Sir Michael, I did not think that I could take a chance." He suddenly saw the two bodies, "The bastard! Are they dead or alive?"

"I know not. You see to Geoffrey and I will see to Charles." I knelt next to my wife's uncle and put my hand to his throat. He was alive. I saw that the sword had cut his head and while there was a lot of blood the cut did not appear to be deep. I tore off some of Sir Maximilian's shirt and grabbed the wineskin. I poured some of the wine on the wound and then dabbed the wound clean. So far as I could tell the sword had not broken the bone, just the flesh. I went to the saddlebag and took out the honey. I smeared it on the wound and it slowed the bleeding. Tearing more of Sir Maximilian's shirt I made a bandage and fastened it around his head. I poured some of the wine into his throat and he coughed and spluttered himself awake.

"What...?"

"The knight is dead and he tried to take your life. He will not stand trial."

He closed his eyes and lay back, "I knew we should have killed him."

Thomas' voice was triumphant as he shouted, "Geoffrey lives. He was struck in the face with something and it rendered him unconscious."

I heard Geoffrey's voice as he said, "The snake headbutted me. Sorry, my lord, I should not have cut his bonds."

"This is not the time for recriminations. We will talk of this anon. Hide the body and then saddle the horses, Thomas. I will see to these two. We must leave now. There is no point in doing what we planned. We ride as hard and fast as we can."

Thomas showed me the body after he had covered it with wood, leaves and dirt. It was hidden but it would be found soon enough. Any delay helped us. I kicked out the fire and then helped Charles and Geoffrey into their saddles. Thomas strung the spare horses together. The two of us would have to do all the work for I could see that the head wounds the other two had suffered meant that they would be of little use to us. A wound to a leg or an arm could be bound but a head wound could come back to haunt us.

"I will lead and you bring up the rear. Charles, keep your horse as close to me as you can and Thomas, watch Geoffrey."

"I am fine, Sir Michael."

"No you are not, Charles, and if either of you feels the need to stop them tell me. I would have the two of you reach Les Pérets with no further hurt."

I led us directly back to the road that twisted and turned through the forest of Belleau. It was still night and dawn would not be with us for a couple of hours. I was confident that we would have the road to ourselves. Once we made the road I headed west. Fate and a cunning Frenchman had thwarted my plans to bring the knight to justice and now we would appear as murderers. With my plans in tatters, I had to think out our escape even more carefully. Senlis was thirty miles away but with three spare horses it could be reached before dark. I wracked my brain to remember what I could about the town. I knew that three hundred years ago it had been a favourite of the French kings but had fallen out of favour. Its position meant that despite having a wall around the town more than twenty feet high it was continually attacked and taken by both sides. The once royal city became almost abandoned. We might be able to play the part of soldiers down on our luck returning from the war in the east. I began, as we trotted along the cobbled road, to concoct my story.

Dawn saw us at the hamlet of Gandelu and we reached it as it was coming alive. There was a tavern but I avoided it and just stopped at the water trough. A farmer was walking towards us leading a horse and he stopped to water his animal at the trough. His beast was a plough horse and dwarfed, Shadow apart, ours. Thomas and I helped down Charles and Geoffrey. Neither had spoken all the way from Belleau and I was becoming concerned about them.

"I see you have been in the wars, my friend. Was there a battle?"

I would have to use my manufactured tale, "No, we were set upon on the other side of Belleau. We gave a good account of ourselves but my two friends suffered head wounds. Is there a monastery or priory close by?"

"Aye, the Couvent de Cerfroid is just three miles up the road." He smiled as a bell began to toll in the distance, "There you can hear them." He looked at the spare horses. "If you are short of money, I could buy one of the horses from you."

I would have sold him one but we needed all of them. A man in my position would have at least considered his offer and so I said, "How much?"

"Five silver coins."

I was relieved for it was a paltry offer and he was hoping to take advantage of us. Shaking my head I said, "We have travelled far with these beasts and we are too fond of them to sell. We shall tighten our belts."

We mounted and headed along the road. The conversation had been necessary but the man would remember us and our route was marked. I owed it to Charles and Geoffrey to have them attended to but it would make the task of any pursuers that much easier.

The monks had finished their service and were tending their fields when we reined in. Holy orders were places of help and healing but the handing over of coins ensured a warmer reception. They did not admit us into their building but Geoffrey and Charles were attended to in the cloister and when I handed over a generous number of coins, fresh bread and cheese were brought out as well as milk from their cows. It was an unexpected benefit although the delay of an hour meant we would have to hurry to reach Senlis. When we left, with the two wounded men tended to by real healers, I knew that I had marked our passage as clearly as if I had made a map and marked it in red ink.

The healer who had tended to them was not worried about Geoffrey's injury but the cut to the scalp of Charles had necessitated stitches and he warned me to be careful if Charles slipped into sleep. Mindful of his words we spoke on the road that continued to weave in and out of trees and then small, cultivated fields. One piece of news was that there was a castle at Neufchelles. The healer had made the comment whilst watching my face. He had smiled as he had said, "It marks the end of the forest proper. When men wished to avoid it, they took a detour through the woods and rejoined the road where they could not be observed." His smile told me he knew that we were fleeing.

"Once past this castle ahead, we have just twenty miles to Senlis. Thomas, you must keep an ear out for pursuit."

Geoffrey had perked up after being tended to and fed, "My lord, I can lead the horses Thomas is better used as our eyes and ears. All of this is my fault for I was too kind. I need to repay the three of you for my laxity."

Having heard the healer's verdict I acceded, relieved that we now had three swords that might be used if we had to fight again. "Charles, are you still with us?"

I turned to look at my wife's uncle. He had not spoken, even when his head was being stitched. "Aye, Sir Michael although it feels as though there is a weaponsmith in my head and my ears are filled with a hissing sound as though I have a nest of snakes in each ear."

"The sword did not kill you, Charles but it makes you an invalid until we reach Rouen. If there is danger and we are pursued then I command you to ride ahead. You are a liability at the moment and if we were watching out for you then we might lose."

"I confess, my lord, that I do not think I could defeat your son, Jean, at the moment. I feel weak."

When we spied the standard fluttering from the top of the castle at Neufchelles I led us into the forest to our left. The healer had said that the road twisted and turned and so it did. We found ourselves riding south with the road to our right. We had to pick our way through the trees and I was constantly turning around to see if Charles was coping. It was necessary but the avoidance of the castle added an hour to our journey. When we rejoined the road there were open fields and the castle was hidden from us by the last of the trees. The others each swapped to one of the spare horses ten miles later but I continued to ride Shadow. He had responded well to the challenges of the road. Once the horses were changed and we had eaten more of the food the monks had sold us we made better time but we were all weary.

There were mile markers along the road and while some had been robbed out or used for building enough remained for me to know, when we stopped for Geoffrey to take a stone from one of the horse's hooves, that we were just five miles from Senlis. I shaded my eyes to look at the sun and estimated that we had about two hours before dark and we would make the town. I had just taken the stopper from the wineskin when Thomas said, "Lord, I hear horses."

We had neither seen nor heard any horse since the farmer in Gandelu. Horses in the plural suggested our pursuers. I looked around. We were close to another wood. I did not know its name but it gave us our best chance of evading the horsemen. If they were harmless, we would have lost nothing. I led my men and horses into the trees. Thomas came last and he disguised where we had entered. I rode forty feet in and then turned. I drew my sword. "Charles, take the horses from Geoffrey. I pray we do not have to fight but we may need to."

He took the rope and Geoffrey drew his sword. We could all hear the horses as they clattered along the cobbles. As they passed us, we saw that they were cloaked and that hid any marks or signs of their master but there were eight of them and they wore helmets. They did not stop but that gave me no comfort. I sheathed my sword and when the sound of their hooves had receded in the distance I said, "So they are now ahead of us and any hopes I might have had of a night in the comfort of an inn are now shattered."

Thomas said, "Sir Michael, when they reach the next town and there is no news of our passing, they will surely turn to search for us."

I shook my head, "I had hoped that when we avoided Neufchelles we might have made them stop and search but they have not." I knew then that the stop in Gandelu had been a mistake. Had we skirted around it then they might have wasted time searching Belleau Forest. The farmer and the monks let them know, albeit innocently, of our route. They could ride as hard as they wished. My only hope was that Senlis would be the place they sought us. I had asked the monks how far the journey was there and that had been another mistake. I was making so many that I could almost hear the despair from the ghost of Sir William. He would have thought he taught me better.

I looked around at the forest, "Charles, do you know this forest?"

His head had been slumped forward and now it jerked, painfully, up, "Not its name, Sir Michael but this part of France has many such forests. The kings of France used to like to hunt here."

"Then we use the forest to escape. We will head south and west until we find a trail and then we shall camp. Tonight we will have a well-earned rest and tomorrow we will take whatever road we find to the south that heads west. Mayhap we shall lose them."

As plans go it was riddled with holes but it was a plan and the three went along with it. The trail we found was a wide one and that worried me. My fears were confirmed when we found a huddle of houses in a large clearing. We smelled their woodsmoke before we were seen and detoured to the west to get around it. It was getting too dark and dangerous to carry on and when the smell of the hamlet had gone, I stopped at the first clearing we could find. We were just unsaddling our horses when Shadow nodded his head and led me to a small watercourse. It was perfect for the horses which had not drunk since the monastery. We let them satiate themselves and then broke out the oats we had brought as emergency fodder. This was the time for the oats.

We made a camp and Geoffrey said, "I shall take the first watch."

"No, we all need sleep and we trust to Shadow's nose and ears. He will warn of any danger."

I had just closed my eyes when Charles said, "Those men will hunt us down, my lord. We have taken away the man who paid them. There will be other masters but until they find one, they will wish to take our horses and whatever we have in our purses. As Sir Maximilian said, they know whence we came and even if we evade them then they will be waiting for us at Les Pérets."

"Sleep, my friend, and let me worry about such things." He was right and now I saw how foolish I had been. To think I could have succeeded with a handful of men was pure arrogance.

We woke before dawn but did not leave until the sun was trying to peer over the eastern horizon. It helped with our navigation. We made good time once we left the trees. We found ourselves on a road that led, according to the road signs, to Beaumont sur Oise. It meant crossing a river and was in disputed land but that could not be helped. I hoped that our night in the forest south of Senlis would have thrown off our pursuers. I was also heartened by the fact that Charles seemed less disorientated and he even commented on the road. "Beaumont has a monastery and a small castle but I do not think that, so long as we cross the bridge quickly and quit the town, we should be hindered."

"Do they keep a watch on the bridge at night?"

He shrugged, "I know not. I crossed during the day and there were guards there then." He rubbed his chin. "The castle is south of the river. If we approach during the evening it may be that we might be able to cross the bridge. After all, their defences will face the northwest and Rouen."

I was not convinced but we had no choice and we rode hard. We passed many farms and through villages and hamlets. If our pursuers wished to know where we were then it would be easy enough to find us. Charles was now fit enough to speak when we asked for water or food but we were easily marked as warriors and the fact that three of us were largely silent would be a clue as to our identity. It was in the late afternoon that we reached Beaumont sur Oise and we halted half a mile from the river to view both the castle and the bridge.

The standard flying from the tower told us that the castle was occupied. That in itself was not necessarily a problem as many castles had just a small garrison. The problem we had was that even a small number of men could hold us up. Charles had still some way to go before he was fully recovered and There was really only Thomas upon whom I could rely.

"I think we will try to get across the bridge when it is almost dusk. By then they should be changing the guards and the ones going off duty will not wish a delay. Charles, you will have to lead. Perhaps the bandage on your head might elicit some sympathy."

"Perhaps."

We could have done with buying some food. We were down to the salted meat we had brought and the last of the wine and ale. The villages and hamlets through which we had passed had sold us ale and wine but they had little enough food for themselves. We tightened the girths on our mounts and fastened our own belts a little tighter. With luck, we had but one more day and we would be close enough to Rouen to feel safe. I nodded when I deemed the time to be right and we mounted. Charles led but I was just to his right. There were a few people on the bridge. Most seemed to be heading towards the castle and town. The walls had sentries and I felt their eyes upon us although we did not look in their direction. The road forked close to the bridge and passed within thirty paces of the castle. I could see that they had just two men on the north side of the bridge for there was no need to have any on the south side. The castle gatehouse acted as a strong sentry post. Charles gave a casual wave to the men on the gatehouse as we crossed the wooden bridge. The wave must have worked for there was no challenge nor the crack of a crossbow. The hooves of our mounts seemed to thunder on the wooden bridge. The base was a stone one and the parapets were also made of stone but the central part was wood. At the far side, I saw the two men discussing something. I guessed that it was us.

As we neared them one raised his hand to stop us.

Charles reined in, "Is something wrong?"

The man smiled, "No, but I am curious and would know why you do not stay in the town or the castle."

"Ah, there you have me. As you can see from my bandage, we have encountered violence some days ago. We were attacked and robbed. Two of our number were slain and they took the horse of our captain. It had our pay in the saddlebags."

"That is a shame. Where was this?"

Charles had done well hitherto and the guards were sympathetic. He then made a mistake although, at the time it did not seem disastrous. "On the Belleau Road."

"Ah, I will mention it to the castellan. He will inform the Seigneur. I hope you find shelter for I think there will be rain this night."

We all looked at the skies and saw that he was right. Charles shrugged, "When a man's luck changes for the worse it always rains."

"Aye, you have the right of it."

I waited until we were half a mile from the bridge and approaching the four houses that made up Persan before speaking, "I fear that telling them we came along the Belleau Road might not have been the best of ideas. I believe we have lost our followers but if they come here and ask about a handful of warriors heading west, we will be identified as the ones they want."

"You are right, Sir Michael and I have put us in peril."

"Not necessarily and we can make good time on this road. We will stop only when it is dark and take shelter where we can."

Our luck must have changed for six miles from Persan we found a burnt-out and abandoned farm just as the sun disappeared to the west. It looked to be a victim of the war in which we had all fought. I spied the heads of bolts and arrows still embedded in the doorframe and lath walls. That the arrowheads had not been removed told me that they had not been English archers. They would have dug them out to sharpen and reuse. English bowmen were ever frugal. The last place we had passed had been Persan and I decided to risk a fire. We found a slightly damaged pot and filled it from the well. Charles picked greens and dug up some roots while Thomas lit a fire. We would eat hot food and that always made a warrior feel happier.

This time we had no choice but to leave before dawn, weary though we were and we headed for the last forty or so miles to Les Pérets. Fleury sur Andelle was thirty miles away and if we could pass that tiny hamlet then we were safe. The road there twisted and turned up a steep ridge. By the time we reached it, our horses would be weary but when we had crossed that last barrier the road would be an easy one to the river.

Gisors was the largest place we passed and we stopped for it was a busy market day. One of the horses was a little lame and so while I bought food Charles negotiated its sale. The money was irrelevant but the abandonment of a horse by shabbily dressed men would arouse suspicion. With drink and food inside us, we pushed on, now with just two spare horses. Only Shadow was still in anything like an acceptable condition but the road was flat and passed through tended fields and small hamlets. This land was friendlier than it had been before Beaumont sur Oise but it was also more exposed. As I glanced back over my shoulder, I saw that it was flat almost all the way back to Gisors. However, I began to hope that our deviations, detours, and trickery had helped to hide us from pursuit.

We were not far from the huddle of houses that was Écouis when Thomas who was still at the rear glanced over his shoulder and spied something, "Riders, my lord, and coming fast."

The land was too open for us to hide. This would be fight or flight and I chose the latter. "Ride hard. When they close with us let loose the spare horses for they might delay the pursuers." I had not asked how many men had been seen. Even a handful might be too much for us. I stroked Shadow's neck and spoke sweetly to him. This was land over which I had ridden and I knew it better than Charles. I took the lead and we galloped through Écouis. The villagers pressed themselves against the walls of their houses as we hurtled along the road. I saw the forest ahead and the road that twisted up its side. Our weary horses, even Shadow, would soon start to slow and if the enemy had better horses, then they would catch us. The village of Fleury sur Andelle lay on the far side. If we reached it then we might have succour but if we had been slowed by the road then we would have perished before then. I glanced over my shoulder, confident that Shadow was surefooted enough not to misplace a hoof. I saw the men. I could not make out numbers but I saw their proximity to us. They had better horses and were now less than a mile from us.

I made a decision. "When we reach the steep ground and the road turns then release the horses. Be prepared to turn and fight but wait for my command."

The three voices did not sound despondent as they shouted, "Aye, my lord."

As we neared the steep climb, I could hear the horses behind as they closed with us. Someone was shouting what sounded like encouragement but I could not make out the words. It mattered not but it showed they were close. I pulled my coif over my head. We had worn mail since we had taken Sir Maximilian. That seemed a lifetime ago.

Our weapons were sharp and we were good warriors but we would be outnumbered. As we reached the climb and the wood, the road turned sharply to the left and afforded me a view of them. There were eleven men and their horses looked fresher than ours. Of course, they had been able to ride along roads while we had often had to cut through forest trails that took their toll. The two horses, suddenly released, galloped for a few strides and then stopped. Each turned to the side of the road to graze and effectively blocked the road. The horsemen crashed through them but it bought us a minute or two as they slowed. We reached the first of the bends and turned right. The horsemen were lost from view. I remembered that there was another turn a few hundred paces ahead and I spied the tiny light of hope.

"When we turn to the left at the next twist in the road then wheel. We will face them there and charge them. I do not intend to fight for long. I want our horses to have a brief rest and for us to give them a shock. No heroics: when I say break then follow me over the crest and towards Fleury."

"Aye, lord."

The corner came and as we turned, I saw that the horsemen were just two hundred paces behind us. We disappeared from view as we turned to continue our climb. I drew my sword and wheeled. Shadow was lathered but not yet panting. The horses of my companions were suffering and would appreciate the rest. The crest of the road lay just two hundred paces from us but this was our only chance to bloody their nose. I could hear voices exhorting them to catch us and, as the leading riders turned the bend I shouted, "Charge!" and dug my heels in Shadow's flanks.

The enemy horsemen were just twenty paces from us and they held no weapons in their hands. We were in no position to be either merciful or honourable. Shadow led the way and I saw the leader, a mailed warrior wearing a helmet try to pull his sword from its scabbard. I swept my sword across his chest and he tumbled over the back of his mount. I lunged at the next man before me. The others would have to deal with the men behind me. The man at arms had almost drawn his sword but my blade sank into his tabard and then his mail. He screamed as the tip found flesh.

Wheeling Shadow through a gap to my right I shouted, "Back!" We had achieved all that I could have hoped and the enemy had been stopped. At least two had been incapacitated and that was all that we could hope for.

It was as we turned that Geoffrey was struck by the axe. It caught him on the shoulder and he kept his saddle but I saw blood.

85

"Charles, grab Geoffrey's reins!" I rode Shadow towards the man with the axe who had raised it to end my man at arms' life. Neither my horse nor my sword let me down and my blow half severed the arm of the axemen, his weapon falling to the ground.

Thomas was facing down the slope and he whirled his blade before him. It bought Charles the time to grab Geoffrey's reins and begin the climb to the crest. Only Geoffrey's cantle held him in place.

A French voice shouted, "We have them. Gaspar is dead! Forget the bounty and let us have vengeance!"

I whirled to my right as I sensed a man coming at me. My sword made his horse veer and Thomas shouted, "Lord, there are too many. Let us ride!"

Reluctantly I nodded and turned Shadow to begin the leg sapping ride to the crest. We had bought enough time to give us a lead of ten paces and that would have to do. I forced Shadow to keep pace with Thomas' horse. I could not allow my brave companion to fall into the clutches of these men. Only two of their men had been eliminated and while I knew I had wounded at least one other the odds were still in their favour. I saw that we were gaining on Charles and Geoffrey whose horses were labouring towards the crest. Behind us, I heard the hooves as our pursuers began to reel us in. I glanced over my shoulder and saw the leading three men leaning forward in their saddles with their swords ready to strike us as soon as we slowed. We were tantalisingly close to safety but I knew we would not make it.

Suddenly I heard the unmistakable sound of a bowstring and as I felt the whizz of an arrow I turned and saw one of the pursuers plucked from his horse. Another three arrows followed in quick succession and three more men fell. My glance back had eased the pressure on my reins and Shadow, now weary beyond words, slowed. I saw the next four arrows fly and they struck the other followers. Four men lay on the ground and the others wheeled their horses and fled. I watched as another two fell from their horses and then the survivors made the bend and disappeared.

Nicholas War Bag and my other three archers emerged from the trees. He was grinning, "We had watched here these last three days and began to despair. Thank God we did, eh Sir Michael?"

"Indeed I will give thanks for I was sure that we were dead."

Just then Charles' voice came like a sudden shower on a midsummer's day, "Sir Michael, Geoffrey is dying!"

Chapter 9

By the time we reached Geoffrey, he was almost gone. Charles had given him his sword to hold and to kiss the hilt. The Frenchman shook his head as Geoffrey looked up at me, "It has been an honour to serve you, Sir Michael and…"

It was not enough and yet as I looking into the eyes of the dying man I knew that no words could ever have been enough. Geoffrey of Yarpole, the warrior from the west, died on the crest of the col close to Fleury sur Andelle. I had thought we would all die there but the death of just one man was too much and I felt tears on my cheeks. Thomas put his hand on my shoulder, "He died as he would have wished, my lord, fighting for you. He often said that you were the best knight and the last knight he would follow. I know he was angry with himself for letting Sir Maximilian almost escape. This was his atonement."

I closed his eyes with my fingers, "He had no need to atone." I stood and turned to Nicholas, "Thank you for your timely intervention but this not the time for words. That willcome later. Fetch the horses and the enemy dead. We will have the locals bury them. I would not want to encourage carrion."

Thomas shook his head and waved a hand at the dead Frenchmen, "The carrion are here already my lord. We have rid the world of a pestilence."

We walked the horses down to the village. There was no church, it was too small for that but we gave the villagers the coins we had taken from the bodies and asked them to bury the dead men. We left two of the horses that were too lame to take back to Les Pérets; they looked to be in need of either a working animal or the food its carcass would yield. We walked on foot for one mile. The only one on the back of his horse was Geoffrey. It was like a funeral cortege honouring a hero and that was as it should be. As we walked Nicholas explained what had happened.

"After we returned to the manor we fretted about you, my lord. I worked out that you would probably come over the Fleury col and we agreed to wait there. It is just ten miles from Les Pérets and we did not mind a couple of nights in the trees. After all, we shall soon be quitting this land and there are parts of it of which we are fond. We heard the noise of the hooves as you were pursued." He smiled, "Few travellers gallop up the steep road and we knew there might be a danger. Had we thought about it we would have waited lower down and then, perhaps, Geoffrey of Yarpole would be alive."

87

I shook my head, "Ifs, maybes and buts are not the words of warriors. We take whatever Fate throws at us. You saved three of us and who knows, had you been lower down the ambush would not have worked as well."

"And you, Sir Michael, what is your tale?"

I shook my head for Geoffrey's death hung heavily on my shoulders and I could not speak; Thomas told him of our adventures.

As the sun began to dip in the west, we mounted our horses to ride the last part of our journey. We reached the manor after dark. I was gratified when the villagers appeared armed and ready to fight as we clattered into the manor's yard. We had no priest yet to replace Father Michel but we had a church and graveyard. We honoured our friend by digging a grave and burying Geoffrey of Yarpole. Thomas and I were the ones who spoke. Thomas had been his best friend and I had fought alongside them both. To those who were not warriors then the words might not have seemed appropriate but Charles and my archers nodded as we spoke of his prowess with sword and pole axe and of his honour. Charles promised that he would have a stone cut and erected. The graveyard would have markers for all those who had died there, Henri, Maud, Father Michel and now Geoffrey of Yarpole. The dead would be remembered.

We rose late the next day for there was no need for us to hurry any longer and we exhausted in every way imaginable. I hoped that we had quashed the desire for vengeance. Only five of those who had pursued us had survived and I doubted that their hatred burned hot enough to risk crossing our paths once more. While Thomas and Nicholas went to the port to secure us a passage, I went over all that Charles would need to know what he needed to be the steward of my manor. On the second day, we rode into Rouen so that I could formerly hand over the management of the manor to Charles. I went directly to the archbishop knowing that we could have a written record. I did not want the Duke of Bedford to find some excuse to take it from Charles. He had earned the right through his blood and his loyalty to be master of the manor.

The night before we left for England I sat with my men and Charles in the warrior hall. Until the manor house was rebuilt Charles would have to share the building with the handful of men and servants who remained with the manor. "And what of the profits, my lord? Do you wish them sent to England?"

I laughed, "I can see you know little about the running of a manor. The only lords of the manor who make a profit are those who abuse their tenants and take more of the crops than they should. No, Charles, if there are profits then keep them safe. Weedon and Iden are richer manors and Sir William left me well off. If things go ill and I need money then I will send to you but use it as you will. The rebuilding of the house will consume the money for the next years and you will need more for then you begin a family."

"A family?"

"Marrying your niece was the best thing I ever did, Charles. Find happiness. You have fought enough and now is the time for you. Make the most of this peace for it may not last."

He nodded, "Will you return to France?"

"I will not say no for I know not what lies ahead but if I do then it will be reluctantly. We cannot win this war."

He nodded, "I am French and if we do win then I will be content for it means that it will be over. I have lost a brother thanks to this pointless war, fought over a crown to wear upon a head." He suddenly looked at me, "You are a clever man, Sir Michael." I cocked my head to one side, "By making a Frenchman a steward then you have the best of both worlds."

"I had not thought of that but if it means that the people of Les Pérets will be safer then I am a happy man. Before war returned to the manor, I was content here and enjoyed the company of my people."

The cog we had hired to take us home contained not only my men, our horses, our luggage and our war gear but also the wine that, somehow, the raiders had overlooked as well as the bottles of Calvados we had bought. We would be travelling, not to London but to Ipswich. It would be a longer journey from the east Anglian port to Weedon but one with less traffic than the London Road and we would be more likely to hire carters and wagons.

As the six of us stood watching the land of Normandy flash by on our journey to the sea, it was with the remembrance of men like Geoffrey of Yarpole whose graves lay in France. I thought back to those days when I had come as a boy with King Henry and we had the excitement of believing we could take France and we had so nearly succeeded. The deaths of a great king and then a great protector of king's ended that dream and now we would all look within England. Foreign wars would be a thing of the past.

I turned to Thomas. I knew that the death of Geoffrey had affected him badly, "And you, Thomas, what of you? Do you wish to serve me still?"

He did not answer immediately but stared at the land, "For the moment, then, aye, my lord, but I found the saddest part of Geoffrey's death was that he had not left his mark on this earth. Oh, we will remember his heroism and his skill but his seed died with him. Had he had children, boys especially, then they would have been great warriors to defend this land of ours. As you advised Charles I will seek a wife. I want a mother for my children and if I do that then I will not go to war again. I will defend your home but if the call comes to fight the Welsh or the Scots then I will decline." He turned to look at me, "Is that a bad thing, Sir Michael? Do you think less of me for this honesty?"

"Quite the contrary. Like you, I no longer wish to go to wars that merely serve to make powerful men even stronger and richer. I would that the duke had left me to watch over the young king. Then I would have been content. I could have shaped his mind. I respect your words and there will always be a place at Weedon. Sir William gave farms to those who had served him and I shall do the same for you."

The voyage back was not a pleasant one. We had to endure an early winter storm and the ship had to fight both the sea and the storm. When we reached Ipswich, I swore it would be a long time before I took a sea voyage again. I would get to my home and stay there. I had done enough for my country. We reached Weedon and the manor house just a few days before Christmas. It seemed to me a perfect time. I would enjoy a family Christmas and catch up with my former squire Jack. As we rode towards Weedon Thomas asked Nicholas about the manor. Thomas had not lived there and Nicholas had.

"Why it is a wonderfully large and rambling house. Sir William and his wife extended and added to it for their family. Sadly, they rarely visited. I think that Lady Isabelle and her sister will easily live there for it is large enough for them to have their own chambers. As for the men at arms, Sir William was of the Blue Company and he ever looked after the interests of men at arms and archers. The warrior halls are large and while they are not chambers as such, each warrior has his own space and yet there are tables for dining. I am looking forward to returning there."

I knew I had spent less time at Weedon than some of the men who followed me. I had spent longer in France on the wars than I had at Weedon. I was looking forward to becoming reacquainted with it.

We did not have the luxury of large numbers and I could not send a message to my wife warning her of my imminent arrival. We spent a night in Cambridge and then pushed on reaching Weedon in the late afternoon. Little Jean clung to my legs and Isabelle sobbed with relief in my arms.

"I was worried that something had happened to you. I know you said you might not be quick but…" she looked up and saw Thomas and my four archers, "is Geoffrey attending to the horses?"

"Geoffrey is dead," I put my arm around her and led her into the large dining hall. "Come I have much to say and to confess."

Jack nodded, "It is good to see you, my lord," his usual smile was replaced by a frown and chewing of the lips, "however when you have time I must speak with you in private for I have a message for you."

I was intrigued but I had to speak to Isabelle first. I sat with Jean on my knee and Isabelle knelt on the rug before the fire. I told her all but I sanitised the story so that it appeared less dangerous than it had been.

She was clever and saw the story beneath the words, "You lied to me."

"No, my love, I never said I would not hunt down Sir Maximilian. It was when we were on the road that your uncle and the others told me that the renegade Frenchmen would still come after us and I am glad that I did. Did you not hear what I told you of Jacques, the one who fought with your uncle? They had plans to come here. I confess I was not as truthful with you as I might have been but you can see that I had to do what I did. And now I am home and we are together."

"No more dishonesty, Michael. Honour me with the truth. I am stronger than you know."

"I swear that I shall." I smiled at my son, "Now then Jack, what tricks have you to show to me?" My son had grown in the short time we had been apart and the hour or so I spent with him before we ate made my heart ache. He was a lovely child and I would do all that I could to make him happy.

The two sisters fussed over the meal and made it seem a feast when it was a hurriedly thrown together concoction. It boded well for the Christmas celebrations to come. When we had eaten and Isabelle took Jean to bed, my former squire said, "Eleanor, I must speak with Sir Michael."

She beamed and kissed him. "Do not be long, husband. Seeing my sister and her family makes me want children of our own."

When she had left us alone, he shook his head, "We try each night for a child and so far God has not sent one."

"Do not worry. She is still young and there is time. Now, what is this news that took the smile from your face when I arrived home?"

"The queen, King Henry's mother, sent a message just before Isabelle and your men arrived back. She asked that you visit with her at Much Hadham in Hertfordshire."

I had not been close to the Queen Mother but we had got on. I know that she had nothing to do with my dismissal. Indeed she approved of the late king's request for me to guard his son. "And she did not say what it was about?"

He shook his head and drawled a long, "No…"

"Jack…"

He smiled, "What I have to say is gossip but fairly common gossip. Queen Catherine and Edmund Beaumont formed an attachment but, as you know, it is frowned on for former queens to consort with nobles, especially nobles with royal blood. The Duke of Gloucester had a law passed forbidding a widowed queen to marry without Parliament's permission."

"And that means his."

"Precisely."

"It is rumoured that she then fell in with a Welshman from Anglesey, one Owen Tudor and that they had run from the court." I remembered a Welshman who had left the court with the queen when I had still been the king's guardian. I had thought his name was different, Maredudd or something. At the time I had been more concerned with the safety of young King Henry than his pretty mother. "The timing is hearsay but she fell pregnant and then, it is said, married Owen Tudor in private. There is a rumour the Welshman fought at Agincourt with Sir Walter Hungerford but none of the men who were there remember him. He shrugged, "Not that it matters, my lord, but you were there. The child is called Edmund. That was three or four years since. She had another child, Jasper a year later and a third. It is said he died soon after he was born." He shrugged, "All is rumour and conjecture, really, my lord for the queen is private and keeps herself to herself but visitors on the London road know that you were the guardian of the young king and they chatter."

I nodded, "As you say, this is all gossip and had, so far as I can see, nothing at all to do with me."

"Except that the Duke of Gloucester is not happy about it. He rules England with an iron fist while the Duke of Bedford, France and Normandy."

"Does she know I was in France when the message was sent?"

"I sent John Morhier with a spoken message to that effect. She said that whenever you landed in England you should visit with her. John said that she sounded desperate."

I sighed. Was I to have no peace? Yet I knew that I had to go. Sir William Strongstaff had always put the royal family before his own life and I knew that to honour his memory, I would have to do the same. "Thank you. I will impose upon you on the morrow and ask that you accompany me. You are more attuned to the politics of England than I." I stood, "Thank you for watching over my manor and my wife and now,

I suppose, I will go and give her the news that I shall be leaving, albeit for the briefest of times."

As we lay in bed I did as she had bid me and told her the truth. She seemed quite calm about it. Catherine of Valois had been a French princess and I think my wife felt sorry for her, having lost her husband so soon after the birth of her son. "And this Much Hadham, is it far?"

"Seventy miles."

"Then you will need to stay overnight. I will find some decent clothes for you. After all, you are meeting a queen." Practical matters always came to the fore of my young wife's mind.

The long journey necessitated an early departure and even my son, who always liked to rise early, was barely awake as he waved me a weak goodbye. Jack led a sumpter with clothes fit for a meeting with a queen and we were well wrapped against the elements. Thankfully the air was dry but the wind, slicing into our faces all the way, came from the east and felt like knives. At that time of day, the road was empty and we could speak without fear of being overhear; it passed the time.

"Jack, I would have you knighted. Perhaps, I should see one of Sir William's sons. They could do this for me. They owe me that much, at least." I was not sure if Sir William's sons resented the fact that I had been left the family home. Certainly, their manors and homes were far grander than mine but Weedon had been Sir William's favourite.

"Sir Michael, I am uncertain if I wish to be a knight."

I turned in the saddle to look at him and felt the relief from the driving wind, "Not a knight, but you are my squire?"

He nodded, "And when I left my father and Weedon I thought that being a knight was all that I wanted. Meeting Eleanor was part of the change but when you sent me back to be steward then I knew that while I am a good warrior, I am a better steward. I like the variety of tasks and the old warriors left by Sir William helped me greatly."

"I am pleased."

"And the other reason is that I do not wish to be at the beck and call of every lord who is my superior. You and Sir William have been taken from your families too often."

"Things have changed now, Jack, a knight can refuse and pay another to go in his place."

Jack laughed, "Sir Michael, when you were sent for this time it was because Sir John Talbot knew that you were the best man for the job and while he has let you return home, if things go badly then you will be summoned and," he looked at me, "you will go."

I said nothing for I knew that I had a flaw in me, I obeyed summons from those who were above me. I looked at Jack and knew that he was adamant and he would not be knighted. Now that I knew the reasons, I would not push the matter. Instead, I asked him about the queen and this Owen Tudor. He told me all that he knew and then said, "You met him, lord, at Windsor."

I frowned. I remembered a Welshman and the scandal in the castle when he and the queen had fled. It had been kept secret outside of the court for neither of her brothers in law, the two dukes, wished the scandal to be known. The queen was rich. King Henry had been generous and had given her many manors. Some were in Hertfordshire but most were in North Wales or the Welsh marches. I remembered then that I had been surprised at her action for Edmund Beaufort had been a constant visitor until the Duke of Gloucester had warned him off. I knew then that I should have spoken to John Morhier to ask him the precise words the queen had used and to ask him about the Welshman. Jack gave me sketchy answers about the politics of court. He knew little for the ripples from court rarely touched my manor.

We reached the huge manor house after dark. There was an imposing gatehouse and a high wall that surrounded it. It had no mailed guards but the men who answered the door looked to know their business and it took the signet ring I wore to gain us admittance. A small Welshman scurried from a chamber to the side, "I am Iago ap Maredudd and Queen Catherine's steward."

The fact that he was a Welshman and not a Frenchman surprised me. "I am Sir Michael of Weedon and just returned to England. The queen asked to see me as soon as I arrived."

He smiled, "Quite so, Peter, take this knight's squire and their baggage to the guest room in the east wing. Davy, see to their horses." He gestured at my cloak, "If you would give your cloak to your squire, I shall take you to her majesty."

Jack nodded, "I will see to the laying out of your clothes." He looked at the steward, "We have travelled all day and had little food."

"Of course, and the queen has yet to dine. I will have extra places laid." He led me along a corridor lit by burning brands in gilded sconces and we entered a cosy chamber where a large fire roared. The queen was with her ladies and one of the three was reading to her. "Your Majesty, Sir Michael of Weedon."

I was shocked by her appearance. When I had last seen her, some years earlier, she had been the most stunningly beautiful creature I had ever seen. She still had beauty but she had aged and her face showed that she was unwell. Her smile, however, was as radiant as I remembered and it warmed me as much as the fire as she held out her

94

hand for me to kiss. "Ladies, leave us." I kissed the back of her hand and she said, "Iago?"

"I will make the arrangements."

As they all scurried off and closed the door, she gestured to the seat opposite hers recently vacated by a lady in waiting. "Thank you for coming. I began to think that I was being shunned." She had spoken in English to her steward but now she spoke in French.

I shook my head, "My lady, I knew nothing for I was in France with Sir John Talbot."

"I heard he had been summoned." She sighed, "Once I was at the centre of all and now…"

I said nothing but I knew that she had chosen this life. She could have forced the Duke of Gloucester to let her mould her son but she had not. I think that she had liked life too much. Edmund Beaufort had been a handsome and dashing knight and I vaguely remembered the Welshman. He too was good looking in a different way.

"You know that I had nothing to do with your dismissal?" I nodded. She had not even been at court so how could she? "Pour us a glass of wine and I will confide in you." As I did so she said, "King Henry trusted you and so do I. Whatever I say here remains between us."

I turned and handed her the glass, "Of course, my lady."

She looked relieved, "I am married although it was a secret marriage and the Duke of Gloucester is unhappy about the fact. Owen Tudor is my husband." My eyes must have flickered involuntarily to the door for she said, "He is in Flintshire, at the moment, but he will return for the Christmas celebrations. I have four children, Edmund, Jasper, Owen and Margaret. My daughter was born only recently and it was a difficult birth. It is the main reason I have sent for you."

Whatever I had expected of the queen this was not one of the many explanations I had concocted in my mind. "Your daughter? I do not understand."

"I never chose my life. I did not ask to be born a French princess nor marry the warrior king of England. Do not get me wrong, Sir Michael, I loved King Henry but he was taken too soon from me. I thought, when I wed Owen, that I would be allowed to live my own life but that is not meant to be. The Duke of Gloucester had a law passed forbidding my marriage and, as you know, Welshmen are forbidden by law from owning land in England." She emptied the wine glass. Mine was still half full. She gestured for me to refill it. "I am barely thirty years of age yet I look ancient."

"My lady, you are beautiful." I handed her the refilled glass.

"And you are a gentleman. The beauty I have is fading and I fear I shall not see forty." She sipped the wine, "You are married, I believe." I nodded. "To a Frenchwoman."

"A Norman, my lady."

She smiled, "A minor distinction. You married for love?"

"I did and my squire married her sister, also for love."

"Then you are lucky. I was chosen to marry King Henry. Women of the nobility are like brood mares especially when they have royal blood. I have no claim to the French crown but my blood might help some future aspirants try to take it. Owen is safe and monks care for him." The way she said he name Owen, her son, made me wonder for she spoke it wistfully. There was a tale there. "Edmund and Jasper are boys and my husband will raise them as warriors and knights. Both will be rich for, when I die, they and my husband shall inherit all that King Henry left to me. Owen," she gave a sad smile for she had seen my look when she had mentioned his name, "is a special child and the monks at Westminster watch over him. He will live a long and happy life beyond the gaze of men. Margaret is different. She is a female and when I am gone, I do not think that my husband will give her a second thought. I want her to be loved."

I thought of my own unborn child and Jean. I nodded, "Every parent wishes that."

"Sir Michael, you swore an oath to watch my son Henry. I know that in your heart you still keep that oath." I needed to say nothing for she was right. I would have you swear another oath, here in my chambers. That none shall know of it save you and I does not matter for you are a knight and an honourable one at that. You keep your word. King Henry trusted you as did Sir William Strongstaff. You and your mentor are above politics and that is what I need. I wish you to swear an oath and be the Queen's knight."

I was stunned for I knew not what she required of me. She had a husband and surely, he could fight for her if she needed it. However, I obeyed, I dropped to my knee and bowed my head, "I shall swear my lady but I know not what my duties shall be."

She put her soft fingers under my chin and raised it so that she could look into my eyes, "Take my daughter and raise her with your family. I cannot give her a manor but I can give one to you so that she will have an income and a family when she grows." I was shocked and she saw it in my face. "You are so honourable, Sir Michael, that you cannot see the black hearts of some of those who fawn on me. I give up my daughter out of love. I can see in your eyes that you are a gentle man and you married for love. I have never met your wife but if you have chosen her then I know that she will be a good mother to my daughter. Take out your sword and swear."

I slid my sword out and held it like a cross. "I swear to be the Queen's knight."

I was about to replace the sword when her hands pressed my hand onto the sword. I felt a tendril of blood as the edge cut into me. She added a codicil to the oath, "And I swear that I will protect all those borne of Queen Catherine of England." I looked up into her eyes and, smiling sadly, she nodded. "All of them! Henry, Edmund, Jasper and Margaret."

I knew I could not refuse. Sir William would have agreed immediately and I owed all to him, "And I swear that I will protect all those borne of Queen Catherine of England."

She beamed and suddenly looked younger, "Now you may rise." She waved towards the chair as I replaced my sword and then sucked the blood from my fingers. The oath was even more binding now for it was a blood oath. "Margaret has a wet nurse. Sarah lost her own child. I think it was the news that her husband died fighting in France. It is a shame for she has barely turned twenty. She is a lovely young woman and she tends to the baby for me. I shall tell my husband and my ladies that Margaret died. Owen wants sons and my ladies are too frivolous to be concerned with a mewling four-month-old child. You will need to stay another day so that I can have my priest make the legal arrangements for the manor. It will be in your name but you and I know that it will be for my daughter."

"Of course, but are you sure about this? Can you give up your child? I know that I could not."

"And that is why you were chosen. I did not ask to be of royal blood and that makes us different Sir Michael. I cannot guarantee my daughter's happiness. You can."

Weedon

N

Blecheley

Haughton Regis

Much Hadham

Colchester

Waltham Abbey

Griff 2022

Chelmsford

Westminster Abbey

Barking Abbey

The Thames

Bermondsey Abbey

Les Pleasaunce

12 Miles

Chapter 10

The Queen had me seated at her right hand when we ate. Jack was seated amongst her ladies and Father Bertrand, the Queen's confessor sat on my other side. The priest was an older man with white flecked and thinning hair. He said little but I saw him observing everything. I have no idea what we ate that night although I suspect it was superbly cooked and delicious. My mind was running through all the things I had to do. Not least amongst the list was how to tell Isabelle that we had a daughter for that was what it amounted to. The queen had told me to raise Margaret as my own and that I would do. I knew how fond Sir William had become of me and that Isabelle and I would be just as loving with the child for that was in our nature. When I had reached England Isabelle had told me she was pregnant. Would the extra child be to much for her?

Before the main course was brought in Queen Catherine stood, "I give a toast, Sir Michael of Weedon who has now agreed to be Queen Catherine's Knight." Although all the glasses and goblets were raised, in the small gathering in the intimate hall, I saw the looks of surprise on the faces of her three ladies in waiting. She had not mentioned it to them. "As payment for his future services I give him the manor of Houghton Regis. It was a gift from my husband and as it lies twixt here and Sir Michael's home at Weedon it seems perfect for we can visit each other."

The reward brought curious looks from all apart from Iago and Father Bertrand. I could see that they were her confidantes. When the food was brought in the queen nodded to Father Bertrand, "And while I get to know your squire a little better, I pray that you speak with Father Bertrand. He is my confessor and my soul is an open book to him." It was a command and not a request.

She turned and I faced the priest who smiled, "I am pleased that you are such an honest knight, Sir Michael, who cannot hide his feelings or mask his emotions. You are surprised and humbled by the gift I can see but you should be proud that you have been chosen." He lowered his voice, "To give up a child is a hard thing but the queen is not well and while she knows that her sons will be protected by their father the fate of an infant girl is less certain."

"Why me, Father?"

"The alternative would be a nunnery. If I was a younger priest, I might see that as the most worthy of vocations but I am older now and unlike many of my fellows, celibate. I can see how attractive a life with the prospect of children might be and from what I know of you, Sir

Michael, your home will be a happy one." I gave him a quizzical look. "The queen came up with this plan when she bore Margaret all those months ago. She was not well and while she may attempt to have more children I am not certain that it is the best of ideas She sent me to Weedon to investigate you. I stayed with the monks at Weedon Bec and I learned that, like Sir William, none had a bad word to say about you. I spoke to your squire's wife in Northampton market and discovered that you had a family and that you were a devoted father. All of this makes you perfect and then, of course, there is your sword."

"My sword."

"You may have to defend, not only Margaret but also Edmund and Jasper." He nodded, "The queen told me of the oath she would ask you to swear. You are a renowned knight and while you do not lead large armies men would follow you if you had to defend her children."

"But who would wish them harm?"

The priest said nothing at first but chewed thoughtfully on a piece of meat. He swallowed, dabbed his mouth and then gestured to the coats of arms displayed around the manor which had belonged to the Plantagenets, "A family with a noble history, eh my lord? They have held to the crown, some might say, ruthlessly."

I caught his eye and the slightest of nods. He was telling me that her brothers in law might well wish harm upon them. They had no royal blood but being borne of the queen were a threat. What had I taken on?

Later that night, my mind aching with all the information I had gathered as we prepared for bed Jack, after ensuring that none overheard, bombarded me with questions. They were all understandable. "My lord, what is this about? You are given a manor and have to protect the widow of King Henry? It strikes me as a dangerous task." Even Jack knew the dangers of the king's uncles.

I smiled, he would know the truth in any case for he would be escorting the wet nurse and the child. "It is more parlous than that, Jack, I am to ask my wife to help me raise the queen's daughter as our own."

Jack sat on the bed open-mouthed and then said, "That is unfair."

"Perhaps but if it was asked of you, what would your answer be?"

He sat in silence for a moment and then nodded, "You are right. The child is innocent in all of this. And the father?"

I shrugged, "That, to me, is the most interesting part of this. He is not here and, from what I have been told, will have little interest in a daughter. I will make it my business to find out more about this Owen Tudor."

I did not sleep well and was glad when a thin sun dawned. After we had breakfasted Father Bertrand fetched Jack and me to a small room on the top floor of the hall. The queen was inside and cuddling a laughing baby. A young woman, I took her to be Sarah, the wet nurse was resting in a chair.

"This is Margaret, Sir Michael and, as you can see, she is a happy baby." I saw Sarah's eyes roll towards the ceiling. "However, she has her moments and Sarah is exhausted after a night of broken sleep." She held the baby towards me, "Here."

Although Isabelle had sent my best clothes to wear I still felt they were too rough for what was a royal baby however I knew how to hold children and I took her in my arms and gave her the silly smile that had always worked with Jean. She giggled and the queen clapped her hands. "See, Father Bertrand, I have made a good choice."

The priest gave an embarrassed look, "When the queen handed Lady Margaret to me the bairn cried."

The queen turned and chastised the priest, "None of that Lady Margaret. She is Margaret for I do not wish attention drawn to her."

I bounced the child in my arms and asked, "There is something I need to ask. How will the baby be explained to the people in my hall? I speak not of Isabelle and Eleanor but the rest of the household."

The queen had thought this through, "You have taken pity on Sarah who is an unfortunate who had a child out of wedlock. Sarah is happy with this deception for she is to be paid an annuity of one hundred pounds a year so long as Margaret is unwed. I asked you to look after them because I knew you were an honourable knight." She looked at the priest and wet nurse, "All is well is it not?"

Father Bertrand said, "Jesus suffered little children to come unto him. I am content."

Sarah smiled, "And I am happy, Sir Michael. I promise that I will not be a burden to you and when Margaret no longer needs me as a nurse I will happily work as a servant."

All seemed happy but I was not sure how Isabelle would view it all. I handed the baby back to the queen, "And now I ask how we spirit the child away for I can see that you have kept these two apart and from the words last night I know that the ladies know nothing of this."

The queen nodded, "It will be a departure before dawn. Father Bertrand will accompany you. It is too great a journey to do in one day and so you shall stay tomorrow night in Houghton Regis. The Father will have the documents you need to take ownership of the royal lodge. He will explain to any in your household the reasons behind the arrival of a baby and its mother." She smiled, "I have thought all of this out, Sir Michael. I grew up in a world of deception, lies and half-lies. I know how to weave a tale." I nodded my acceptance. "Your squire will have to lead the horses with all that my daughter and her nurse needs. I apologise for that but the fewer who know of this the better." She held her child tightly to her bosom and I saw a tear trickle down her cheek as she said, "I want my daughter to have a good life and if that means that the years remaining to me are sad ones, then so be it. When I was a child my mother told me of the sacrifices I would have to make as the daughter of the King of France. I never thought my own child would be one of them but my son Henry is lost to me and those who watch him are less honourable than you Sir Michael, so I am content."

"What will they say when you tell them that your daughter is dead?"

"I am a queen and they will just think me heartless that I do not even have her buried." She gave me a sad smile. "Sir Michael. it is just another part I play. A queen does not cry in public." She put her hand on father Bertrand's, "Father Bertrand is my confessor and my conscience. He approves."

The old priest nodded and I saw in his eyes how he had wrestled with the dilemma.

"Sarah, can you ride or shall we have a wagon?"

"I can ride but not whilst carrying a baby."

Father Bertrand said, "And I am too old to bounce around on the back of a horse. A small wagon or even a cart would suffice."

"Would you go and ask Iago to find one. I confess I had not thought of that."

"It will be easier, my lady, for this way Jack will not need to lead horses."

The baby began to cry and the queen handed her to Sarah, "I think we should leave now. My daughter is ready for a feed and while I do not wish to waste one moment of my time with her, she needs to feed. This night I will spend with Sarah and Margaret. You shall dine with Father Bertrand and my ladies. We will tell them that I am ill. It has happened many times lately. They will believe it."

As we left, I felt inordinately sorry for the queen. To the rest of the country, she would appear to have a lovely life with no worries or fears about food, a roof and being protected from danger but the reality was that there were other parts of her life that one would not wish on their worst enemy. Jack and I went to the stables to check on our horses and there we met Iago. "I will have horses and wagon prepared for you but," he hesitated, "One does not like to speak ill of a man of the cloth but Father Bertrand is not the best with animals. He is no St Francis. Perhaps, young master if you could drive and…"

Jack smiled, "Aye, I can do that."

Relieved Iago said, "I will come for you at Lauds, my lord. There will be hot food but it will be served in the queen's small dining room. There will be no guards when you leave. I shall be chamberlain and bodyguard until dawn." He turned to go and then faced me once more, "What you do, my lord is a good thing. That none will know of it and yet you still do it speaks well of you." He left.

It seemed by a moment before I was shaken awake. Jack and I dressed for the road. We would not need mail but put on extra layers. We went to the wagon first. Iago himself was attaching the horses. He was a resourceful man and I could see that he was devoted to the queen. There was a story there. How had a Welshman become so attached to a French woman? Even as I headed to the small hall having deposited our gear in the wagon, I knew the answer; she beguiled men. Although no longer the beautiful princess of which troubadours sang her eyes bewitched and entranced men. I had felt it too.

The short walk to the stables and back was enough to chill me to the bone and I hurried to the smell emanating from the hall. The food was hot and plentiful. Father Bertrand was eating for two and it was the queen who cuddled her daughter, probably for the last time. Sarah, as I came to realise was an eminently practical woman and she was eating food, which if she had not been a royal wet nurse she could have only dreamed about.

All too soon it was time to go. I felt evil as I mentioned that time was passing. The queen nodded and handed her child to Sarah, kissing Margaret gently on the lips. Sarah said, "I swear, my lady, that she will be happy and that she will think fondly of you."

The queen shook her head, "No, Sarah. She can be fond of the queen but she must never know that I was her mother. I know from my own country that distant relatives can come to untimely ends just for being a relative."

She was right. I remembered the story of a Breton princess who had been incarcerated in England just because her children, had she had any, would have enjoyed a claim to the crown.

The queen looked at me. "I announced that you were my knight, Sir Michael, I may call upon you to visit. I pray that you heed any such call with alacrity, not because of my position but because if I send for you then it will be urgent."

"And I shall come, my lady, for I swore an oath and I will never break an oath."

"I know." She stood on tiptoes and kissed me on the cheek. "No, go for when you are departed such tears will flow that my hall may become moated."

Sarah swaddled the baby and then donned a fur which the queen herself handed her. We hurried out into the chilly December morning. Iago had thoughtfully made a nest in the back of the wagon with furs and soft pillows. He had rigged a cloak over the top so that the nurse and her charge were not only protected from the elements but hidden from the gaze of folks on the road. A basket of hot food wrapped in straw was placed close by and Sarah would be comfortable for the thirty-mile journey ahead. Jack fastened his horse to the rear of the wagon and then helped the portly priest into the seat. He climbed up and took the reins. We needed no words to send us on our way and we slipped away from the manor like thieves in the night. We had a long day of riding ahead and an even longer one the following day. Anonymity was the key. Iago had assured us that we had good horses to pull the wagon and that there were spares at Houghton Regis. I hoped so. Normally a wagon moved at the pace of a walking man. I intended it to be slightly faster. We did not speak until dawn broke. I peered in the back and saw that Sarah and her charge were asleep. That was good. I rode next to Father Bertrand.

"Father, I do not wish gossip nor do I wish you to break your confessional but there are things I need to know if I am to be the queen's knight."

He nodded, "If I can answer then I shall."

"This child, Owen, what is his story?"

"You have heard the rumour that the queen married in haste because she was with child?" I nodded, "Owen was that child but it became clear that he had, shall we say, problems. Healthy enough physically, he would never be a warrior and his father asked me to entrust him to those who might care for him. The queen wanted a happy life for him. The monks at Westminster were a good choice. The child is now five and I see him when I visit London, he is happy and content. The monks believe him to be my child and I do not disillusion them."

"Then he is not the son of Edmund Beaufort?"

"That was a scurrilous lie put about by the enemies of the queen. She has many. While King Henry lived, she was accepted but she is French and the daughter of the French king who is inexorably recovering his lands. It did not cause her illness but has made it worse."

"And Owen Tudor, what of him?"

The priest was silent for a while and then sighed, "The queen is enamoured of him and he is a personable young man but I fear his ambition."

He glanced to the rear of the wagon and I shook my head, "She sleeps and you can trust Jack."

"Welshmen, as you know, cannot own land in England. The queen has used what little influence she still has to gain him denizenship. He is now accepted as an Englishman and can keep the manors that the queen has given to him. He is devoted to Edmund and Jasper. He will ensure that they are Englishmen and he will have them trained to be knights." He shook his head, "Girls cannot inherit and so the queen has done what she has done."

I began to piece together the story in my head. That there was an illness was clear. There had been doctors at Much Hadham and the queen had been whisked away to see them twice in my short stay there. She was a clever woman and could not guarantee that her daughter would be cared for. Her decision to use me and my family, unlikely though it had seemed when it was first broached, now made perfect sense.

"This puts my family in danger, does it not?"

When the priest was silent, he confirmed my fears. We plodded along with just the sound of hooves on the road to mark the time. He peered into the back to ensure that the nurse and Margaret still slept and then he said, "I do not wish to tell you what to do, my lord, but I would beg you not to upset the Duke of Gloucester. He is the enemy of Owen Tudor and only the queen's protection saves him. She is the mother of the king and Humphrey, Duke of Gloucester is wise enough not to alienate the king. He is very fond of his mother."

"Despite the fact that he was abandoned at an early age?"

"I think that abandonment made him put his mother on a pedestal for he believes she did it for his sake. He may never be a warrior king like his father but he sees the machinations of politicians and understands how these things work. No, Sir Michael, while the queen lives then the world is in harmony but when she dies…"

I saw then that I would need to use my men at arms and archers as guards and protectors. I had allowed the numbers of my retinue to fall. Now I would use Thomas of Chester and Nicholas War Bag to recruit more men. I now had the income from Houghton Regis and using the money to protect not only my family but the queen's seemed a good use of the funds. I would need men who could fight. These would not be major battles. I would not fight another Verneuil or Agincourt but the men I hired would have to be able to handle any combat. Thomas had shown that he was a perfect leader for such a band of warriors.

We managed to reach Houghton Regis not long after night had descended. With days just five hours long that was no mean feat. The letters we had brought from the queen ensured that we were admitted and while Sarah and Margaret were taken to a bed in a room with a good fire and Jack saw to the animals I spoke with the steward, Ralph of Dunstable and Father Bertrand.

"Queen Catherine has given this manor to me, Ralph and I will be making use of it."

He nodded and then said, guardedly, "It is a royal manor, Sir Michael."

Father Bertrand handed over a parchment for the steward to scrutinise, "And now it is Sir Michael's. All was done legally."

The steward looked relieved, "I just had to be certain, my lord, no offence."

"And none taken. To put your mind at rest I have no intention of removing you from your office. You know this manor better than any. We will leave early tomorrow before the sun is up and I will need to replace the draught horses."

"I can replace the two with four, my lord, to speed your journey. This is winter and we need them not for the fields."

I beamed, "Then you and I shall get on famously, Ralph for I can see that you are a resourceful man."

He nodded, "And when I was younger, I served for a time with Rafe Red Beard and Sir William. If you were named as Sir William's heir then you are a good man."

I was even more relieved to know that I had a former warrior who knew Rafe. The ties that bound us were strange and defied logic.

All that I had time for was a rapid tour around the hall which was larger than my own manor ar Weedon. Being a royal residence it had been used by kings who brought with them a large entourage. The accommodation for servants was sumptuous compared with most that I had seen and the manor boasted twelve chambers for sleeping. Not all were large ones but the one used by the kings looked big enough to joust in.

The steward's household, mainly his wife and children, cobbled together a hurried meal for us. His wife, Marianne, asked, "Will you be living here, my lord?"

At first, when I had been told of the gift, I had no intentions of moving but the more I had thought about it the better the idea sounded. I was cautious in my reply, "Perhaps but I must speak with my wife first." The three of us were left alone. Sarah was a quick eater and she had eaten while Ralph's wife had nursed, what seemed to me, a very easy going and affable baby.

Marianne was happy to heat water for a bath and so the three of us finished off the bottle of wine and discussed the next day. "It is forty miles to our home, Jack, but do you think that with the two extra horses we can do it in one day?"

"I think it is imperative, my lord. If we risk another night somewhere else then the identity of the babe might become known. If you wish my opinion then we need to have Margaret as part of your family as soon as possible. In addition, we said we would be home this day. I know that both our wives will worry."

Jack was right and before we retired, I asked Ralph to wake us well before dawn. He was intrigued by Sarah, "The girl and the baby with you, my lord, what is their tale?"

The question made my heart sink but I knew that I needed an answer for it was one that would rear its head for quite a while. I would have to speak to Sarah when we travelled the last part of our journey but I came up with the story for Ralph for if we returned, he would need to believe that we had adopted Margaret.

"She is an unfortunate young woman who needs our help and the baby has to have a loving home. When the queen made her gift of this manor, Father Bertrand asked me if my family could help. I go to ask my wife."

"That is very Christian of you, my lord. If there is aught that Marianne and I can do..."

"Keep what I have told you to yourself and your wife. We all know how hurtful can be gossip. If I visit or come to stay here then the child, hopefully, will be my foster child."

He tapped his nose, "I understand, my lord and you can rely on our discretion."

The next day, as we rode, I discussed the matter with Sarah. She was a pragmatic young woman. "Since my husband died, my lord, I have little prospect of family life. I am happy to go along with the lie for the queen was kind to me and I love little Mags as though she was my own. My life means nothing compared with hers."

Father Bertrand had listened to our words and he said, "Do not be so willing to settle for a lonely life. There are many men who would find you more than attractive as a wife and mother."

"You are a kind man, Father Bertrand, but I will keep my ambitions low. A happy life alone is better than a sad one and I shall try to make my life as happy as I can."

The Duke of Bedford fought wars in France for many reasons but one side effect was that men died and women like Sarah were left as widows and I could not see the reason for it.

Chapter 11

Halfway to our home, we came to the farm at Stony Stratford that had been the first manor of Sir William and Lady Eleanor. It now belonged to Sir William's son but I knew the steward, Richard for I had visited the manor on a number of occasions with Sir William. We stopped so that the baby could be changed and we enjoyed a warm by the fire. Richard had fond memories of Sir William and he did all that he could for us. The hot food, potage, that his wife Anne served to us enabled us to push on further than we might have without a rest.

Weedon's welcoming light was like a beacon in the night as my horse wearily clumped his way into the yard. The door opened and a shaft of light showed Isabelle and Eleanor looking anxiously out, "Thank God," She turned and shouted, "Sister, it is our husbands!"

Isabelle rushed out as I swung a tired and aching leg over the cantle. "You said one night!"

I kissed her and said, in her ear, "It could not be helped and the queen has given me a task. It involves you and the whole family so, I beg you, wait until our guests are settled in their rooms before I am beset by questions."

She stepped back, the hostess in her coming to the fore, "Guests?"

"Father Bertrand, the queen's confessor, Sarah and a babe."

"A babe and you are leaving her out in this cold! Have you taken leave of your senses?" She held a hand out and said, "Come, I apologise for my husband!" Sarah carried the swaddled baby from the wagon and as she passed her my wife said, "Men!"

Sarah smiled as she passed my pregnant wife and said, "Lady, you are lucky and you have a good one."

Isabelle gave me a funny look. I had much explaining to do. The arrival of the guests caused such an upheaval that there were no questions before we all wearily trudged off to our beds. It was in my warm and comforting bed that the interrogation began. I should have initiated it for Isabelle had devised her own explanation. "This child is yours, is it? And you boldly bring her here for me to raise with Jean and our unborn child?"

I squeezed her closer to me and kissed her. My words were gentle and soothing, "Until I visited the queen, I had never seen Sarah and knew nothing of Margaret." I sighed, "She is the queen's daughter and we have been asked to raise her as our own."

The silence that ensued showed that I had stunned my wife. Rather than answer questions that might not get us anywhere, I told her all that I had been told. I even spoke of Owen, the child who would be a monk.

The silence when I had finished told me that my wife was now thinking about what to do. Eventually, she squeezed my hand and said, "Sarah is right and you are a good man but what you can do to protect Margaret's elder brothers I know not. My child is due in a month. When Christmas is over, we should move to this new manor at Houghton Regis."

That surprised me, "You would leave Weedon and your sister?"

"This is Eleanor's home and to have two mistresses in one house is never a good thing. I love my sister but there would be words and I would not have that. The new baby and the secret makes the move necessary." There was a sudden intake of breath, "She will have to know of this will she not?"

"I fear so. We have to keep the babe's identity a secret but there are some who will know all. You may be right. If we move to Houghton Regis then there will be fewer questions. You are wise."

"The manor is a good one?"

"I know not the income but the hall itself is palatial compared with Weedon."

"And Sarah, the wet nurse?"

"She will live with us until Margaret no longer needs her care."

My wife was practical, "She could be a nurse to Jean and my new baby too. We could pay her as part of our household."

I thought about the idea and it appealed. By the time we had talked enough, we had planned our future and our story. I wondered if Jack was having a similar conversation with his wife.

The next day Isabelle and I spoke with Father Bertrand and told him our plans. His smile told me that he approved.

Isabelle asked, "Will you stay with us and celebrate Christmas, Father?"

He shook his head, "I had planned on leaving this day to return to the queen. She will be anxious to know how her daughter was received. I can tell her that this is a loving home and family. Last night I saw it while we ate. My silence enabled me to observe you all and I am content."

I looked at Isabelle, "And I should ride with the father to Houghton Regis. If we are to go there in a couple of months then Ralph and his wife will need to know that. There are preparations to be made."

"Christmas is but three days hence, husband."

"And while the journey there will be a day I can ride back far more quickly. I will take Thomas and two of my archers with me for they will need to view the new manor. I hope to take some to live with us there but I know that some of them have put down roots here at Weedon."

We left soon after breakfast and I knew that we would arrive at Houghton Regis well after dark but that could not be helped. We were aided by the fact that the wagon was now empty. Father Bertrand would have to travel the next day on the back of a horse but that was a sacrifice he would have to make.

I rode with Thomas and Nicholas, who both had questions. "A royal manor is a great honour, Sir Michael, are you to be elevated?"

I knew what he meant. I was a banneret. Thomas wondered if I would become a baron. I shook my head, "I am the queen's knight, that is all." I looked at the two men alongside whom I had faced death many times. I dared not tell them the truth but I needed their help. "I pray that if there are questions about the babe, Margaret, you will respect my wishes. She is now part of my family and shall be accorded the same rights and privileges as Jean who now becomes her elder brother. As far as the world is concerned she is our child. You know that she will be a foster daughter. Let others speculate but you must be consistent in your story."

Nicholas nodded, "There were rumours as soon as you arrived back last night, my lord. Your men are loyal and know that there can be nothing dishonourable in your actions but there are questions. We will honour your wishes but when men are in drink there will be talk and wild theories."

I know but hopefully, this will be a seven-day wonder and when my new child is born then Margaret will just be accepted." They both nodded, "And you should know that we are moving to Houghton Regis and it will be after twelfth night. I need to know which of my men would come with me. I will not uproot any who are happy at Weedon."

Thomas laughed, "We have not had time yet to settle. I for one will come with you."

"And I another."

That made me happy for the two men were as close to me as brothers. Indeed that is what they were, brothers in arms and far closer to me than, say the two dukes who between them, ruled England and France.

There was a village in a clearing in the forest just twelve miles from Houghton Regis. Blecheley had just ten houses and a deserted manor house. We were forced to stop there for the wheel on the wagon threatened to come off. The village had a smithy and Robbie Red Fletch was able to repair it. Seeing the priest the smith's wife fetched us ale that had been heated with a poker and infused with butter. Although not to my taste it would have been churlish to refuse.

I mentioned that I had been given the manor at Houghton Regis and her face darkened a little. I wondered why. "I have lived all my life here in Blecheley and I have never heard of the king or the queen visiting Houghton Regis. I suppose it needs a lord of the manor."

"What happened to this manor?" I pointed to the old manor house which was derelict.

"None have lived there in living memory. It is said that the last lord of the manor who lived there upset King John and he was blinded as a punishment. When he died the manor was abandoned." She shrugged, "That was the tale I heard."

Father Bertrand asked, "And to whom do you pay taxes?"

She shifted uncomfortably, "I know not, you should ask my husband." She took our empty beakers, "And now I should get on. I pray you to have a safe journey. The woods are not safe places at night." She hurriedly disappeared.

Was that a threat or just friendly advice? She had clearly said that which she should not.

The wheel fixed we hurried on. I rode next to the wagon to speak with the priest, "I liked not that last comment, Sir Michael, the one about danger from the trees. The sooner I am delivered the better." He waved at hand at the trees that seemed to encroach upon the road. It was now getting on to dark and they seemed more threatening.

"Aye, and I can see that she was hiding something, the question is, what?"

It was Ralph, my new steward who enlightened us, "Blecheley has long been a thorn, my lord. The people there should pay their taxes to the Sheriff of Bedfordshire but they do not. The village lies close to Buckinghamshire and as there are bandits in the forest then tax collectors rarely travel that far. The ones that tried it were robbed and they would risk it again. It is not worth it just to collect a few pennies. The folk in the village make a living and have no responsibilities. They tolerate the bandits who prey on travellers." He shook his head, "I fought for this country and it galls me that there are men who did not and yet reaped the rewards of our victories. They enjoyed the peace that good King Henry won for us."

Father Bertrand said, "I will speak to the queen and, when we next visit the king in London, I shall tell him. He is young but he should know these things."

It struck me that the Duke of Gloucester should be the one to take action. I knew that I would have to present myself at some time to the duke to inform him of the gift from the queen. I wondered how he would take it. I was also aware that I needed to speak to the king for my role as the knight of the queen, his mother, ought to be explained to him. He was now thirteen years old but had not yet, despite his two coronations, declared himself old enough to rule. I wondered how his two uncles would view that. Until he did so they were effectively ruling the lands of their nephew.

Ralph and Marianne were more than pleased with my news and keen to know the exact time of our arrival. "I cannot say precisely but once twelfth night is over then expect us."

We ate another quickly cooked but satisfying meal and the priest was happy for Thomas, Nicholas, and Robbie to join us. In truth we had all dressed the same on the road. The only thing that marked me as a noble was that I rode Shadow and as my three fellows had horses almost as good as mine then it was an indiscernible distinction.

"Will you head back to Much Hadham in the morning, Father?"

"Aye, Sir Michael but it will not be as early as you rise. My days of rising for Matins and Laudes is in the past. The queen keeps much more reasonable hours than you."

The four of us laughed and Thomas said, "A warrior learns to rise early in case some enemy is sneaking up."

Marianne had just fetched in more fresh bread and she said, "Surely that is no longer true for you are in England and peace rules this land?"

I said nothing but Father Bertrand answered for me, "So long as we have a child king and men seek the crown there will be no peace. Richard, Duke of York, has blood in his veins that takes him back to the Black Prince's brothers, Lionel, Duke of Clarence and Edmund, Duke of York. Thus far the young man has shown no desire to make a claim for the crown but that does not mean he will not or that some other might choose to use him. And do not forget the French. I know from my time with the queen that the French often seek to cause problems in England to relieve pressure in their home. So long as Paris is ruled by Englishmen then there will be war."

She shook her head, "I am glad we live in such a peaceful backwater as this, my lord and the sooner you and Lady Isabelle get here the better."

I was tired when I went to bed for the last few days of hard riding had taken its toll. When I woke I was still groggy and bleary-eyed. We bade a quick farewell and headed along the road that would take us home. We were four miles down the road before I realised that I had left my signet ring in the room we had used.

"I will go back for it, my lord."

"I am sorry, Robbie, to have inconvenienced you. I feel a fool but I need the signet ring."

He said, cheerfully, "I will enjoy the ride, my lord and we will see how swift Mary is!" He had a palfrey that had been sired by Storm. Thus far he had plodded for he had not yet taken her to war. Now was his chance to see how fast she really was.

The wind was icy again and there was the threat of snow in the west. We pulled our hoods over our heads and tightened the fastenings on the cloaks. I wished I had worn my rabbit skin hat. I had spent too long in Normandy which had a more benign climate. We reached Blecheley and I decided to wait there for Robbie. It was not fair to make him rise too far alone. The houses seemed deserted and that surprised me. Perhaps they were late risers and almost as soon as the thought entered my head, I knew it was not true. We dismounted and watered our horses. The smithy was cold and that, too, was a surprise for in winter a hot smithy drew villagers just to chat and gossip. Shadow suddenly neighed. Had we been at war I would have known there was danger but Marianne had been right; this land did feel at peace.

Stroking his head I said, "What is it, boy?"

Suddenly an arrow slammed into the cantle of my saddle and our hands went to our weapons. Nicholas' bow was still in its case but his hand went to his sword. A voice shouted, "The first weapon that is drawn will see a bloodbath. Raise your hands and step away from your horses."

Thomas and Nicholas looked at me. They were both ready to take their chances but I shook my head. There was a time and a place for action and we had no idea how many men we faced.

"Do as he says."

We moved but I kept the horses between us and the voice. Five men emerged from the trees. They stopped just twenty paces from us. Two had bows with nocked arrows and the other three all wore brigandines. They each had a mail coif about their heads. The leader carried a long sword. It was the kind that was best wielded with two hands but the man looked to be strong and held it easily.

"Why do you ambush peaceful travellers on this road?"

"Let us say that while I have no title, I regard Blecheley as my domain as well as the other villages and houses in this forest. You spoke of taxes and you were with a priest. I wanted to let you know that if the tax man comes here, he will die and then so shall you if you set foot on my land again."

I laughed and saw his eyes narrow, "You are a brigand, a robber baron with delusions of grandeur. You cannot prevent travellers using this road."

It was his turn to laugh but there was no humour in it, "Few folk travel this path, my friend and those that do pay a tax to me. I am in a generous mood this day and will just take your horses, purses and swords. Your lives you can keep but come not again lest you forfeit them."

Thomas had endured enough of this and he growled, "Let you and I stand toe to toe, bandit and you shall have just as much ground as your body."

"Fool! I have two archers with strung bows. Why should I risk injury when at the snap of my fingers two of you will die and I am sure that three of us can finish off the one who remains. You tire me, Oswald!"

One of the archers pulled back his right arm. Thomas was about to die and while it had not been the right time before, it was now. If we moved then we might be able to reach them. "Now!"

I drew my sword as did the two others and we ran at our enemies. By closing the range we stood a better chance of survival for we might panic the archer. The arrow did not leave Oswald's bow for a red-feathered arrow sprouted from his chest. The other archer and the three men looked around for danger but Robbie Red Fletch was too good to be easily spotted. The distraction allowed us to close with them. Nicholas rammed his sword into the guts of the other archer while Thomas and I took on the two nearest bandits. Their leader simply disappeared. I brought my sword down and the bandit I was fighting blocked it. I knew that his brigandine would give more protection than my cloak which, if anything, hampered me. It was too late to get rid of it and I merely threw its folds over my shoulder. The man lunged at me as I did so and I barely blocked the blow. He had been a man at arms and I wondered at the events that had brought him so low. I could hear the other bandit exchanging blows with Thomas and I shouted, as I slashed at my bandit, "Robbie, Nicholas, get after the leader."

"Aye, my lord!"

The bandit, realising, perhaps that there were just two of us swung his sword at my unprotected head as he whipped out a rondel dagger. I was wearing leather gauntlets and I grabbed the blade while punching at his head with the pommel of my sword. I caught his sword and the crosspiece scored a red line down his cheek. I saw fear in his eyes and I said, "Surrender and I shall get you a fair trial!"

He laughed and brought back his coifed head to headbutt me. I had learned how to fight roughly by Rafe and as the head came at me, I simply fell backwards. I was clutching his left hand with mine and his momentum carried him towards me. He could not stop. My own reaction was to release his hand and use my left hand to break my fall. I succeeded but my action meant that the bandit fell onto his own dagger. I saw the life leave his eyes as he fell. The blade must have entered his heart.

I pushed his body from me and stood. Thomas had slain his man and I saw Nicholas and Robbie emerge from the woods shaking their heads. "He had a horse, Sir Michael and he fled. We could follow him if you wish."

I shook my head, "We were lucky. When the time is right, we will bring all our men and scour the woods of this parasite. Robbie fetch your horse and thank you for your timely intervention."

He grinned, "When I saw your hands in the air, my lord I knew there was danger. You are more than welcome. And I discovered that Mary is as fast as any horse I have ever ridden. All is well."

I was angry and after wiping my sword on the dead man's breeks I sheathed it and then cupped my hands around my mouth, "Villagers of Blecheley, show yourselves. I will count to ten and if you are not here then we will fire this village!" Anticipating my next command Thomas and Nicholas went to the smithy where there would be the embers of a fire. "One, two, three, four…."

"Stop, my lord! We come!"

They had all been inside their homes and they sheepishly came forward. Their hung heads told me of their remorse even before I had begun to speak to them. "That you knew there were men waiting to ambush us, steal from us and, perhaps kill us are grounds enough for me to haul you to the nearest Sheriff and demand justice but I am a merciful man. Speak, leave nothing out and I may well reconsider."

The smith stepped forward, "We are hostages to fortune, my lord. The bandits use us as though we were their tenants and take what they will. Any of us who complain are beaten and we have no recourse to the law for there are no lords of the manor close by."

"There is now." They all looked up at me. "I am the new lord of Houghton Regis and in the absence of a lord here, I shall be available to dispense justice and maintain the law. Tell me, smith, how is it that you manage to make a living in a settlement of less than a dozen houses?"

He hung his head and it told me all that I needed to know.

"Is it not the case that you make and repair their mail and weapons." He nodded. "Who is the leader of this band that causes so much trouble that men shun this road?"

"You met him, my lord, he was the man with the long sword. He calls himself The Taxman which he is except that he does not come but once a year but whenever it pleases him. I am surprised he brought but a handful of men. More than twenty live in the forest. They have built dwellings."

"And they just raid this road?"

"No, my lord. They also raid the road on the far side of the forest. Perhaps he had men taxing the travellers on that side of the road."

I mounted Shadow. "I will be taking up residence in my new manor soon. When this bandit leader returns and returns he will, then tell him that Sir Michael of Weedon will be hunting him." My men mounted, "When he is gone then this village will pay their rightful dues once more and you will enjoy the protection of the law."

The smith nodded, "And that is all that we want, my lord."

As we headed north and west, I said, "We will speak with Richard at Stony Stratford. He may be able to shed more light on the matter."

Richard did, indeed, know more about the man called The Taxman. "He has not harmed us, my lord, for we live beyond the reaches of his forest home but I know that fewer travellers use this road and some, who have passed, told us that they had been robbed. They went to the lord of the manor at Buckingham but he was unable to help." He looked at me nervously, "I suggested that they go to Northampton and speak with Sir William's son, Sir Thomas. He told them that it was too far for him to venture."

As we rode the last part of the road to Weedon I began to realise why Sir William had left the jewel that was Weedon to me. His sons had larger manors but they had not turned out to be the knights he hoped. He had been part of the Blue Company and knew hardship. His children had, thanks to the business acumen of Lady Eleanor, enjoyed the rich lives of pampered nobles. That they had not fought at Agincourt told me much. Even Sir William's former squire, Sir John of Dauentre was not the knight he hoped he would be. I shared much in common with Sir William. I came from common stock and my father had been a sword for hire. I was determined that whatever happened, I would not change and my son would learn the right values. He would not be pampered. It was at that moment, as we entered the village of Weedon and passed the weaponsmith, Martin's workshop, that I truly began to see what I had taken on by becoming the queen's knight. Isabelle and I had to mould Margaret, born of royal blood, into a woman who would have to live in the world of ordinary folk. It would not be easy.

Just before we entered my cobbled yard I said, "And not a word about the attack to any. We wait until we are settled in Houghton Regis before that happens."

"Aye, my lord."

As I threw my leg over the cantle I said, "And if any of you wish to reconsider your decision to follow me there then I will understand."

Nicholas Warbag shook his head, "Quite the contrary, my lord, it has made me more determined. I wish to hunt this bandit. I am not a man to be threatened by the scum of the earth."

Peter, the ostler, hurried over to take our horses, "Feed them well, Peter, they have earned their food these last days."

"Aye, my lord."

The door gaped open and Isabelle stood there, glowing with joy, "Now, husband, we can begin the Christmas celebrations. We close the door on the outside world with all its attendant problems and the manor of Weedon will enjoy a happy Christmas."

Chapter 12

And it was, indeed, a joyous Christmas. We were all safe inside the manor and hunkered down as a blizzard swept in from the west blanketing the land in white. That it was two days before Christmas and the morning after we had returned seemed ordained by some higher power. Eleanor and Jack seemed keen to make it a good Christmas for they knew they would have their home returned to them and with Eleanor also now with child the two sisters had more in common. Sir William had taught me well and we maintained the tradition that the whole household ate together in the huge dining hall made by Lady Eleanor. Sarah had been used to eating alone but she dined at my table with those men at arms and archers who were not wed. There were but eight of them. She was an attractive woman and the unmarried archers and men at arms fluttered around her attentively bees around a newly opened flower.

Jean seemed fascinated by the baby, Margaret. Although still an infant, Christmas Day was the day my wife and Sarah began to feed her what Thomas called proper food. Mashed up beans and tiny shredded pieces of duck were fed to her. Most seemed to end up on the floor and when the dogs were allowed in later they would enjoy the feast. Jean was now allowed to sit at the table with us, bolstered by cushions and he giggled at his mother's attempt to feed Margaret tiny mouthfuls of food.

"She does not know how to eat!"

Isabelle smiled at Jean who but a year or two earlier had been the same, "And like all babies, she has to learn how to do such things. You can help your sister, Jean, for as she grows, she will look to her big brother."

Jean turned to me, "How is Margaret, my sister?"

A hush fell upon the table. They say that out of the mouths of babes and infants come awkward questions and they were right. This would be a good test. My wife answered it with consummate ease, "Margaret was sent to us to care for. You remember the story of baby Jesus and the stable?" He nodded. The stories his mother told him at night were from the Bible. "So, if the baby Jesus, along with Mary and Joseph came here we would give them shelter would we not?"

"Of course."

"Then we do that with Margaret but lacking a mother and a father we have to give her a family. You would like to be her family would you not?"

"Of course, but is not Mistress Sarah her mother?"

The silence was deep enough to cut with a knife and I shook my head, "Sarah is her nurse for she is a kind lady but now Margaret has a family and Mistress Sarah can look to her own life."

It was as I looked up that I saw Thomas of Chester with a strange look on his face while he watched a smiling Sarah. Was my man at arms finally succumbing to the charms of a woman?

The moment passed and the feast continued. Of course, Jean, as all little boys do, continued to ask questions but, thankfully, few were about Margaret. His favourite word appeared to be '*why*' and to try to answer each one was impossible. He was fascinated that he might have another brother or sister when my wife gave birth, after we had eaten and Robbie began to sing Christmas songs, his questions were about the words of the songs. When his head flopped onto the table Sarah and my wife took the two of them to bed.

Thomas stood, "Let me carry John, my lady." Like me, Thomas anglicised my son's name. I smiled for I knew the reason Thomas did so was to allow him to follow Sarah who did not seem averse to his silly smile.

We celebrated St Stephen's day too although the feast was more informal as we ate the remains of the Christmas meal. Thomas began to court Sarah. I remembered the conversation we had in Normandy and how he wished for a family. He had told me he might give up his sword and perhaps she had chosen Sarah. I just hoped that she would not reject his advances. I was given, by Isabelle, Margaret to amuse.

"You missed Jean when he was a babe but soon there will be another and I would have you comfortable with the holding of a child."

I did not mind for Margaret seemed to enjoy the faces that I pulled and the silly noises that I made. I saw the looks of amusement on the faces of Robbie and Nicholas but I cared not. The baby's smiles made me content and that was enough.

That night I spoke of Thomas' words to me in Normandy, "I think he will court Sarah. Is it not a little sudden?"

"No, husband and it is a good thing. I like Thomas but he always seemed so serious and sad, especially after Geoffrey was killed. He smiles now and his gentle words speak well of his thoughts. Do not worry about Sarah. When you were away, we spoke at length. She loved her husband and misses her own child. Margaret helped her as much as Sarah helped the baby but she wants a life of her own. I, like you, watched the two of them and while she may not love Thomas yet, she likes him and he makes her smile. That is a start. I do not think that she will dismiss him."

"And how do you feel about this move which will soon be upon us?"

"At first I thought it hasty but I have spoken to my sister. Now that she is with child, she is content." My wife waved a hand above us, "She has lived here longer than I have and she feels that this is her home. I know that it is yours but you know what I mean. A woman likes to leave her mark on a house. I never met Lady Eleanor but I can see her hand in every part of this home. When I get to Houghton Regis then I shall do the same but Eleanor wishes this to be her home. She will miss me but we can visit can we not?"

"Aye, we can." Even as I answered my wife, I knew that first I had to rid the road of The Taxman.

More men wished to come with me than to remain at Weedon. All the single men chose a life at Houghton Regis and two of the archers chose to uproot their young families. I knew that was partly because Nicholas and Robbie had told them of the attack. I knew this because the day before we left Isabelle faced me, "You were attacked?"

"There are bandits in a nearby forest. I shall scour the woods of them and you need not worry, you shall be safe. Houghton Regis is a royal manor. They would not dare to do it harm."

She did not look convinced but having made the start of the move she would not go back on her decision. We took two of the wagons from Weedon. I knew that there was one at Houghton Regis and we could return one to Jack. His manor had more need of wagons than mine. When it was harvest time Weedon supplied many cereals to Northampton market. When I had left Weedon the last time it had been to go to France to fight for England and I had known that one day I would return. This time it was unlikely that I would and our parting from those who worked the land was sad. Men who had followed Sir William to Agincourt and the French wars had seen me grow up and now we were leaving. As they all came to bid farewell on an icily cold January morning, it brought a tear to my eye. They were old men now with families of their own. Some had already said that when their sons were old enough, they would have them join my retinue. Jack had let all know that he had given up the sword. I hoped I would never have to go to war again and certainly not for the failed one in France but I knew that so long as there was a throne in England and a crown to be wrested from a king's head, there would be wars. I had chosen my side by accepting the Queen's offer. I would defend the House of Lancaster and the children of Owen Tudor.

The wagons and the families could not be pushed in the same way as warriors and we stayed overnight at Stony Stratford. My family were given rooms in the large house Lady Eleanor had built while the rest crowded cosily in the barn. Mindful of the bandits Nicholas had the archers ride in the forest when we passed through it. They would be an early warning and they rode with strung bows. We were not harmed. The Taxman was not a fool and he would choose his battles. When I rid the world of him it would be through force and my men would have to seek him.

That Isabelle was impressed by the royal manor was clear for her mouth gaped open as we soon as we saw it. The gate and high wall through which we passed were as impressive as many small castles and there was a herb garden in the centre of the cobbled yard that lay before the main doors. Yard was the wrong word for it was more like the courtyard of a grand palace. The buildings that serviced the hall were all discreetly hidden behind the two wings of the building and the small inner wall that allowed many flowers to grow in their lee. The man who had designed it, many years ago, had not wished to spoil the southwest view the front enjoyed. While my family entered the main house the rest rode around the building to the rear of the hall. There would be their homes. I had yet to ascertain how many vacant houses and farms there were but I knew from Ralph that there were some. I knew that the first days, perhaps weeks, would be confused as order was brought to the ants' nest we had disturbed.

If I thought that Ralph and Marianne were at all discomfited by our arrival, those thoughts were dispelled by the smiles that lit up the warm and comfortable hall. Marianne gushed, "If you would come with me, my lady, we are blessed with many servants." She suddenly looked across at me, "If his lordship cannot afford their pay…"

I smiled, "Fear not Mistress Marianne, there will be no changes in the arrangements. There are funds and I intend this to be a working manor."

Relieved Marianne led my wife off and Ralph said, "My lord, it was dark the last time you came. Allow me to give you a tour of the house so that you may see all."

It had been a house in which kings could entertain small numbers of lords and ladies. I gathered, from Ralph, that it had been used as a hunting lodge. Ten lords and their ladies or mistresses would have stayed. That meant the stables were large enough to accommodate all my horses and there was a warrior hall for the men who would protect the king. There were two dining halls. Once was large enough to feast twenty odd people while the smaller one was for half a dozen. Both had fireplaces and I knew which one would be used the most. There were other chambers on the first floor as well as a large kitchen and a cellar that appeared to be the size of the hall. It was enormous and boasted not only a buttery, wine store and beer store but also an armoury. While some of the weapons were old most were high quality and I appreciated them. Cedric of Barnsley would like the array of billhooks and halberds. He now had four men he led and they would act as guards and sentries for the hall. He had grown very close. He and Robert, the other original billman, were determined that Isabelle, Jean and now Margaret, would be safe no matter what. The land to the north of the outer wall was pasture. The hall boasted four milk cows, two goats as well as sheep. They were there for their milk. I saw it as a perfect place for my archers to set up their marks and train each day.

Satisfied with what I saw I joined my wife in the small hall, "Well, my love, are you happy?"

She beamed, "More than happy. We have a large bedchamber and the small one that is attached, I assume for the chamberlains of the king will make a perfect nursery. Marianne, who is a kind lady, is already moving a cot and a small bed there. Sarah is happy to share the room with the two until they need it. Jean has already picked out a room he would like when he is old enough."

"Where is he?"

"Thomas took him to explore the hall."

"Thomas?"

She gave a cheeky smile, "Aye, he appeared when you were having your tour and asked if I needed help. I think it was to be close to Sarah."

Those first two weeks in the hall were frenetic and I had little opportunity to think about The Taxman. However, as January drew to a close and winter bit Ralph added more information about the bandits. "You say, my lord, that the villagers called him The Taxman?"

"Aye, do you know him?"

Shaking his head he said, "I knew that there were bandits in the woods. There are bandits in every wood but they are merely a nuisance in most places. No, when I was a warrior, I served on the Welsh borders for the Mortimer family." The Mortimers were an important family and related to the king. I had heard of them. "They had a warrior who was most cruel and he would often ride into Wales to devastate small villages. He said that he was taxing the Welsh for the privilege of being ruled by England. Eventually, his excesses became so bad that Sir Edward forbade his forays. When the warrior abused a young Welsh girl Sir Edward ordered his arrest. He killed the two men sent to arrest him and fled."

"You believe that this is the same man?"

"Your description, my lord, and what I knew of him leads me to believe that it is. Since you first spoke to me about the attack it has been on my mind and it was a conversation with a carter yesterday that put the thought in my head. He came from Wales and it was when he spoke of the Mortimer family that the connection was made. I may be wrong but…"

"No, Ralph, it all makes sense. The man I fought had skills beyond those of a brigand or a bandit. He knew how to lead and understood how to lay a good ambush. What was the man's name?"

"Eustace of Hereford."

"Then I will store that information."

"Beware, Sir Michael, he is a cunning and a cruel man. None of those in the garrison liked him but we all feared him."

I would not take my victory for granted. When I hunted him, I would plan it as though planning a chevauchée.

We chose a day to hunt them when the ground was frozen solid but there were clear blue skies. Men living in the forest would need fires on such a day and the clear skies and lack of clouds would help us to both see and to smell them. I had twenty-two men who would accompany me. I knew that the bandits might well outnumber us and so we went mailed and plated. With helmets upon our heads, we would be well protected. I rode Storm and he was also mailed. We did not have far to ride and I wanted to protect my most valuable horse. We had spoken at length to Ralph and he knew the woods. One of the gamekeepers from the manor, Osric, came with us as a scout to take us through trails he knew into the forest. We would avoid the road. Once we neared them then Osric would retire and act as a horse holder. Thomas and I, along with John, William and Edward, carried lances. The young warriors who had never been men at arms carried javelins. There is an art to using a lance.

As soon as we neared the woods, three hours after sunrise we saw the smoke spiralling from within it. As soon as Osric saw it, he nodded, "It is a clearing in the middle with a small hummock of a mound. There is water close by." He shook his head, "It has been many years since I ventured into that part of the woods but I remember it from my youth. The deer and wild pigs would gather there. I think the fourth King Henry was the last to hunt here and his party killed the last wild pig. It is sad."

"Were you old enough to remember him?"

"My father was gamekeeper here before me and he told me."

He took us down a trail we would not have found ourselves for the entrance was overgrown and, had we been on foot we would have struggled to negotiate. Bushes and shrubs had grown over what was clearly a hunters' trail. For the first twenty or so paces it was hard going and small branches brushed and scratched our horses' flanks. Then we found where animals had used it and it became more of a game trail. Inevitably it would lead to water but we followed Osric. If you had an expert, it was as well to use him.

After half a mile he stopped and came to join me. He spoke quietly, leaning over from his own, small horse, "It is about a mile away, my lord. Should I continue to lead?"

It was a brave thing to say for he only had a hunting bow and dagger for weapons. "Does the trail continue?"

He nodded, "It becomes wide. See, my lord, there are boot prints and that means men have used this recently for the ground is frozen."

"Then stay here and guard the archers' horses." I waved over Nicholas. We had more archers than men with lances and spears. "Take your eleven archers and get as close to you as you can. Spread out on both sides of the trail and if you think that they will fly then release your arrows. We will come down the main trail and rely on our plate and mail."

"Aye, my lord." He signalled for the dismount and I turned, "Thomas, you and Edward follow me. Put the new men at the back."

"My lord…" I knew that Thomas thought he and Edward should lead.

I smiled, "I wear the best plate that money can buy and I doubt that they will have bodkins. Storm is mailed too. I do not take risks but I would not have one life wasted for these men who prey on the weak." Hoisting up my shield, I couched my lance and lowered the visor on my sallet helmet. A hunting arrow could still blind me and I would endure the limited vision that I would have.

The archers disappeared as only those skilled in woodcraft can and I pointed my lance and urged Storm forward. I think that a good warhorse learns the signs of war. The shutting of the visor, the raising of the shield and the couching of the lance, each action told my horse that he was to go into battle and I had to fight to keep his speed steady. The hard ground had one disadvantage for us. It amplified the sound of the hooves and the bandits would know we were coming. I heard a horn when we were just a hundred paces from the clearing. The first two arrows sent at me, although hurriedly released, managed to hit. One struck the shaffron on Storm's head and the other smacked into my breastplate. I had made the right decision to lead.

I spied, through the opening in the visor, men hurriedly arming themselves and loosing as quickly as they could. I saw The Taxman; he had four warriors with him and all had helmets and mail. They were what passed for bodyguards. I dug my heels in Storm's flanks for we were now in the clearing and there was little risk of his tripping on a rogue root. I felt Thomas and Edward close with me as they made their horses gallop to protect my flanks. Even though I was concentrating on the five mailed and plated men I was aware of arrows flying from behind me and slamming into the bandits who were attempting to send their own arrows at us. Another arrow hit the greave on my leg but, once again, it was not a bodkin.

The Taxman was not a fool. If he ran then our horses would chase him down. I spied his horse and the other two that the bandits had tethered close to a crude log hut. It was not saddled and flight would be difficult. He stood at the front of his four men, three of whom held long spears. It would deter most horses but Storm was a warhorse and had mail about his chest. More importantly, I knew how to use a lance from the back of a horse. This was not like charging another horseman. I did not need to brace myself against my cantle. I could stand and strike down. I was aided by the fact that I managed to slow Storm down and that allowed Thomas and Edward to ride boot to boot with me. The bandit leader was a big man and he swung his long sword, two-handed at me rather than my horse. As it came towards me, I braced myself and guided Storm to his left. At the same time I thrust with my lance and the head struck the mail of the man next to the leader. It had a tapered point and the end ripped through his mail. I put power behind the strike and I was helped by Storm's speed. It entered his chest and I felt it scrape off his breastbone. His scream was feral and he fell clutching the lance. I let go of it aware that Thomas' horse had managed to hit The Taxman and knock him to the ground. My move had made him miss me and end the life of one of his warriors. His sword had barely managed to strike me and I was grateful to Thomas.

I wheeled Storm and drew my sword. The bandit leader was quick to rise and he swung his sword one-handed at me. I jinked to his right to enable me to block his strike with my sword. They rang together but used one-handed his blow was not as powerful as mine and with my added height it meant I forced him back. I pulled back on Storm's reins and he reared. His mighty hooves clattered down on the breastplate of the warrior. He was big and he was tough but such a blow would fell the fiercest of foes. He landed heavily and it was all that I could do to pull Storm to the side so that he would not smash the skull of the bandit. I stilled Storm and raised my visor. The bandits were finished. The ones who had not been slain dropped their weapons and raised their arms. It was then I saw that there were not only men but also women and young girls. There was even a small boy.

I dismounted and Thomas took my reins. I walked over to The Taxman and took off my helmet. His right hand still clutched his sword and I pricked his chin, for his helmet had fallen and I said, "Yield and face judgement for your men have surrendered and you are at my mercy."

He released his sword and sat up. His face looked pained, "Had you faced me like a man and not on a horse then the result might have been reversed."

Thomas laughed, "Do you not know yet that this is Sir Michael of Weedon who was appointed king's champion for his skill. The result would have been the same."

I sheathed my sword.

"It was still a trick and I dispute your view. Your hand, Sir Michael."

I put my hand out to help him to his feet. I knew how hard it is to rise wearing plate. He held out his left hand and as I was pulling him I heard Thomas shout a warning. The evil grin on his face told me that he had murder in mind and I saw the bodkin blade come at my eye. I could do nothing about it and I would either die or lose an eye. The four arrows that slammed into him came over my shoulder and three of them hit his head not only killing him but driving him back a good four paces. The fourth embedded itself in the bandit's shoulder.

Nicholas said, "Never give a snake the benefit of the doubt, my lord, it will bite every time."

Thomas snarled, "And this is a nest of snakes! Let us butcher them all! It is nothing less than they deserve."

"Hold!"

I saw the five men who had survived look up in terror at Thomas' words. Two of the women stood protectively in front of two of the bandits.

"We take them back to Houghton Regis. I will hold a court and they will be judged."

One of the women shouted, "And what kind of justice will that be? You will hang them!"

Nicholas shouted, "Hold your tongue, crone, for who is to say that you are innocent?"

I kept my voice calm but authoritative as I ordered, "Bind the hands of the men. Are any of ours hurt?"

Edward shook his head, "One of the horses has a nasty wound but we are all whole. Your plan worked, Sir Michael."

I looked up at the sun and saw that it had passed its zenith. We would be lucky to reach Houghton Regis before dark. "Robbie, take three men. Take the mail and the plate from the dead and place their bodies on the fire. Burn them. Put the weapons and mail on the three horses and follow us."

"Aye, my lord."

I led the motley band of warriors, bandits, and women back to Osric who held the horses. "Osric, ride back to the hall. I need fetters for five men and somewhere to hold the prisoners; ask Cedric of Barnsley to arrange it. Tell Lady Isabelle that we are well."

It was almost dark as we entered the gates of my new manor. I had Cedric and the billmen secure the male prisoners and place the women, girls, and the child in the barn. There was just one entrance and I had it well guarded. We would feed them. If any chose to run we could not stop them but something made me think that they would not.

"Nicholas, have food brought. We will give them food and drink."

Isabelle was concerned for she had seen the women and girls brought into the barn. "What will you do with them?"

"I know not. The men are easy. They have committed a crime and will be punished."

"Death?"

I shook my head, "They are guilty of banditry and I have a mind to let them live but the punishment must make them change their ways. As for the women?" I shrugged, "I will hear their stories and then make my decision but that will be tomorrow's task. I am hungry, I last ate at dawn and my stomach thinks that my throat has been cut."

Isabelle did not smile at the jest and I knew that she was upset by what she had seen. She was too kind.

I did not wish to prolong the agony and so the five men were brought before me in the large hall that we had thus far failed to use. I had Ralph sit next to me as well as the priest from the handful of houses that made up Houghton Regis. Normally the village would have been too small to merit a priest but as there was a small chapel in the manor Father Baldwin ministered to the villagers.

The men who were brought in looked fearful. I had my men bring in the women and the child. Before I began, I addressed the women. "Are any of these five related to the women here present?"

One young woman said, "I am Susanna, the wife of Peter there." She pointed at the youngest of the five. I made a mental note of that and wrote the name of the man on the wax tablet before me.

The loud and aggressive woman said, "And I am Betty, the wife of Robin." She pointed at the oldest man amongst the bandits. He had the beginnings of grey hair sprouting from his thinning thatch.

After writing his name I pointed to the young woman with the boy, "And you?"

"I am Elizabeth and this is my son, Jack. Jack's father died some weeks ago."

Here was an intriguing story. If her partner had died, why had she stayed with the bandits in the middle of winter?

"You other three, what are your names?"

"Robert the Scot." His accent identified his origins even before he told me.

"Dick the Wanderer." He shrugged, "I should have wandered more."

"Ned of Sheffield."

"Do any of you deny that you were bandits?" They hung their heads and said nothing. "And is there any justification for your crimes?" I was desperate to give them a way out.

They looked at Robin. As he was the oldest, they looked on him as a leader. "We all have stories, my lord. Some fell out with their parents and fled their homes. Some liked to drink more than work and found it easier to prey on travellers than earn an honest crust. My wife and I chose the life for my father disapproved of my marriage and threw me from the family farm."

I nodded, "Thank you for your honesty." I leaned back to speak to Ralph and Father Baldwin quietly, "I am tempted to be lenient. Disfigurement or branding seems a little harsh."

Father Baldwin said, "They did prey on travellers, my lord."

I nodded, "And there will be a punishment. Will the two of you allow me to choose the manner?"

Ralph smiled, "You are the lord of the manor and need not our approval."

"Yet I would have it for I am still young and would appreciate any wisdom you have to share."

They looked at each other and nodded. Ralph said, "Whatever you deem appropriate, my lord."

I looked at the men. They would be relatively easy to deal with but only two of the eight women appeared to have a connection with them. What would I do with them? It was interesting that none had run during the night. They had not been closely watched. Why had they stayed? I thought I knew the answer but I would have it confirmed later.

"I could have your right hands taken or have you blinded if I had a mind. When I served with King Henry in Picardy, he had those who stole as we marched, hanged. Death is also a punishment." The one called Peter looked almost ready to bolt although my armed men would have made that impossible. "However, I have a more merciful punishment in mind." I was acutely aware that all eyes were on me." I glanced up at the minstrel gallery that ran along one end of the hall. I saw Isabelle there watching. "The five of you will be kept here for six months and you will work for six days each week to repair the cobbles on the road. At the end of that time, you will be free to leave so long as you quit this county and find another place to reside. If you run before the sentence is finished you will be hunted down and hanged." The relief was palpable. They were not fools although they had behaved foolishly and they knew that they would be fed and housed while they worked off their sentence.

Ralph leaned towards me, "That will be an expense, my lord."

I turned, "Does the road need to be repaired?"

"Of course, Sir Michael, we have to mend it each year."

"Then it is not an expense for the men who do this will not be paid, will they?"

Ralph smiled, "I bow to your wisdom, my lord. You need no white hairs to be clever."

I looked at the women, "And now I come to the matter of the women and the child before me. I have not heard of women being involved in any banditry and so your crime was that of caring for the men with whom you lived."

One woman, who had not spoken before, burst out, "Not all of us were there by choice, Sir Michael, some of us were taken by force and used."

I glared at the men. This shed a different light on their crimes, "And were any of these five perpetrators of such crimes?"

The two women Susanna and Betty shouted, at the same time, "Our men are innocent." Betty added, "He would not have dared to touch another!"

I saw Ralph smile. I continued to stare at the woman who had made the accusation, "Well?"

She shook her head as did another two of the women, including Elizabeth, mother of the boy, Jack, "No my lord, you slew them at the camp and for that we thank you."

I was relieved. There would be no further punishments. I looked up at the minstrel gallery. Isabelle was still there and watching. "If any of you women wish to return to your homes then my men will escort you. You will be clothed and fed. For the rest, if you need a home then there is one here but it will not be a home given freely. For the privilege of a roof and food, you will work," I looked up at the gallery, "under the supervision of Lady Isabelle." I saw her nod and then disappear. "You need not make your decision yet. I know that it needs consideration. Ralph will find beds for you and you can tell him of your decision. Father Baldwin will make himself available in the chapel for any who wish to make a confession. If there is to be a clean start then better to make one in the eyes of God as well as the law, eh?"

Father Baldwin's emphatic nod told me that I had said the right thing.

Perhaps God rewarded us for our mercy. Four days after the trial Isabelle gave birth to our new child, Maud, named after Isabelle's mother and it was, as Isabelle herself said, an easier birthing than Jean had been.

We were somewhat cocooned from news of the outside world but major events did reach us. That year saw a major blow for England. The news we had in the middle of the year was that John Duke of Bedford had died suddenly at Arras and, even worse for the country was that Burgundy had now deserted the English camp and joined the French. Sir John Talbot would struggle to keep the little of France we still held. When the Duke of Bedford's brother, the Duke of Gloucester, was summoned to defend Calais I wondered if that made life safer or more perilous for the two sons of the queen. Richard, Duke of York, who was a belligerent man who also had a claim to the throne, took command of the army in France and I saw a shift in the balance of power. The Yorkist faction now commanded the English Army in France. In England, there was now just one uncle. He had, to some extent, been kept in check by both the council and his brother. One was gone and the other was under his control. His palace at Greenwich was now the centre of power in England. He proved to be an able deputy for his dead brother and he successfully defended Calais and returned to England by the autumn of that year. Of the queen, we heard nothing and I took that to be a good thing. Any news that we had would be bad news. No news meant that she still lived and I began to hope that there might be some cure for her malady. I confess I was looking for an easy life; it was not meant to be.

Chapter 13

Houghton Regis 1436

The year passed quickly for we had a new baby, two if you counted Margaret and a new house. There was a great number of adjustments to be made. The men left us at the end of their sentence. I suspect that some of them might have asked to stay, had they had the courage. I would have said no for although I had forgiven them they had been watched constantly during the time they had worked on the road. Within a moving of our arrival Sarah and Thomas were wed. My wife had been proved correct and they each saw in the other something that was lacking in their lives. When Sarah delivered a son to Thomas nine months after the wedding we knew that God blessed the union too. That simple act of two lost people finding each other seemed to make the whole manor more harmonious and at peace. That summer was one of the best I could remember. We seemed to have little rain, enough to water the crops and that was all. The harvest for the villagers was one of the best and the trees and bushes were laden with fruit. The hives produced the tastiest honey any of us had tasted and all was well. My son grow, seemingly by inches and Margaret learned to walk when she was but fourteen months old. That brought with it attendant problems but they were ones with which we could live. And then the summer drew to a close and we had a wet autumn and as winter took hold the ground was gripped in ice. The idyll had ended.

I was summoned to Bermondsey Abbey just before Christmas. The Queen was ill and asked to see me. The rider, a Welsh warrior, arrived not long before noon. It was not Father Bertrand who came for me but a bondsman who served Owen Tudor. "I am Iago ap Maredudd and the queen sent me to ask if you would visit her. She says that she knows the journey will be hard but begs the company of her knight." His eyes pleaded as much as his voice.

I could not refuse but the winter had been the hardest in living memory. Chalk turned to dust and the herbs all froze. I nodded, "She is unwell?"

Iago was a soldier and had the scarred face of one who has fought in war. He looked at me sadly, "I am no doctor but if you were to ask me, I would say that she was dying. I pray that I am wrong for I love the lady dearly as we all do."

"Then we will leave immediately." I waved Ralph over, "Have this man fed and then ask Thomas to prepare two horses. We ride for London."

I found my wife. We had converted one of the downstairs' chambers into a cosy room where the children, all three of them could play, and my wife and her ladies, sew. It was a joyous room filled with the chatter of ladies and the laughter from children. Jean, Margaret, and my daughter, Maud, all played happily together. Sarah nursed her new babe, Thomas. As soon as I went in my wife sensed, from my look, that something was amiss. I was never any good at hiding my emotions.

"What is wrong, husband?"

All eyes were upon me and I had no time to fabricate a story, "The queen has sent for me. She is dying."

Sarah's hand went to her mouth and tears sprang forth. My wife leapt to her feet and put her arm around Sarah. She made the sign of the cross, "Then you must go and we shall pray that she is not dying and that the messenger was wrong."

The three children continued to play. Margaret did not know that it was her mother of whom we spoke.

I said, "I am sorry for the manner in which I gave you the news but I must leave forthwith. Sarah, I take Thomas with me."

She had herself under control and she nodded, "I pray you to tell the queen that she is ever in my thoughts."

"I will."

Isabelle linked my arm as we left the room, "I will pack you a bag. You must be presentable when you meet the queen."

She was ever concerned about such things.

The road was hard packed with ice. I had given Iago one of my horses and we led the one that had travelled north with him. We said little as we headed for London. It was more than thirty miles away. "When did you leave Bermondsey, Iago?"

"Yesterday at the third hour of the afternoon. The queen's condition worsened and Father Bertrand begged me to ride."

"Not the queen's husband?"

He shook his head and said nothing.

"We will ride as long as our horses allow. You have a spare, Iago, and our mounts are good horses." I turned to Thomas, "I am sorry to drag you away from your wife and child, Tom."

He smiled, "I would not have a wife and child but for the queen and you. This is right, my lord and I have done little since the fight in the forest. I need this."

He was right. After we had eliminated the bandits the women had become part of our manor. Sarah and Thomas had soon wed and my wife's prediction had been accurate. They wasted no time in starting a family and joy entered my man at arms' life, probably for the first time.

The time had been a happy one for us all. Margaret fitted in well and as she became first a toddler and then one who could begin to articulate words so Jean and she became inseparable. The manor had been a hunting lodge and with the new folk living in the manor, we soon began to make it a working manor. My men at arms and archers were given plots of land. They still worked at their skills but with land came an attachment to the land. The time had passed well and we were cocooned from the outside world.

"How is Iago, the steward?" I suddenly turned, as we rode on the frozen road, "He is not a relative is he, I mean your names…"

He shook his head, "No, my lord. My family name is Maredudd. He was my father. Old Iago died at the start of this harsh winter. He slipped on some frozen stones and broke bones. He was old and he died a week later. We all miss him for he was the queen's rock. I confess that her conditioned worsened when he was taken from her."

The road we rode was the main one to London and we were not the only ones who braved the winter to travel it. There were inns and taverns along the way that were open and we used them if only to rest the horses. It was when we stopped that we were able to speak to Iago. "Whence comes the illness, Iago? I have not seen her since she gave me my manor and whilst she was unwell at that time, I did not think that she would be close to death. She is not old, is she?"

"She has seen barely thirty-five summers, my lord. She is a great lady and I have been honoured to know her these last years."

"And your master, her husband?"

He gave me a look that suggested that he would not brook any criticism. I kept my face neutral. "He loves the queen if that is what you mean."

"I would hope that was true but I wondered about his position." I looked around. We were the only ones in the inn. The man who had served us drinks had taken our money and now dozed before the fire that he kept alight. "The Duke of Gloucester is known to be a man who has voiced his disapproval of the secret marriage."

Iago looked relieved, "He knows that his position will become more parlous without the protection of the queen."

I lowered my voice, "And the king, what of him?"

"The king?"

"Aye, the queen is his mother, has he been informed?"

My words seemed to take him by surprise, "I had not thought of that. I know not. Perhaps."

He would have to be told and I wondered if that was the reason for my summons. I was unique in that I had a connection to both the queen and her son, King Henry.

The most difficult part of the journey was the crossing of London Bridge. There were watchmen there who questioned the three cloaked and armed riders. My spurs afforded me more courtesy than Thomas or Iago might have enjoyed and we were, eventually, allowed to pass. We reached the abbey not long after dawn. The Benedictine monks were all awake having held services during the night. The monk who took us to the stable told us that the queen was still poorly but she would be able to receive visitors later in the morning and he suggested that, as I was to be presented to the queen, I should clean myself up and change. The clothes I had worn for the journey had been chosen to keep me warm. I was now able to change into clothes that were finer and more suited to meet a queen.

Father Bertrand came for me at Terce, "It is good to see you, Sir Michael, although I could have wished for better circumstances."

I nodded, "And the queen?"

"She has moments of despair and then at other times, like now, she appears to be almost healthy but her doctors say that is it merely a matter of time. If she sees next year then it will be a miracle." I nodded and felt inordinately sad. "And how is…" he looked around. Iago was on the table with Thomas and a monk was serving them porridge, "your charge?"

"Healthy and loving life. My wife treats her like one of the family and to speak truly, she calls me father and Lady Isabelle, mother. I hope that we have done all that the queen wished of us."

He beamed, "Of that I am certain. When I saw your home and met your wife then I knew we had chosen well."

I lowered my voice, "And her husband?"

Almost whispering Father Bertrand said, "Ready for flight. He knows that those that hate him are only awaiting the death of the queen."

"And the boys? For I know well the oath I made."

"The queen has made arrangements for that. Jasper and Owen have been given places at Barking Abbey where the abbess, Katherine de la Pole is willing to give them an education. There they will be safe. Their belongings and treasures were sent when Iago came to summon you."

It was then I realised that Margaret was the only one of the queen's second family who would have anything like a normal life. It made me even more determined to see that the queen's wishes were carried out.

When the queen was ready to see me I was fetched by a monk. Father Bertrand accompanied me. As we reached the door, I saw a man leaving. I knew it had to be Owen Tudor, the anglicised Welshman. He was not a warrior. You can tell a man who has fought in battle by the way he carries himself. Owen might have been at battles but he would have been one of those who managed to avoid shedding blood and incurring a wound. I knew few warriors who did not have a scar or two. Having said that I could understand the queen's attraction. King Henry had been a warrior but he had borne a disfiguring wound from the battle of Shrewsbury. Owen Tudor had fine features and when he spoke his voice was pleasant to the ear,

"You must be Sir Michael. I am Owen Meredith ap Tudor I am glad that you have come and I pray that you will hear my wife's words for we are in need of your help."

His words told me a number of things, titles and names meant much to him. He had used his full name. Secondly, this was not just a courtesy visit, I would be needed again.

The physicians and her ladies took themselves to the far side of the chamber as we entered to leave us as close to alone with the queen as could be managed. It was like looking at a body laid out for burial. The room had the odour of death in the air. The queen was still beautiful but it was a pale beauty, almost blue as though she was about to become a wraith. She gave me a sad smile. I knew from Father Bertrand that she spoke English to her husband but to me, she spoke French.

"Yes, my gallant knight and protector of my children, I am close to death. I was not granted the time on this earth that I wished. I will make my will, later this day and then I will await the summons to," she looked at Father Bertrand, "heaven?"

"Without a doubt, my queen."

She nodded and I saw that even that effort was too much she beckoned a long bony finger and I went closer to her. I knelt next to her bed. Father Bertrand stood but within hearing distance, "How is Margaret?"

"She is a delight and can walk. My poor wife and Sarah are beside themselves when she suddenly lurches from one chair to another."

I was glad she had asked and that I had told her for a glow came into her face, her eyes lit up and her tinkling laugh made the priests and doctors turn. "Thank you for telling me and I wish I could have seen it. Let know that…" She shook her head, "She must never know. This is harder than I thought." She squeezed my hand and I felt the chill of her fingers, "When I go, then the protection for my husband goes with me. Humphrey, Duke of Gloucester, my brother-in-law is only waiting for that moment to pounce. My husband," she sighed, "I can do no more for him but my children, they are different. Edmund and Jasper are both here. Once my funeral is over then they will be in danger. I have secured a place of sanctuary for them and I want you to take them there." The effort of speaking appeared too much and she sank back but her hand beckoned Father Bertrand.

He leaned down so that only the queen and I could hear his words, "When the queen is laid in her tomb then it will take the duke time to summon the council and to bend them to his will. When you hear the date of the funeral announced then return here for you must take them immediately that the funeral is over before they can be used."

The queen opened her eyes, "I want you to take my sons to Barking Abbey. I have ensured that they are beneficiaries of my will and I buy my sons' safety. It is the journey to Barking that will be dangerous. You will need to take enough men to protect my sons but not enough to arouse suspicion about your intent." She gave a sad smile and her cold hand gripped mine, "I know I set you an impossible quest but I also know I can rely upon you." She slipped a ring from one finger; the finger was so thin that it came off easily, "King Henry gave me this ring when he came back from Agincourt. He took it from the body of Guichard Dauphin, Lord of Jaligny, Grand Master of the King's Household." She smiled as I took the ring, "A pompous man whom I did not like but my husband thought it a pretty ring. I give it to you. In my will, you and Margaret will be looked after." Her hand dropped to the bed, "I am tired and I say farewell, Sir Michael. I shall never look on your noble face again but I will die happy knowing that my children, all of them, will enjoy the protection of the last true knight in England."

I felt unmanned as a tear trickled down my cheek. Clutching the ring I kissed the back of her hand, "And, my lady, I repeat my oath, here on your death bed. I will give my life to protect your children."

"I am content."

She slipped back and Father Bertrand, after waving over the doctors, helped me to my feet. "Come, we must see the boys. This will be your one day here for the end will not be long in coming and the death of a queen will bring others who do not have such benign motives as you, Sir Michael. It would be better if they did not see you for an association with the queen might bring about suspicion."

The two boys, who looked to be about five or six were with their father and Iago along with a second man at arms, in the refectory. Thomas was speaking with them. I kept the ring in the palm of my hand. I was unsure how Owen Tudor would view the gift. I did not know the man.

It was Father Bertrand who took command, "Boys, this is Sir Michael of Weedon and he is the knight of your mother, the Queen's Knight. He has sworn an oath to protect you. Whatever happens in the future you can trust this knight above all others."

Both he and the boys looked at Owen Tudor. His answer told me that the queen had made her wishes crystal clear. He nodded, firmly, "Aye, Sir Michael will be your rock and I trust him completely."

I wondered if Iago had spoken to the Welshman.

I sat on the bench next to them, "The next time I see you then we shall be riding hard and quickly. Tell me truly, can you ride?"

Their looks told me that they were not confident. Edmund, the elder said, "We have ponies that we used to ride but since we came here, we have not had the opportunity to practise."

"An honest answer. Know that I will always appreciate such honesty and I will never lie to you. My word is as true as my sword. Then when we leave, I shall have men to take you on their horses. My men are all like Thomas here, warriors of England who know how to fight."

I had insulted the Welshman but it had been unintentional. I was not a man who understood the nuances of polite conversation. I spoke from the heart.

Edmund spoke, "We will be ready, my lord, and my brother and I thank you although we do not understand why we are in danger."

His father put his hand on his son's shoulder, "Nor do I but your mother is right to appoint a protector for we swim in a sea filled with predators and we shall all need the armour of Sir Michael and his men."

The boys were whisked off with Owen and Father Bertrand who returned to the queen's chamber. Thomas went to fetch me food for we had ridden all night and I had not eaten since a tavern on the London Road.

Iago said, "This is my shield brother, Rhodri. We are to my lord what you are to her sons."

I nodded as Thomas brought me a bowl of potage and half a loaf. I nodded as I broke a large piece of bread from the half loaf to dunk in the steaming soup. "I do not need to know the details but just as the queen has made plans for her sons has your master made plans?"

They looked at each other and Iago said, "If the queen trusts this man with her two sons, then so should we."

His words told me two things; he knew nothing about Margaret and assumed I was only protecting the sons of Owen Tudor. I did not correct him.

"The closer we are to London then the more danger we are in. Wales is where we have support and we are secure. That will be our sanctuary."

Thomas had a beaker of ale and after wiping its froth from his mouth said, "If you can get there. If I were you, I would have a second plan."

I quickly ate the food and then stood, "We had better return to my home. Father Bertrand is quite right. Our presence here endangers the queen's plan." I held out my arm to Iago, "Farewell, Iago, and I hope that fate favours you."

"And you, too, Sir Michael."

Our horses had been given oats and had a brief rest but, as we mounted, I said to Thomas, "We need not flog our mounts to death. We shall cross London Bridge and find an inn, north of the city."

Fate intervened almost as soon as we left the Abbey. Riding from the east and, presumably from his palace at Greenwich came a gaggle of knights and I recognised the one in the middle as Humphrey, Duke of Gloucester.

We reined in and awaited them for to simply ride off would have inspired suspicion. I was mindful of the words of Father Bertrand. The duke frowned as he recognised me. The recognition surprised me for I was not wearing livery and my riding cloak was not richly made. "Sir Michael? Sir Michael of Weedon, what brings you here?" He looked beyond me. We were less than two hundred from the abbey and he nodded in its direction. "You have been visiting the queen."

I nodded. I would have to come up with a realistic version of the truth, "As you know, my lord, I was once the protector of the queen and the young king. I never forgot the oath I took to protect them. I heard that the queen was unwell and I have been to pay my respects. She is a great lady."

"Indeed she is and, from what I hear, soon she will enjoy God's protection in heaven. As for the king, he no longer needs your protection for I and the council are here for him." He was, as he had done all those years ago, putting me in my place.

"I am a loyal Englishman, my lord, and as I fought for his father, so will I fight for his son, against all enemies."

The duke's eyes narrowed, "I have heard you have a new manor, a royal hunting lodge. You have done well for the son of a sword for hire."

I was being insulted but I let it slip from my back. "Fate and the queen have been kind to me. Does my ownership of the manor cause a problem, my lord?"

He waved a dismissive hand, "La Pleasaunce at Greenwich is more than sufficient for me. I just hope that the manor does not give you ideas above your station."

I smiled, "Oh no, my lord, I know my place and, more importantly, my duty."

"Good. Then fare ye well."

We had left London and were on the road that led, eventually, to Wales before we spoke of the meeting. It took until then for the road to become quieter. When the road ahead and behind was deserted and we passed along empty fields, Thomas said, "You have made an enemy there, my lord."

I shook my head, "He was never my friend and the line is a fine one between one who is not your friend and one who is an enemy. I swore an oath, Thomas, two if you count the one I made to Sir William and King Henry. The Duke of Gloucester and his brother forced me away from young King Henry so that I could not fulfil my promise. I now have the opportunity to do so." I stroked Storm's neck, "We need to think who we will take with us when the word comes."

"Four men at arms and four archers, my lord. The queen showed that she has an eye for strategy. I spoke with the monks in the abbey and they showed me a map. It is only ten miles between the abbeys but we have to pass through London. What if they are seen?"

"You and I will have to carry the boys on our horses. We will have two saddles made that will accommodate them and we will wrap them in cloaks."

"And if we have to fight?"

"That is unlikely in London although it is quite likely that we will be seen and even if the boys are not recognised then we will be. You are right in one respect. The duke now feels we are enemies and London is his city. He will have men watching for us from now on."

139

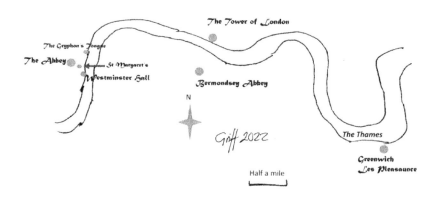

The Tower of London

The Gryphon's Tongue

The Abbey

St Margaret's

Westminster Hall

Bermondsey Abbey

N

Griff 2022

The Thames

Greenwich
Les Pleasaunce

Half a mile

140

Chapter 14

The queen died on the 3rd of January. It was Iago who brought us the news. He stayed the night and told us that while her end was peaceful, it was fraught with fears for her husband's position. "The funeral is to be held on the 3rd of February at Westminster Abbey. That is when Father Bertrand asked you to be at Bermondsey. He will accompany the boys to the abbey after the funeral."

"Not their father?"

Iago smiled, "One advantage of Westminster is that there it affords sanctuary and, to be honest, Sir Michael, the attention of the duke. The boys may well be invisible."

An idea sprang to my mind. If this was a battle and we knew an ambush was coming we would try to avoid it, "Suppose we met Father Bertrand, not at Bermondsey, but at Westminster. As soon as the funeral was over then we could find a way to take the boys directly to Barking." He looked dubious. "If we accompany the boys to the funeral then we will be identified. Let my men and I be invisible."

"It is a longer journey."

"Two miles but we would not have to cross the river. London Bridge is an easy place to spy and to stop us. We cannot afford a battle and we could skirt the walls of the city if we take the boys at Westminster." The more I thought about it the better and the safer it sounded.

Thomas was with us and he nodded his approval, "We could disguise ourselves as pilgrims. If we carry the cockleshells of a pilgrim then our attendance at the funeral might be seen as the first step on the way to Canterbury. Of course, once we headed northeast and not southeast then they would know."

"We can ride to Barking from Bermondsey in under two hours. If they think we are heading back across the river then it delays pursuit." I looked at Iago, "Your master could help by drawing attention to himself."

Iago laughed, "I do not think that will be a problem. Already the duke's spies watch us constantly. I left before dawn and crossed the Thames far upstream from London."

"Owen should enlist the help of the king. While he is still young his mother's death will have most definitely have affected him."

"Perhaps I will suggest that to my lord but he is a man, Sir Michael, who listens to himself more than to others. He acts more quickly than he should sometimes." He was telling me that Owen Tudor was reckless.

"Then when you return tell Father Bertrand that my men and I will be in London on February 1st and he need not seek us, we will find him. There will be nine of us."

Thomas asked, "You have a plan, my lord?"

"You have given me the bones and now I have a week or so to hang the flesh upon it."

Iago counselled, "Be careful my lord lest the hanging is of your neck. The Duke of Gloucester has made it quite clear that he views the boys as a threat to the crown. I do not think that their lives are at risk but the Tower of London has many chambers where they could be hidden."

I nodded, "I remember the Maid of Brittany and I would not wish her fate on the two boys." I saw him remembering the tale of the maid who was locked up until she was an old lady. "You know this part of London?"

"I do."

"Then give me the benefit of that knowledge and I can let the priest know where to meet us."

We spoke at length and long into the night. We soon had a through picture of the place. We also learned much about Iago. He envied Thomas and his life. He told us that he was no longer a young man and when his master safe he would seek to leave his service and find a wife. "I think, Sir Michael, that once he is allowed to live in peace he will also seek a wife and live peacefully in Flintshire. At least that is my hope. I like not this intrigue."

Iago left the next morning. He would be back in London quicker than he had reached us as he could now risk London Bridge. I had spoken to Isabelle of my task the night before. She more than understood. She had become inordinately fond of Margaret who was a delightful child. The thought of the girl's elder brothers being incarcerated filled her with dread. The thought of my going to war for a king did not meet with her favour either but she was happy for me to risk my life for two children. I had no arguments from her.

The choice of men was easy. They were the ones I had led into the woods and who had served with me in France. We gathered in the large hall and I had Cedric and my billmen act as guards on the doors. I trusted my people but we now had more strangers living amongst us than hitherto. We restricted the access to none and I could not risk our plans being overheard and then repeated, even, innocently. It was not just our lives that were at risk but those of Jasper and Edmund.

"We do not wear mail, save, perhaps, a coif. We do not wear my livery and we carry no shields. You archers will carry your longbows in cases and sheathed swords only. My wife and her ladies are making cockleshell symbols that will identify us as pilgrims. We will not travel together as that would draw attention to us. I will travel with Thomas and Nicholas. The rest of you should travel in a group of three. We can travel together until we reach Yling and then we split into three groups and each one takes a different route." I looked around the faces and saw confidence oozing from them. "The funeral is at Westminster Abbey on the 2nd of February. The abbey and the palace are almost two miles from the walls of London. We will find inns where we can stay on the 1st. Thomas, Nicholas and I will be the ones who meet Brother Bertrand and bring the boys to the inn called The Gryphon's Tongue. It is a low place and close to the river. Two of you will be there to watch for danger and when we leave you will act as a rearguard to spy out any enemies."

"Where will we leave our horses, Sir Michael?"

"You can leave your horses at St Margaret's in Westminster. With the crowds at the abbey, it will be deserted. We can take the boys into it so that any who spy us think that they are lighting candles for their mother. It will allow the mourners to leave the area around the abbey. When we leave I would do so with as few people watching as possible. We will take our horses and head for Barking. You six will get your horses and follow. I do not fear anything ahead of us but there may be pursuit. Better if you are behind us. All you need to know is that we shall go from the abbey to the inn and then to the church of St Margaret. It will throw pursuers off the scent."

We went over the plan several times and they clarified all the problem areas. "Although we will not be going there, we tell any who question us that we are heading for the Tabard Inn in Southwark. It is the place pilgrims normally meet for the journey to Canterbury. Now go, choose your clothes and your horses. We have at least a fortnight before we leave. I will be letting my hair and beard grow for I wish to change my appearance. I shall find old buskins to wear and the horse I take will be neither Storm nor Shadow. They are too well known. If the preparations are right then all will be well."

Our rescue of the two young boys made me even closer to my three children. Margaret was not of my blood but that did not matter. I had seen her since she had been a swaddling baby and I loved her as much as Jean or Maud. When I was not preparing my equipment, I was playing with them.

All too soon it was time to leave. I wished to be on the road before daylight. I was not sure if any of the duke's men were watching the hall but if they had been it would have been a daylight watch only for the nights were still icily cold. By leaving before dawn we guaranteed reaching London before dark. We rode in our three groups. Whenever we spied men approaching in the opposite direction, we spread out so that none would know if we were one large group or three smaller ones.

We reached Yling a couple of hours before dark and we watered our horses in the tiny village. Robbie led his group off and then Edward took his. I waited until they were out of sight before I took my two companions on the road to Westminster.

"This new saddle feels strange, my lord."

I nodded. With the front wooden cantle removed it felt as though we would slip off. It was nonsense of course but if we had to fight then we would be at a disadvantage. I shook my head and smiled to myself. There would be no fight for Thomas and I would be holding on to a child and they dared not be endangered.

"Remember our story. We have returned from the French wars and wish to atone for any sins we might have committed. We watch the funeral of the queen of our good King Henry and then we travel to the tomb of Thomas Becket. After that, we hang up our swords."

Thomas laughed and patted the old Norman sword we had found in the armoury of Houghton Regis, "And this blade is so old that it needs a funeral itself."

I laughed along with him. We had left our good swords at home and had taken old, though still well-made swords so that we could appear as warriors for the working day and not men who had fought and captured Jeanne d'Arc. Anonymity was the key. I had decided to take rooms at The Gryphon's Tongue. Iago knew it and told me that it was a warren of tiny rooms many of them little better or bigger than the hovels we used when on campaign. We would find a room but we would be paying far too much for it. Westminster was outside the city walls and there were fewer inns close by than in the city proper. The palace had a wall around it but that was all. We dismounted when we passed the abbey. It was not only a sign of respect it allowed us to view the security. There were men outside with halberds and I saw that they wore the livery of the Duke of Gloucester. There might be a council running England but the man who ruled the council was the younger brother of King Henry V[th].

The road dipped down to the river and we headed for the inn. I saw that it was a ramshackle wooden affair and it seemed to me that it had been added to over the years. There was a stable and an ostler. Remarkably there were few horses in the stable.

When Nicholas asked why, with an important funeral the next day, the ostler said, "It is not those who ride horses who come to view the spectacle of the funeral. Those who cannot afford a horse also wish to attend and we are cheap. There are many who think ill of the dead queen and come here to ensure she is dead. She was French."

"And how cheap is cheap, my friend? We are poor pilgrims heading for Canterbury."

"Oh, you can afford the prices they will charge you but expect to have more company when you sleep than you might like." I cocked my head to one side and he laughed, "There is much wildlife in the chambers." He nodded towards the river, "There are more rats within than without." He smiled, "Your horses will be better looked after than you, I fear, for I am Hob the ostler and I look after my charges." I slipped him three pennies. The inn would charge us for the stable and the fodder. The coins were a tip, He knuckled his head, "I will look after these tired-looking beasts for you." We took our blankets, cloaks and swords and headed for the inn's entrance.

That he had seen nothing remarkable about the horses meant we had chosen wisely. I had wondered if he would comment about the two adapted saddles but he did not. We entered the inn. It had a small door and we all had to duck to enter. Such an entrance was cleverly devised for customers could not flee quickly if they tried to avoid payment. Inside it was smoky as it was lit by tallow candles on upturned wooden barrels. The seats were of the same design. There were fewer within than I expected but then again it was early. We strode over to the trestle bar.

"Yes, my good fellows, what can I do for you?" The small greasy looking man had a ready smile and, I did not doubt, a blade ready to hand. I knew the type and had we not needed the anonymity of the inn I would not have come with a mile of it. "I see that you are pilgrims, welcome. One day I shall make a pilgrimage. I am Septimus Bartry."

"We seek a room for the night. We have come to see the funeral of the queen. We followed King Henry to France."

"Ah," he scrutinised me, "and you must have been young then."

"I was a boy and learned my craft in Picardy and Normandy."

"I have a room. You have horses too?" I nodded, "Then for the three of you that will be a shilling." It was too much and he added, hurriedly, "For that, I will feed you this night and give you a breakfast before you leave to view the spectacle."

I took out the mean looking purse and peered inside. I took out the coin as though it was the last one I had."

"Agnes, take these three to their room." He gestured to the stairs. I was just grateful that it was not one of the rooms below ground level. The ostler's words about rats had worried me.

The woman called Agnes looked ancient and appeared to have lost half her teeth but I knew that she might only be thirty years old. The women who worked in such places had a hard and a short life. I often wondered why they endured it. Of course, for many, they had made the wrong choice of man when they were young and were then used and abused.

"Come with me." We ascended stairs that were so narrow that Nicholas' broad shoulders barely fitted through them and so rickety that I feared they would not take our weight. Thankfully, we were on the first floor. The door was also narrow and Nicholas barely made it through. There were three straw-filled mattresses and an unlit tallow candle on the wooden lintel of the wind hole. The crone smiled her graveyard smile and said, "You will not need blankets for the heat of your bodies will suffice. I hope you get on with each other!" She cackled as she left us and I saw what she meant. The three of us would fill the room.

We had brought our own blankets with us and we laid them out before descending. We returned to the main room downstairs. The food was unremarkable and had more greens in the stew than meat. As Thomas commented, they had shown the stew a ham bone but that was all. My two companions wrinkled their noses at the ale. The shilling bought just one ale each and we stood after the platters had been cleared. It was not good food but men such as we would have cleared them.

"More ale, lads?"

"We had a long ride today. We will walk to the abbey."

He shook his head, "They will not let you within. The Duke of Gloucester fears that men may wish to hide inside and do harm on the morrow."

I adopted a puzzled look, "Why?"

"The duke is very popular in London but there are people travelling from all over the land to attend the funeral. He takes no chances."

"And do you like the duke?"

He gave me a suspicious look and then smiled, "The duke likes his pleasure. You know that he has called his home at Greenwich, La Pleasaunce?" I nodded, "And that he married his mistress, Eleanor of Cobham, a real beauty she is."

"I did not. We have been in France."

"Ah, she is an enchantress, but it is said, she studies the dark arts. Some say she is a witch." He gave a lascivious grin, "I have seen her and she has the looks that make a man's loins itch. I think the duke is lucky and when he passes, he is generous. I live in London and not England. The duke can do whatever he likes so long as we are not heavily taxed and left to our own devices."

As we headed into the now dark night I reflected on the words. The duke was popular and we would have to bear that in mind. The populace would be on his side and not ours. We said nothing as we headed to the abbey. The guards peered suspiciously at us as we walked beyond it. I saw that there were many of them although four of them did not wear the livery of the duke. I wondered at that. I did not wish to risk returning quickly and so we headed along the road that led north and then turned to come around the rear of the abbey and the complex of buildings. We headed back towards the inn. To our left was St Margaret's church and to the right, Westminster Palace. The church had no guards and I nodded towards it. This was where we would meet our men and I was keen to see within it. When we neared the doors, that were obligingly open, I gestured to the left and right. My two companions nodded. They would wait and watch.

I entered the church which was lit by candles. I spied a couple of shapes knelt in prayer. I knelt, made the sign of the cross and then went to the place where they had candles. I took a penny from my purse and dropped it in the box next to them. It struck other coins. I lit a candle and placed it amongst the others. As I knelt, I had the opportunity to view the interior. It was a small church and largely unadorned by silver and gold. It was probably the very antithesis of the abbey.

Another penitent came and knelt next to me. I was about to rise when Father Bertrand's voice spoke, "Stay Michael. I need to speak." He spoke in hushed tones and I merely nodded. "The plans will have to change. The duke has men he has set to watch the boys, me and Owen Tudor. The queen's husband is fearful of his life. The men set to watch are killers. There are some Swabians hired by the duke and they are the ones to fear. They do not wear the duke's livery. To create a distraction Owen will seek sanctuary at the Dean's court. In the confusion, I will bring the boys in here for their safety." He had his hands together as though in prayer and he pointed, "There is a door at the rear. You will need to have your horses outside. Do not worry there are trees and it is hidden from view. I fear your escape will, perforce, be faster than you might like. Remember, the moment Owen makes the break for sanctuary is the time to save the boys. I will bring the boys here. It is a short way from the abbey but you will need to be quick and decisive."

147

I said, quietly, "And afterwards, what about you?"

"The queen asked me to watch over her husband. I am to be his chaplain. I will join him in the sanctuary. If nothing else I can be a witness to whatever deed the duke has planned."

He stood and left the church. I waited until I could no longer hear his feet and then I stood. When I emerged my two men stepped from the shadows, "Was that Father Bertrand?"

"It was and we have a problem. The men who watched at the abbey were they Swabians?"

Thomas nodded, "At least four of them were."

"And it is they who will try to take both Owen Tudor and the boys. They are killers. Let us go to the river where we can talk." Pulling our hoods up we headed towards the river. The trees would hide us from scrutiny and we would be able to ensure we were not overheard. The dark river was flowing slowly and the trees were silent. With no one around I began and I told them what Father Bertrand had said. "I fear that my plan, cunning though it was, may come to undo us. I have no way of knowing where the other six are. We will have to adapt it. Nicholas, you will have a strung bow and wait by the horses behind the church." We had seen the place where the horses could be tethered unseen and we had our route to the north-eastern road already plotted. "Thomas and I will wait as close to the abbey as we can. I do not think that any attempt will be made to take any of them until they have left the precincts of the abbey. Owen Tudor, and his men, will race for the Dean's yard and it is then that Father Bertrand will bring the boys to the church. You and I, Thomas, will have to deal with the Swabians. I hope that Owen Tudor will be the greater prize but if there are six then two or even three may well come after the boys."

Thomas asked, "We use deadly force?"

"Not on those who wear the duke's livery for that might be deemed treasonous in these strange days but the Swabians? Aye, for we use the oath I took to the queen. We say we were protecting the boys from unknown attackers."

Thomas smiled, "I am content but I wanted to be clear."

"Nicholas you are the backup plan now. Robbie will be at The Gryphon's Tongue. We may see him and be able to give him the changes but we cannot guarantee that. In order to deter pursuit you will have to nock an arrow and try to release it from the back of a horse."

He nodded, "The range will be short but do not underestimate Robbie and the others, my lord. You chose well and they can think for themselves. You mentioned St Margaret's church and they will head for it but you are right in one respect, this will be harder than we thought."

We headed back to the inn and after checking on the horses, entered and found that it was now rammed with customers. It was clear to me that there was little competition for the inn and Septimus Bartry was making money while he could. We did not bother to buy more ale and went directly to our room. We realised there that our room would be very noisy. We had thought having just one flight of stairs was a good thing but we now realised that we had been given the worst room in the inn. Once we were in our beds then the door could not be opened as our feet were there. Agnes had also been correct for in spite of the wind hole and the chilly night we were far from cold as the heat from the room below rose to warm us.

I slept fitfully and I guess that the others had the same problems that I had. The result was that when I heard the bell from the abbey for Laudes, I sat upright. My movement woke the other two. Thomas picked at something and he held the louse between two fingers to crush it, "I will need to burn these clothes and bathe before I approach Sarah. She cannot abide lice and nits."

"Let us rise and breakfast. There is nothing to be gained from waiting here. We will head to the church while it is quiet."

It was neither Septimus nor Agnes who was downstairs but an old white-haired man with one hand. The room was empty but stank of sweaty bodies, tallow and split beer. Luckily I also smelled the fresh bread and he nodded, "Aye, you do right to rise early. You have the choice of bread. The ones who are tardy will have black bread." He poured us three ales and said, "Take these and I will bring you your breakfast." He chuckled, "Septimus is not the most generous of hosts but it is the early bird who might fill a hole!"

We sat at a table by the ground floor wind hole so that the smell of the beer might be moved. The night man only had one hand but he was strong and he carried the tray one handed, supported by the stump of his other.

"If you would take the platter from the tray."

There were three small white loaves, some thinly sliced ham, a larger portion of cheese, a good knob of butter and some pickled onions. I had endured worse and, to be fair, the cheese and ham were tasty. The warm bread and the slathered butter were delicious and we picked the crumbs off the platter when we had done. It would be an hour or so before the sun rose but there was little point in staying in the inn. We rose and waved to the man before heading to the stables and the ostler.

Hob was asleep on the hayrack above the horses. He heard us enter and peered down. He laughed, "I see that the other residents of the rooms helped you to rise. Would you like me to help you saddle them?"

I knew that it would involve the exchange of more coins and we had the time, "No, thank you. You may sleep a little longer."

We walked the horses from the inn, past the palace, along the river to the place we had spoken the night before. Then we headed for the church. The doors were open and candles were lit. The priests were getting ready for the first service of the day. We went around to the back. Nicholas tethered the horses and then took out his bow. He would not string it until he had to.

"We will head for the abbey but I have no intention of being the first to arrive. We will join the first of the crowds." I had been at royal funerals and weddings. I knew that they would draw not just spectators but those who made money from such events. When the hawkers and traders arrived to set up their stalls and pitches then we would wander up. By being early but with the crowds, I hoped to become invisible. This was, as Edgar White Streak had once told me, like hiding in plain sight. I wished the old man was with me now for he had more battle sense than anyone I had met, excepting Rafe and Sir William, of course.

Chapter 15

I heard the chatter as we neared the abbey. There were people there already. I realised why when I saw the man and the woman lighting a fire. They were heating chestnuts. There was another couple who were erecting an awning and a table. They looked to be selling beer. As we wandered up the woman called out cheerfully, "We'll be ready soon, my sweet. The finest ale this side of the river."

There looked to be about fifteen people setting up stalls. The liveried sentries ensured that they did not encroach on the cobbles where the hearse would pull up and the mourners enter the church. Soon there was the smell of chestnuts augmented by the smell of rabbit and squirrel meat warming up. A local baker had brought his wares, covered by a cloth and I recognised the smell of honey cakes, spiced buns as well as bread. He would charge a pretty penny for them and I doubted that his wares would last long. The aroma of such pastries and cakes would draw a large crowd.

Thomas and I seized an opportunity when a solitary old woman attempted to erect a small awning over her marchpane stall. We helped her and it must have made the sentries think we were with her for we were ignored afterwards. The old women grunted when we had finished, "Thank you for your help although I could have managed and as your assistance was not sought do not expect marchpane from me. It is too expensive for the likes of two out of work soldiers." Our disguise had worked and we were invisible.

I smiled and gave a mock bow, "I fear I do not like marchpane but as pilgrims, we have promised to do a good deed each day. We thank you for affording us the opportunity to do so early and now, if you do not mind, we will stand close by to get a good view of the proceedings."

She sniffed, "Stand where you will but if customers come then shift yourselves."

She was hardly the most gracious of ladies but I suppose she had to make coins where she could and we had now managed to appear to be part of the hawkers and stall holders. As dawn broke so those who wished to get a good view of the funeral arrived. I knew that amongst them would be cutpurses and thieves but enough Londoners arrived to swell the numbers of those we did not have to watch.

The guards we saw yawned. They would be relieved by even more sentries once dawn broke. Indeed even as we watched we heard the tramp of feet as the new guards came. The liveried guards would not be a problem. The duke would have used the men who guarded his palace and they would not know the difference between an innocent visitor and

and an assassin. When the Swabians arrived Thomas and I stiffened. We had spoken of the danger such mercenaries presented. I knew why the duke had hired them. They would obey every order and do so ruthlessly. They cared not for any save themselves and they were a formidable foe. They wore plate and mail and although they wore no helmets, they had coifs atop arming caps. Their helmets would not be needed but they would need clear vision to ensure that the proceedings were not disrupted. They had the long two-handed swords favoured by these most feared of warriors. They were the nemesis of horsemen for their long swords were more than capable of taking the legs from a charging courser. Even worse was the fact that I could see them scanning the faces of the people who were gathering. They were professionals and knew the signs to look for. Thomas and I knelt as though we were removing a stone from our boots and we disappeared below those people waiting before us. We had allowed shorter people before us. A mother and two girls were a perfect distraction before us for the woman was quite comely and the liveried guards had come to her to speak to her. All of this helped our innocent look but the Swabians were a different matter. They would not be distracted.

It was Terce when we heard the trumpets sound from the palace. It was the signal that the funeral cortege was on its way. The sentries and the Swabians flanked the route and they faced the crowd. Even the hawkers and the stallholders stopped what they were doing to watch as the black horses pulled up with the coffin aboard. Riding behind were the chief mourners. The king was there as well as his uncle, the duke, and the council. Owen Tudor and his sons, along with Father Bertrand had walked and stood a respectful distance from the council and the king. The archbishop awaited them. Six men, probably the queen's guards, all dressed in black walked towards the coffin and they were accompanied by six boys, also in black, who carried a black velvet canopy to cover the coffin. The coffin was adorned with silver bells as was the canopy and there was the most lifelike effigy of the queen on the coffin. Our position meant we had a good view of it as it was taken from the hearse. At a signal from the archbishop, the six coffin bearers raised the coffin and, in perfect time walked into the abbey. Negotiating the steps was not easy but it was much harder for the six boys with the canopy who had to keep it above the coffin bearers. They managed it. The king and his uncle with, I assumed the duke's wife followed, then the council and only after they had passed was the queen's family allowed in. I had seen Father Bertrand surreptitiously scanning the crowd and knew that he must have seen me although we had not made eye contact.

As soon as the last mourner had entered the abbey there was a flurry of activity as the people who would remain to watch the mourners come out, sought to buy wares from the hawkers. They crowded around the marchpane stall and the old woman gave us a baleful look so we moved away from her. I put my head close to Thomas, "Head to the inn and see if you can find any of our men. I would be happier with more of them here. Those Swabians look to know their business."

"I do not like to leave you here alone."

"The service will take at least an hour. You can be there and back quickly."

He nodded and I waited. The horse holders stood closer to the dean's yard and I wondered if they would return to Westminster Hall or if the duke would take a boat to Les Pleasaunce at Greenwich and the king ride to the Tower of London. They had all come from Westminster Hall but that did not mean they would return there. Some of the crowds began to move away. Most had come to see the queen and her coffin; I do not think it had disappointed for it had been even more magnificent than her husband's. The ones who remained wanted a glimpse of the king and, perhaps, the duke. It was as the crowd thinned that I spied the leader of the Swabians. He identified himself by walking along the line of sentries, liveried and his men and he spoke to each one. Most just shook their heads while two or three shrugged. None nodded. I had commanded the bodyguard of the queen and the baby king and knew what he was doing. He was asking if they had seen anything suspicious. I kept my eyes on him. He was a large, broad-shouldered man but then that could have applied to most Swabians. He was slightly taller than the normal warrior but what marked him was the bent nose and the scar running down his cheek. It disappeared into his beard but the white close to his eyes marked its direction. The man had almost lost an eye. The crowds continued to thin, as did the stallholders. Some had sold all their wares and they were leaving. The old woman was still there for her marchpane was one of the more expensive items and she still had some to sell.

"I would have thought you had seen enough, pilgrim."

The old woman's words drew my attention from the scarred Swabian, "Aye, I have but as I served in France, I would like to cheer the young king when he comes out for his father was a great man. It did not seem seemly to do so before."

She nodded, "He was a great king but he does not rule this land now. It is ruled by his uncle and I am not sure that they will let him have the chance to become great or even good." She was looking beyond me,

"Your friend has returned." She cackled, "He cannot hold his water, eh?"

I laughed with her but headed towards Thomas. I did not want our words overheard. The ever-thinning crowds helped although they also made it easier for us to be spotted. He nodded and put his head close to mine when he neared me. "I found Robbie and John. Robbie is going to find their horses and he and John the Fletcher will join Nicholas. John is close to St Margaret's church. If we can take the boys, he will slow down any pursuit."

It was as I nodded and studied the crowd to see John that I also spied Edward Poleaxe. I could not see any of the other men he had with him but I now had three men at arms and our chances of success had just doubled.

We spied the doors open and I knew that the mourners would emerge soon enough. The crowd had thinned to a single line of spectators and Thomas and I left the old woman to move closer to the doors of the abbey. With thinner crowds then we were easier to spot but the scarred Swabian, fortunately for us had headed towards a man who had moved from the line of spectators and was moving towards the horses. I had no idea what his purpose was but it allowed us to get as close to the abbey steps as we could without arousing suspicion. The scarred Swabian manhandled the man and hurled him away from the horses to the ground. There was a cheer from the spectators as the man, protesting at his treatment, fell to the cobbled floor. This was entertainment and all eyes swivelled to take in the spectacle as the Swabian drew his sword and beat the man's back with the flat of his blade. The unfortunate man crawled and scrambled to disappear into the crowd and when he did so there was a cheer. The incident kept the last of the crowds there.

We moved closer to the steps and the path that led to St Margaret's. The first to emerge from the church was the young king. He had grown since last I had seen him. We all bowed so he would not recognise me but as I raised my head, I saw that he was now a personable young man and he had with him three young knights. He was gathering his own household. The duke and his bodyguards came out next and I noticed that the king gave just a cursory nod to his uncle before he and his companions mounted their horses.

There were cheers and cries of, "Good King Henry!" Thomas and I joined in. A couple of people shouted for alms and I then knew why the man had risked the ire of the guards by approaching so close. He wanted coins. The king nodded and one of the young knights took a handful of coins and tossed them to the ones who were poorly dressed.

It made the now smaller crowd lurch forward and the guards drew swords to make a barrier. The crowds cheered and the king waved before turning his horse and heading with his knights, east. They were going to the Tower of London.

The event allowed Thomas and me to make a larger space before us. I knew that John and Edward were somewhere behind me and I did not need to worry about them. The duke and his entourage did not move but studied, assiduously, the doors. The scarred Swabian was summoned and he and the duke spoke for some moments. I was glad for it meant he could not look for danger at the steps and Thomas and I were now isolated. If he saw us, it would look suspicious.

It was Owen Tudor and his two companions, Iago and Rhodri who came out first and I surreptitiously drew my sword. As he emerged, he looked at the duke and shouted, "I claim sanctuary!" He, along with Rhodri and Iago ran as fast as they could towards the dean's yard. If he had wished he could simply have stayed in the abbey but he was doing what his dead wife would have wished, he was making a distraction for the sake of his sons. He was buying us the time to rescue them. The Swabians all reacted and ran to try to stop them. The difference was that the Swabians were plated and mailed and the three Welshmen were not. In a foot race the three Welshmen would win.

Father Bertrand shepherded the two boys down the steps towards the path to St Margaret's and Thomas and I simply stepped behind them. Our cloaks and bodies would hide them from view for a few precious moments. I heard the old priest exhorting them to run. Once the Welshmen made the dean's yard then all attention would switch to the steps and the duke, along with his Swabians would seek their secondary prize, the sons of Queen Catherine. I saw, ahead of me, Edward and John stood on either side of the path that led to St Margaret's.

I said, "Father, take them into the church and out of the back door. My men are waiting."

I heard shouts behind but I knew, from Rafe, that if you are pursued then the worst thing you can do is to turn around. All that would be seen, until we did so were two nondescript cloaked men hurrying from the abbey. We might have been innocent. Turning faces would mark our guilt.

The duke's voice rang out above the pandemonium. "The boys are being kidnapped! Take them."

As we passed Edward and John I shouted, "Get around the back of the church. Draw your swords and they will follow you."

The two men nodded and drew their swords which sparkled in the sun. Thomas and I were merely walking fast and the two men with drawn swords that ran drew the attention of the pursuers. We had gained almost a hundred feet and we tumbled into the darkness of the church.

"Hurry boys. There are men waiting with horses." The priest knew the church and led the boys unerringly to the back door.

I knew we had a slight advantage in that we knew what we were doing and the Swabians did not. They would have to split their forces and some would follow us while the rest followed John and Edward. Our cloaks had ensured they the boys had been hidden; they had vanished from sight. I knew that there were three archers waiting with strung bows. They were my edge. I also knew that if the duke identified me then I might risk his anger. Was I putting my family in danger? It was too late for that now and I would have to trust in God. I contemplated sheathing my sword when we entered the church for it seemed to me sacrilegious but we had enemies behind and I could hear their plate rattling as they lumbered towards the open door. There were people in the church and they pressed themselves at the side as we followed the priest and his charges. The rear door was already open and I saw the horses beyond. William of Hereford and Mark the Bowyer held the reins of our two horses and I saw Father Bertrand lift Edmund into the saddle. I sheathed my sword for I would need two hands for the reins. I heard the clash of steel from the far said of the church and knew that Edward and John were fighting.

As Father Bertrand lifted Jasper into the saddle and I began to haul myself behind Edmund I saw my three mounted archers draw back on their bows. Nicholas shouted, "Hold there, Swabian or I shall release."

The man must have moved for Nicholas' arrow whizzed over my head and as I swung my leg over the saddle saw that he had pinned a Swabian to the church door. A bodkin released at less than twenty feet will penetrate plate as though it was parchment.

I shouted to William and Mark, "Go and aid Edward and John." As Thomas mounted his horse, I said, "Farewell and good luck, Father. Thomas let us ride." This was not time for a long goodbye.

Two more arrows flew over me and I heard them smack into the door. They were a warning to those pursuing us. I wrapped my right hand around Edmund's waist and kicked my horse in the flanks. I saw Mark the Bowyer send an arrow at a Swabian warrior. Two other Swabians had suffered wounds and William led the two horses of John and Edward. The arrows had an effect and the Swabians took shelter. Even in plated armour, they now knew the follow of facing an archer who was just thirty feet away. Having done the deed we were in the hands of God. We all knew my plan and Thomas and I led the way. My men would understand what they had to do; delay the pursuers and not get caught. This was no time for heroics. The archers would keep nocked arrows to buy us time to get along the road a ways and my men at arms would be ready to ride down any opposition. The Duke of Gloucester would be angry and he had a choice. Either pursue us with his knights or get his killers mounted. I knew not which he would choose although I suspected the latter as he would first apprehend Father Bertrand and then attempt to winkle the Welshmen from their sanctuary. We did not have far to go and our horses were rested. I kept my heels digging into my horse's flanks to get as much speed as I could on the well-made cobbled road. Each step we took closer to Barking guaranteed the safety of the queen's sons. If it was the Swabians of the duke's knights who followed us we were safe for they wore plate and we did not.

"How are you, young Edmund? I hope this is not too fearful for you."

I heard the excitement in his voice, "Mother said we could trust you and that you had the safest hands in England."

"Good."

"Is my mother with God now?"

I suddenly realised that in all the planning and the plotting I had forgotten that this day had seen him bury his mother. He was still a very young boy. "Surely and she is now without pain."

I saw his head nod, "And for that, I pleased. I wondered if she was being punished for when last I spoke to her, her face was drawn and haggard." He was silent as we ate up the miles to Barking. When he did speak again his words surprised me, "I had a sister once and I thought she died but my mother, when she spoke of her, did so as though she was alive. Should I speak of my mother like that?"

"If it helps and gives comfort. I often speak to comrades alongside whom I fought and who are now dead. I believe that they are in heaven and having their spirits close to me cannot hurt."

"Good for I know that while the nuns of this abbey will be good people else my mother and Father Bertrand would not have entrusted my brother and to their care, they will not be my mother. They will not tell me stories at night and they will not be able to comfort us in the same way that she did."

"Aye, she was a great lady and a good mother. You cannot replace her, none of us can but we honour her by doing what she wished. For my part, that means the protection of you and your brother."

He was silent again. I was beginning to see what a clever boy he was, "The king is my brother, sort of, is he not?"

I hesitated for I was out of my depth now. Then I remembered that the oath I had taken had been to protect all the queen's children and she would wish to them to know the truth. "You are his half-brothers and, as such, you need to be mindful that men may try to use you for their own ends."

"But not you. Mother told us that we could trust you above all other men." He paused, "I think she meant my father too but he is a brave man, is he not and he sacrificed himself for us."

"He is."

The thundering of the hooves was all that I heard for a while. Jasper, it seemed, was too engrossed in the ride for conversation and I risked a glance over my shoulder. There were riders half a mile behind us. I recognised the blaze on Edward's horse. They were my men.

"What of the nuns, Sir Michael? The abbess, can I trust them?"

Once again, I was in a difficult position and I constructed an answer that would, I hope, be the right one. "They are there to educate you and to protect you but they should not try to use you for their own ends. Never agree to anything immediately. Think about it and ask yourself what your mother would have said."

"Or Father Bertrand."

"Aye."

"Or you."

I was touched by the trust but also worried by it. If the boy thought I was important then what might others, the duke, for instance, think? I thought about the duke's position now. His brother, the Duke of Bedford had died childless and he himself was childless. That should have made the position of King Henry secure but he was just a boy and until he married and sired children then the crown was also insecure. King Richard had died childless, in fact, both of the kings called Richard had died without an heir. If King Henry failed to produce an heir or died then it would be the York side of the Plantagenet house that would be heirs to the crown. Would Edmund and Jasper be hostages to fortune? Would they be used by the Duke of Gloucester for his own ends? This was all too complicated for me and as I saw the walls of Barking Abbey loom in the distance I hoped and prayed that my involvement was over.

We galloped through the gates and a handful of nuns appeared. One ran back inside and I waited on my horse. I would not dismount until my men or the abbess arrived. I turned to speak to Edmund's brother, "How are you, young Jasper. Were you fearful on the ride?"

He shook his head and his eyes were wide and filled with excitement, "No, my lord, it was the best experience I have ever had. I would be a warrior like Thomas here!"

Nicholas and my men reached us before the abbess. "My lord, they are but a mile behind us."

I kicked my horse on and said to the nearest nun, "Are there stables?"

"Why yes, sir, around the back."

I shouted, "Follow me." We hurried around the cloistered building and when we were out of sight of the gate, I relaxed a little. We passed through a gate in the wall which, if this had been a castle, would have been the inner bailey. I spied the stables and we headed for them. I dismounted and helped Edmund from the saddle. The rest dismounted. "Guard the boys and I will find the abbess."

I knew there had to be a way into the complex from the rear and I ran to the wall that surrounded it. Sure enough, I found a gate and entered it. I found myself in a vegetable and herb garden. The nuns there stood in shock when I appeared. With my unruly hair and wild beard, dressed in cheap clothes I did not look like a knight. I hurried towards the abbey itself and entered a door that led through the kitchen. There were screams and squeals as I passed. I walked through the empty refectory and found myself in the cloisters. Ahead of me, I could see the main entrance and I saw some nuns there. I slowed and moved through the building, keeping to the shadows until I was in the entrance hall close to the open door. I could hear the conversation.

"As I said before sir, although your manners tell me that you are not a gentleman, that we are a simple order of nuns and no one has entered through our doors this morning. You are the first men and riders I have seen. Is that not simple enough for you?"

The guttural, accented French told me that it was a Swabian who spoke, "Lady, we have followed nine men who abducted the sons of Queen Catherine and they entered the gates of this abbey. We saw them."

"Then perhaps they carried on. There is another gate and the road heads north and east. Now I must return to my devotions."

"Tell the men who hide within," he raised his voice to a shout, "that they have hurt three of my men and they shall pay. Günter of Brabant has a long memory and is the most patient of men. There will be blood."

"You really are an irritating man. Go for you are giving me a headache!"

I heard the hooves as the men left the abbey. I knew that they would not go far and they would be watching for us. The abbess entered and did to seem surprised when she saw me. She smiled. Katherine de la Pole was a beautiful young woman. I was surprised how young. "Quite an entrance, Sir Michael. I expected you and, I presume the boys, but not in such a fashion."

"I am sorry, my lady but events conspired against us. The Swabians you just sent away were seeking the boys. I do not know if they intended to harm them but I swore an oath to protect them and I keep my word. I left the boys at the rear near to the stables and they are guarded by my men."

"So I have heard." She turned to a nun, "Sister Beatrice, go to the stables and fetch the boys."

I shook my head, "I will have to go with them for my men will not allow your ladies to take them without my command."

She laughed and it was like the tinkling of the bells on a Maypole. It made my heart sing. "I can see that Queen Catherine chose well." Her face became serious, "We have said prayers for her and we will continue to do so. Sister Beatrice, go with Sir Michael and bring the boys and his men to the refectory. Sister Maria, have food prepared. Sir Michael, we will feed your men but they must stay in the stable this night. I assume you wish to stay for a night?"

I nodded, "The Swabians will be waiting for us and I would have a night of rest."

She nodded, "And I hope they have a cold night for the man was rude and aggressive. Foreigners!" She leaned over to me, "You know, Sir Michael that I agree with my father, the Earl of Suffolk, we do not need France and we should not waste our time in war with them."

I liked the abbess and as I followed the nun, I felt happier about the choice of sanctuary for the boys. They would be safe.

My men sheathed their swords when they saw me approach with the nun. "Stable the horses and then come with us. We will be sleeping in the stable but we are to be fed in the refectory." They all cheered.

As we walked towards the abbey Edmund said, "I know that our mother said we would be safe here but could we stay with you, Sir Michael? You and your men had shown yourselves to be more than capable of protecting us."

"For that, I thank you but it was not just protection your mother sought but an education. We cannot give you that. Let us honour your mother's memory by obeying her wishes."

He nodded.

The abbess made a great fuss of the boys. I saw then that although she had a position of great power, she had given up the chance of children of her own. She would never have sons. The way she looked at the boys and spoke to them told me that they would be loved and cared for. The queen had chosen well. Father Bertrand had sent the boys' clothes ahead and the abbess took the boys to their new chambers. The nuns fetched us mead, bread and cheese while the food we would be given was cooked.

Thomas shook his head, and gestured towards Edmund, "How old is the boy?"

"Six or so."

"He speaks like a grown-up."

I nodded, "Aye, but he was not brought up like us. The two had tutors and the queen spoke to them as adults. I hope that our children have a better chance of normal lives."

When the hot food came and the nuns had left, I spoke of our dilemma, "We have hurt the Swabians and their leader is determined to have vengeance. They have lost the boys and, I dare say will lose any money due to them. They will wait until we leave. One advantage we have is that they do not seem to know who we are. My plan is for us to leave tomorrow before dawn and to head for Colchester. It is in the opposite direction to our home. They may well follow us and we will try to slow them down and discourage them."

"If we hurt three, my lord, then we outnumber them."

"Aye, Nicholas that would appear to be the case but, Robbie, you were at the rear. How many men pursued you?"

"At least twenty but there were more men in the distance. It might well be more."

"Then we are still outnumbered."

Thomas nodded, "It is a good plan and we ever trust your judgement."

Chapter 16

We slipped away while the nuns held their first service of the day. I had bidden farewell to the boys and told them that no matter what happened in their lives I was still their protector. Their mother was dead but I was still the queen's knight. Poor Jasper was quite tearful as he was led to bed by Sister Beatrice. The abbess reassured me that I would always be welcome but warned me that the villagers had told her that there were more than twenty armed men camped in the woods beyond the village. They were all well-armed and, alarmingly, none wore livery. That made sense for the duke would not wish it to be known that he had hired mercenaries to hunt down the sons of Queen Catherine. It was not just the Swabians we had to deal with. Günter of Brabant led others.

Our scouts went first and we followed just a few minutes later. I knew that they would have men watching the rear but we could not spend our lives in the abbey. I knew we had caught their watchers by surprise when there were shouts from the trees next to the main road to Colchester. The passing of our archers had alerted them. I doubted that they had a horse already saddled and we had until they had saddled it and then rode to their main camp. I had no intention of riding forty miles to Colchester but I wanted to pass through Romford and head along the Chelmsford Road before turning off the main thoroughfare. The Swabians would question those in the villages through which we had travelled and I wanted them to become over-confident and try to predict our movement. The sun was well up when we rode through Romford and people looked up as the horsemen galloped through. We would be remembered. We were not riding our horses at their fastest speed but we were moving faster than most travellers. They would notice it and tell the Swabians. The old Roman road crossed the road we were using and we turned on to it to head due west before we reached Brentwood. The miles they would ride before they discovered we had deviated from our original route might buy another half an hour. The road would take us to Cheshunt and then we would have many choices of road. My original plan was to head north and spend the night on the Bedford Road. It meant we could then make the last part of the journey from there in less than a day and, I hoped, confuse our enemies.

We stopped at some small, nameless hamlet and let our horses drink from the pond there whole my archers strung their bows. We remounted and hurried along the road. We were not far from Waltham Abbey when the trap was sprung. Had Günter of Brabant employed English archers it might have succeeded but he did not. He relied on four men with crossbows and the twenty odd horsemen he had brought. Nicholas War Bag, who had a nose like an alaunt halted us before the trap could be sprung. How he knew they were there I know not but know he did and raised his hand and made the signal for danger. My archers were off their horses and stringing their bows almost before I realised where lay the danger. Their arrows were in the air before the four crossbows cracked and released their bolts. The missiles were sent hurriedly in the direction of the horses and archers and as my archers had used the horses for shelter then the bolts hit saddles and cantles rather than flesh.

We had no mail and they outnumbered us but I knew that we had to be aggressive if we wanted to survive. With that in mind, I pulled up my coif and drew my sword. "Charge!"

My archers had left a gap in the centre of the road and we hurtled through it. I led four men and once we had passed our archers, we spread out to hit the enemy together. It would have been better if we had been able to use spears but we did not. Nicholas and my archers continued to send arrows at their targets. They were now clearer to me and as Günter of Brabant had set his mailed and plated men to stand in the middle of the road so that they could block us then my archers' targets were even easier. I saw one Swabian fall, clutching the bodkin arrow that protruded from his chest. The red flights told me that was Robbie's arrow. A second was hit in the thigh. They were being thinned. The Swabians relied upon their armour but my longbowmen were too good for them. A single crossbow bolt came in our direction. I heard a cry and knew that one of the others had been struck. A white fletched arrow hit the crossbowman and he fell from cover, an arrow in his head. John Morhier was on the extreme right of our line and I saw his arm as it swept out to take the spearman who stood before him in the side of the head. As I looked, I saw that William of Hereford now sported a crossbow bolt in his left arm. Not a mortal wound it would slow him. The surviving Swabians held the centre of the road but they were flanked by men with spears and swords. They were hired men. Some wore mail but I knew that they were like the brigands we had fought in the woods. They had fought in battle and knew how to use weapons but they were not the best of warriors. The Swabians in the centre were the greater danger and they already had their swords raised to sweep them across our horses' legs. Nicholas must have seen the danger for more arrows were sent at the Swabians and another was hit.

When we were just twenty paces from them, I shouted, "Break left and right!" I spoke in English. I knew that the Swabians would be able to understand the words but it was not their first language and there would be a delay as they processed that information.

163

Thomas moved to the left and I rode to the right. The surviving Swabians had already begun their swings and where they swung it would be air and not horseflesh. The men who stood on their flanks saw the heavy horses hurtling towards them and I saw fear in their eyes. I swung my sword at the Swabian while Edward used his sword to cleave in two the skull of a mailed swordsman. My sword hit the neck of the Swabian. Had I used the sword that hung in my hall he would be dead but even with the old sword, I used it had sufficient strength and power to knock him into the side of Günter of Brabant. Thomas managed to use his sword to stab into the face of a third Swabian and when his body hit that of Günter of Brabant, the mercenary leader lost his footing and fell. William and John managed to hit their men and the result was that the rest of the hired men ran away from the hooves of our horses. They raced towards their horses. I saw that they had not hobbled them but loosely tied them. We reached them and I slashed the ropes that held them and my men slapped their rumps. Most of them ran and we followed. Some were tethered and they would be used to follow but there were too few now to make the pursuit anything more than an attempt to recover some pride. We had hurt them. My archers mounted and followed us by using the fields along the side of the road.

We reined in at Waltham Abbey. Nicholas was removing the bolt when a priest came out. "We were ambushed on the road."

He nodded. "I am a healer, I will fetch my tools." While he went I sent Robbie back down the road to see if we were being pursued. William's wound had been cleaned, stitched and bandaged by the time he returned.

"They are not following, my lord."

The priest looked up for there were no spurs on my boots. He said nothing. "Then let us ride while we can. I thank you, brother."

"The man should rest, my lord."

I handed the priest a silver coin and said, "And rest he will but not until we are nearer to our home."

In case they followed us to the abbey we turned north as soon as we were out of sight of the abbey and stopped for the night close to Much Hadham. I might have risked the manor of the queen but there was too much danger attached. We knew the land thereabouts and found a dell and an old cow byre where we spent the night eating the cold fare the nuns at Barking had prepared.

The men were in an ebullient mood. One wound was a small price to pay for the victory over better armed and armoured professional soldiers. Only I was silent, listening to their banter and the recounting of the battle. They talked of blows and blocks, slashes and stabs. The archers spoke of cleverly flighted arrows that descended unexpectedly to smash holes in their defences. I appreciated every word that they said but something was nagging at my mind.

It was Thomas who noticed. I had been with Thomas more often in battle than almost any other man. It was he who had been with me when we had brought the child from the queen. "My lord, what is amiss? We won this day and, by rights, we should have lost. Our archers' skills and your bold charge won the day. You should be happy."

I nodded, "I am sorry, Nicholas that I have not lauded you enough but I am distracted."

"We archers need no plaudits, my lord, for we know you hold us in high esteem. We have lost our foe and this time tomorrow we will be safe within the walls of Houghton Regis."

I was silent for a moment and then I said, "I ask you this, how was it that they knew where we would be? We wore no identification for them and yet despite the tortuous route we took they got ahead of us and blocked our road home."

Robbie ventured, "They were lucky."

I shook my head, "They knew where we were headed." I let that sink in, "I think that they have a suspicion about our identity and that means they probably know where we live. The Swabian might have gambled but it paid off and they found us. This is not over."

The happy mood evaporated like morning mist as they saw the danger. Thomas rubbed his beard. Like me most of my men liked to be clean-shaven and when we returned home the first thing we would do would be to bathe, remove the wildlife we had accumulated at The Gryphon's Tongue, and then shave. "But Sir Michael, the duke cannot have cause to punish us. We merely escorted the boys to the place they were intended to go. He may be unhappy that we thwarted his plans and stopped him from having the boys to bargain with but he cannot go to the council or the people with that."

"His brother is dead and King Henry has not yet taken up the reins of a ruler. There is no one to hold him in check. All that I heard of his pleasure palace on the Thames leads me to believe that he sees himself as the ruler of this land. He has power and as we all know, power changes a man."

"Not good King Henry."

"You are right Robbie but kings like that are rare. From what I have heard the first two King Henrys and the first King Edward were great kings but the rest? Sir William served more than most men and the only one he had time for was the one who led us at Agincourt. Until our king chooses to rule alone then the Duke of Gloucester is a threat." I saw them take that in. "However, it is not he who is the real problem. Günter of Brabant has been hurt by us. He will not care that we did it by fair means, indeed, we gave him all the advantages of weapons and armour but that will not enter his mind. We hurt his men." I smiled, "I might not be as vindictive but if any of you were hurt…"

Nicholas nodded, "Aye, look at The Taxman. We were all keen to have our revenge on him for merely attacking us. You are right, Sir Michael but how many men can he have? We hurt him, as you say and a bodkin wound to the shoulder does not heal overnight. He has, perhaps three hale and hearty Swabians left and that includes him. As for the rest…"

"You are right and yet if he comes, when he comes, it will not be as it was today. They will not have to face charging horses. They will choose their moment to come at us. It is more likely to be a knife in the night rather than a bold attack in the day. Remember Les Pérets."

Realisation set in. They had seen what could happen if a peaceful manor was attacked at night. They had seen the devastation that had been caused.

"And you say three Swabians but there may be more. Some of those wounded could be healed. They are mercenaries and have mercenary pride."

"Then, my lord, we have to be vigilant. It means having men watching all night for the foreseeable future."

"Aye, Nicholas and while Houghton Regis is a more solid hall than was Les Pérets, it is no castle. We have work to do but," I leaned forward, "it will not help our womenfolk if we fill their heads with fear. It is we and the men we left behind who must bear that burden. You are what Sir William would have called my oathsworn. You, I can trust more than any other men in England. We shall be discreet. We do not speak of Swabians or hired swords sent by the duke but that we are concerned that, at some time, the bandits may return and we wish to be safer. There is no ditch around our wall. I suspect that the kings who built it did not wish to spoil the look of the place. We will dig a ditch but we say that it is for drainage and that is not a complete lie. The gates on the outside wall need to be replaced; we say it is not for defence but that they are old."

Thomas nodded, "Aye, for you can bet none of them has ever examined them."

"And why should they for they are always open."

Nicholas interjected, "And one good point is the small watchtower on the northwest corner of the hall. It is the only tower in the hall but it has a good view of the land to the north and west. We can move four archers into that tower. They can be the ones who keep watch at night. Two men would have a good view of the gate, the walls and the entrances to the hall."

They were all thinking now, of our home and Robbie said, "Ralph has done a good job with the hall but he has allowed ivy and other climbing plants to roam the walls. We should cut it down."

"But not, Robbie Red Fletch, the brambles. The spiky plant may not hurt a mailed man climbing over but they will tear and tug where ivy will not. We say that we keep them for their autumnal bounty."

Robbie grinned, "Aye, my lord."

As we headed along the road, the next day, we continued our planning. We knew how to attack enemy strongholds and we put our minds to the problem of attacking our own home. By the time we reached Houghton Regis we were all of one mind and knew what we had to do.

Chapter 17

We had the warmest of welcomes when we reached my manor. William's wound made my wife frown but I dismissed it lightly, "We knew that there would be opposition to what we did but we obeyed the queen's command and William will soon heal."

She was not convinced, "Beware this Duke of Gloucester. I like him not."

"From what I saw at the funeral the king has little time for him for he did to tarry to speak to his uncle. I pray that the king assumes power sooner rather than later."

It was almost as though the king had been listening at our eaves for a couple of months later, he dismissed the council of regents and took the reins of power in his hands. He immediately set himself on a collision course with both the Duke of York and the Duke of Gloucester for he began to negotiate a peace with France. I spied both hope and danger in that. The young king was asserting himself but he was making himself a target of his enemies. From what I had heard the Duke of York, who was descended from King Edward on both his mother's and father's sides, had his own ambitions. Did they include the crown? Perhaps my promise to the queen would mean I had to defend the King of England once more.

The duke was not important to my wife but the hall and the village were. Once she had ascertained that William was not badly hurt and my involvement seemed at an end she gushed about the children and what they had been up to in the short time we had been away. "Maud is such a character and mischievous beyond words. It is good that Jean and Margaret are so patient with her. She would tax a saint." I smiled and she suddenly said, "A saint! I have forgotten some important news, my husband, we have another priest."

I frowned, "Father Baldwin has gone?"

"No, you goose. He has an assistant, a young priest called Friar John. I thought you would have known and perhaps you had asked for one."

"I have been far too busy on the queen's service. What is he like?"

"I have only met him twice and he seems very personable. Father Baldwin is set in his ways and the extra work of the new men you brought, my ladies and the women from the forest have made his life harder. When it was just the village and the hall, the old chaplain had an easy life. We have doubled it. He appears happy that he has someone who can visit those in the manor who need a priest."

We had changed Houghton Regis and I hoped it was a change for good. Not all changes are.

We were far from idle in those icy months as Spring warmed the land. My men and I began to work on the ditch as soon as the freeze ended. Ralph was surprised, "But why a ditch, my lord? It is not as though we need to defend this hall."

Marianne was not there and so I felt I could confide in the steward who had once been a warrior, "Ralph, I have made many enemies. I will not tell you what we have done but just trust me when I say that it was honourable and the queen commanded it." He knew who I meant and he nodded. Travellers on the road brought news of events further afield and all that they had to say was that Owen Tudor was still in sanctuary. No mention was made of his sons. "If those enemies come then we must make this hall as secure as we can. The ditch will make it hard for an enemy to scale the low wall. The stronger gatehouse will resist attack and the men who keep watch in the towers will give us warning of an attack."

He smiled, "I wondered at that, my lord, for the northwest tower is the coldest in the hall and none would willingly choose to make that his nest." I nodded. He turned to view the hall, "And we do not tell the women for we do not wish to alarm them."

"Just so. War is the work of men. My sword is by my bed and my men are the same. I know that you are no longer a warrior but I would sleep happier knowing that my steward had the means to defend himself."

"Of course."

It was fortunate that, one week later, we were no longer working on the ditch for it was raining heavily when we had visitors. I recognised the livery as the twenty riders approached. It was Sir Richard Langton and he was one of the Duke of Gloucester's closest companions. Most of the men he led were also the duke's men but, to my dismay, at the rear rode Günter of Brabant and five Swabians. We had been warned of their approach by the archers in the tower and so I prepared a face to meet them. As they reined in, rainwater dripping from their cowled cloaks, I saw recognition on the face of the Swabian. Any doubts the mercenary might have had were now dispelled. My archers had just said that riders were approaching. Their livery was only identifiable when they dismounted. Isabelle immediately ordered the servants to fetch food and drink. It was the Christian thing to do but I was wary. The look of surprise on the face of Günter of Brabant told me that he had not expected me to be here and so I was curious as to why the Duke of Gloucester would send so many armed men.

I knew Sir Richard for I had met him in France when I served Sir John Talbot. He had brought a message from the duke. That seemed a lifetime ago. He took off his cloak and shook it outside. His men waited without. "Sir Michael, I apologise for this intrusion but I come on the orders of the Duke of Gloucester and the council."

"You are more than welcome. Will you be staying? I can have…"

He shook his head, "This will be, I hope a brief visit." He hesitated, "You are known to be an honourable knight and although I was asked to search this hall, I would rather take your word."

"Search my hall?"

He nodded, "I will ask you directly, my lord, do you harbour Owen Tudor here? The duke knows that you are the knight of Queen Catherine." He gave a wry smile, "Perhaps it was you who spirited away the two boys, I know not but is Owen Tudor within these walls?"

That was an easy one to answer for I had not seen him since the queen's funeral, "I swear on all that I hold dear that Owen Tudor is not within these walls and so long as I have lived here, he has never set foot across my threshold. As far as I know he is still in sanctuary at the abbey."

I was telling the truth and I saw the relief on the face of the knight, "Thank you, Sir Michael, we were ordered to visit this manor to seek him. I did not think he would be here but the duke was insistent."

I shook my head, "Sir Richard, you speak in riddles. The last I heard was that Owen Tudor was in the sanctuary at Westminster Abbey. If he left sanctuary then what was the reason?"

He nodded towards the small chamber just off from the main corridor, "Could we speak there?"

My wife and the servants hurried up the corridor, "My husband, why do you let these poor men wait without? One would not send an enemy out on such a day."

I smiled for Isabelle was kindness personified, "I will speak here with Sir Richard, take the men into the Great Hall if you wish my love but they are wet."

"We can mop up the water." She waved an arm, "Come gentlemen, leave your cloaks here in the entrance. We had a fine fire and I have ale and food for you."

The English amongst the liveried men thanked my wife and I closed the door behind us as Sir Richard and I went into the room normally used for those who kept watch at night in my hall. "Owen Tudor left sanctuary when the king summoned him. He spoke with the king and then, with his chaplain, Father Bertrand and two others left London." I could see that the knight was uncomfortable about something. "The duke was not present at the meeting but after my lord met with the king, he came to me to tell me that Owen Tudor had broken the terms of his parole by leaving London. I was asked to come here first and if he was not here then to follow him to his estates in Flintshire and Anglesey."

"What does the king say?"

Again the knight shifted from foot to foot, "I know not, my lord. I was just ordered to bring him back."

This was not the king's command but his uncle's. "You said he was with just three companions, why so many men? As far as I know, Owen Tudor is not renowned as a warrior." I really wanted to ask about the Swabians but to have done so would have caused the knight to be suspicious.

"The duke was worried that, if he reached his homeland, then there might be support there amongst the Welsh and he wishes to forestall an uprising." As excuses go it was the weakest I had yet heard and whilst the Welsh were sometimes truculent it had quiet since the time of Owen Glendower.

"Then I hope you catch him before he reaches his manors for it would be unseemly if he was hurt for merely breaking parole. The men you lead are good men?"

"I know most but the ones the duke sent after us I know not. They are Swabians," he shook his head, "I do not like mercenaries, Sir Michael but the duke commanded..."

"Just so. I wish you well and if he comes here then, now that you have told me of his crime, I will detain him and send word to you but I do not think he will. Now, come, Sir Richard, my wife will chastise me if I do not let you partake of her hospitality."

We went into the Great Hall and the drying clothes made it seem steamy. We would have to fetch in rosemary when they were gone to rid the hall of the smell of damp. Isabelle came over with wine for the knight, fresh bread, ham and cheese. While we chatted, I watched Günter and his Swabians. They were standing apart from the others and I saw not just recognition on his face but also animosity. When he had entered the hall, it had been dark but here, with the fire and burning brands in the sconces he had a good view of my face. I had shaved my beard and trimmed my hair but he saw that I was the one he had sought. Perhaps that was why the duke had sent them. This would confirm who had absconded with the boys. Our disguises at the funeral meant that they could not be sure who had thwarted the Duke of Gloucester but now they did and, worst of all, they had seen inside my hall. They had an idea of the layout. If and when they returned, they would have knowledge I wished that they did not.

They stayed barely an hour and then headed north and west towards Wales. I hoped that the four Welshmen would reach the safety of the Welsh mountains for I did not trust the Swabians. Sir Richard seemed an honourable man but the Swabians were killers. They could dispose of Owen Tudor and make it appear like an accident.

When they had gone and while my wife and the servants cleaned up the mess left by our damp visitors I went with Nicholas and Thomas to the tower. I said nothing while we watched the riders disappear into the distance and then I said, "The Swabians might have suspected where we lived but now, they have confirmation. I hoped that they would have been given other tasks, perhaps abroad, but the duke, it seems is using them to hunt those he sees as his enemies. We have until they apprehend Owen Tudor to not only make my hall secure but try to obviate the knowledge that the Swabians gained by their visit."

"What do you mean, Sir Michael?"

"I saw them in the Great Hall. They were examining the room. I do not doubt that some took the chance to make water and would have searched other parts of the ground floor. It is what we would do if we planned to attack somewhere. They know the layout of the hall and that can only help them. We have to change the entrance."

"What will Lady Isabelle think about that, my lord? My wife, Sarah, has told me that Lady Isabelle thinks that the hall is perfect as it is."

"Leave that to me, Thomas. I have a plan."

That evening, as we ate, discussing the flight of Owen Tudor and the visit of Sir Richard I said, "You know, my love, it struck me that the visit today has shown me some deficiencies in our hall."

She frowned, "Deficiencies?"

"The hall became much colder when we opened the door and they came in. It took more than two hours for your ladies to clean up the mess. I was thinking of having a stone entrance built. We could have hooks for cloaks and it would be large enough to accommodate say, twenty men. It would make the hall warmer in winter and cooler in summer."

She sliced a piece of duck and placed it in Maud's mouth, "It would have to fit in with the rest of the hall. I would not wish two different types of stone."

"There is a good supply of stone in one of the outbuildings. Mark the Mason does not have much work at the moment and I am sure that he and his sons could build it in a fortnight or so."

"Soon it will be summer. Why the haste?"

I smiled, "We will have the summer to plant flowers around the entrance. You have been asking for climbing roses for some time. This way we will have a perfumed entrance."

She smiled, "You are right. The red roses that were already planted are lovely but we need more of them and you are right, Michael, they should be perfumed. I am lucky to have such a thoughtful husband."

I felt pangs of guilt that I was deceiving her but it was necessary. I would confess my sins when next I spoke to my priest.

While half of my men worked on the ditch I rode with the other half as far as Blecheley. Ostensibly it was to exercise the horses but I wanted to watch the road and to check The Taxman's confederates had not returned. When we stopped to water the horses, the village had a different feel to it. Not all the women we had taken from the bandit's lair had remained with us. A couple had taken up with young men in the village and were now married. Although they now paid taxes to the Sheriff, the villagers were more content for the money that they had paid to The Taxman had been the thin edge of the wedge. The food and services they had supplied had also impoverished them.

Egbert the Smith left his workshop to greet us. On a chilly damp day such as the one, we were enduring it was the best place to be. He shook his head as three of the village children jumped into the puddles and squealed with delight at the simple pleasure, "Children, my lord, it does not take much to make them happy, does it?"

"No indeed, nor the village it seems. Your homes look better maintained and I see smiles on the faces of your people."

"We had neglected our homes for we always thought that one day we would be driven from them by the privations inflicted by the bandits. Your coming brings us stability and order. We feel safer."

"This is not my manor."

He smiled as his wife fetched us ale, "And yet, my lord, you are here."

I nodded, "I came to see if the bandits had returned."

"No, Sir Michael. Now that the bandits no longer control the forest we can enter and forage." He hesitated for there were punishments for taking from what was the lord of the manor's domain. It mattered not that there was no lord of the manor, a crime was a crime. "It is just the fallen branches after the storms, my lord and mushrooms."

I shook my head, "I do not think it matters if you take the odd rabbit or squirrel, Egbert. Until there is a lord of the manor then you need to manage the land. When autumn comes, I will bring my men and we will cull the deer. You and the men can be the beaters and share in the bounty."

Delight showed on his face. The staple diet of the people was beans and greens. Meat and fish were rarities. I felt guilty for we had fishponds that were overflowing. I decided that I would have Ralph send some fish to the villagers. The village of Houghton Regis was well fed by comparison.

We did not ride the same road every day but three times a week men from my manor would ride the roads and showed our presence. Mark the Mason was a good builder and even though the new entrance was a functional build he made it as attractive as he could. This had been a royal lodge and well built. Mark was too good a mason to do anything less than his best. As he told me when he worked, the better the foundations, the part that you could not see, then the more solid would be the part you could see, the building. "I am using similar construction to the one you would use on a castle, my lord. There will be two sets of faced stone and infill between. It will give you a stout entrance and will also be more effective at keeping out the drafts. I have some good, seasoned oak for the lintel and door frame and I have Much the Carpenter making an oak door that will withstand both the weather and any attacks."

"Attacks?"

"My lord, do not take me for a fool, I pray you. We all know what you did to scour the woods of bandits and those kinds of people have twisted views of the world. If they should return to do you harm then this will be secure." He lowered his voice, "Do not worry, my lord, Lady Isabelle does not suspect." He laughed, "Besides, you are paying me well enough to give a good dowry to my eldest daughter who is to be wed at Easter."

"Who is the husband?"

"William, whose father Edward, farms Tithe Farm. Edward is getting old and while William is his youngest, he has no other sons. Three died in France and he does not wish to leave it to his daughters. They have married well. The dowry will help them for Edward has not been in the best of health lately and William needs to hire men to help him."

I nodded. I had not known that and as Tithe Farm was part of my manor then Edward was one of my tenants. I would speak to Ralph. I needed to be more involved with my manor. Isabelle could run the house but the manor was different. Isabelle was not like Lady Eleanor had been. Sir William had often told me how lucky he was to have a wide who knew how to make his manors yield so much profit.

It was my men who brought me the news that Sir Richard was heading down the road. They had been spotted in the distance and

Thomas was clever enough to know that they would call. Lady Isabelle needed to know that they would be arriving. As soon as she was told then she and Sarah became a pair of whirlwinds. I said to Mark, "You and your men can have an early finish for we will have visitors."

He nodded, "It is good my lord for we have just finished the outside shell for the new entrance. I fear it will not look attractive for we will have to cover it with oiled sheets to keep out the rain and the damp."

"That does not matter for the visitors are warriors and will not notice such things." I was glad that the work would be disguised. I did not know if Günter the Swabian and his men would still be with Sir Richard but if they were then I did not want them to know what we were doing.

Mark and his men had gone by the time Sir Richard and his men appeared. I saw that the Swabians were still with them and that they had apprehended Owen Tudor. Father Bertrand, looking as uncomfortable as ever on the back of a horse, was with them. The rain that Mark the Mason had feared had arrived and I said, "Better hurry inside, Sir Richard."

He turned to his lieutenant, a scarred old sergeant at arms, "Sergeant, take the men to the barn and I will arrange for food to be sent to you."

"But the prisoners, my lord."

The young knight smiled, "Sergeant, I am sure that Sir Michael has men enough to watch and besides our prisoner has had the chance to run before now and yet he has not since we apprehended him."

"Yes, my lord. You heard his lordship! Shift yourselves, I can feel my mail rusting just standing here."

Father Bertrand and Owen dismounted and entered the roofless new entrance. They both shook their cloaks and handed them to Ralph as they stepped into the old entrance.

"Good to see you again, Father Bertrand."

"And you Ralph, it is just a pity it is not under better circumstances."

"Ralph, have food and drink taken to the barn."

"Yes, Sir Michael."

After taking the cloaks of Sir Richard and his squire he hurried to the kitchen.

"Come we will use the small hall, it is cosier."

There were five chairs but Sir Richard's squire did not take one. He was well trained. He would only sit if he was told. My wife and Sarah led the servants in with the food. "Ralph told me that the rest of our guests were in the barn. We could have lit the fires in the Great Hall."

Sir Richard shook his head, "We muddied your home the last time we came. It seems we are ever the harbingers of poor weather. We will not be staying long and food and ale will suffice for them."

My wife turned, "Sarah, take the food to the barn. I will join my husband and our guests."

She left and Owen Tudor spoke for the first time, "And I thank you for your hospitality, my lady. You have a lovely home and I feel civilised once more. Here I do not feel as though I am a prisoner for you are, I hope, friends."

"Of course we are, my lord."

I turned to Sir Richard, "And whence will you take him?"

I could see that Sir Richard was uncomfortable, "Newgate Prison, Sir Michael."

I was shocked and it showed, "But he was the husband of the queen. If he is to be incarcerated then surely the Tower of London would be a better home for him?" The Tower had chambers that were almost palatial and most royal prisoners were held there."

It was Father Bertrand who answered for the knight, "We are being punished, Sir Michael. The orders have come from the Duke of Gloucester. I fear he wishes us harmed."

"That is unfair, Father Bertrand." Sir Richard did not sound convincing.

Owen Tudor's voice was filled with anger as he burst out, "Unfair? Then why were Iago and Rhodri slain before they could even think about drawing their swords?"

His words shocked even me, "Iago is dead?"

"Aye, Sir Michael. Those damned Swabians had their swords out and the mercenaries hacked them to pieces before the poor boys could blink. Had not Sir Richard intervened then I think that Father Bertrand and I would have suffered the same fate."

"They would have killed a priest?"

Sir Richard's voice showed steel for the first time, "Do not worry, Sir Michael, I have my men watching them now and when we reach London, I will let the duke know of their crime and he will punish them."

I caught the eye of Father Bertrand; we both knew that was not true and the Swabians had been sent with Sir Richard to end the lives of the man he saw as a threat to the crown. I felt a shiver run down my spine. I prayed that Edmund and Jasper were safe in the convent. Then I realised that my family and my home were at a greater risk.

While we ate, I pondered the problem. The Swabians had seen the oiled cloaks but they could not possibly know what lay beneath. However, we would only have a week to finish the work for they could easily get to London and then return in that time.

176

I was still planning when Owen Tudor said, "I did not get the chance to thank to for helping my sons to escape those killers. I am ever in your debt although I do not think that you will derive much benefit."

Father Bertrand smiled, "Sir Michael is an old-fashioned knight, my friend, when he gives his word, he keeps it and duty is all. I never met Sir William Strongstaff but I think that we see here before us, a fair copy of that great man and protector of kings."

I felt Sir Richard's eyes upon me and I turned, "Aye, you were right, Sir Richard, my men and I did spirit away the boys and knowing the fate of Rhodri and Iago then I am happy."

Isabelle had been listening to all and taking it in. I had seen the shock on her face when we spoke of the threat to Father Bertrand but now, hearing that Margaret's two brothers had been threatened she could not contain herself, "The duke sent killers after those two boys! He should be held accountable!"

Sir Richard was the duke's friend and I feared that Isabelle was getting out of her depth. The duke would demand the truth from his friend and Sir Richard would tell him. "My love, there would be no proof that the duke ordered the Swabians to kill the boys. He would say that they were there to protect them from us and I am sure that Günter of Brabant will say that Iago and Rhodri drew their weapons."

I saw the nod from Father Bertrand and Sir Richard said, "You are right, Sir Michael but I would pray you to curb your tongue. Neither my squire nor I will breathe a word about the comments we have heard here in this hall but you know that if others were to report to the duke, then…"

I gave the knight a sad look, "Yet he is your friend."

"I thought he was a friend but a friend would not have sent me with hired killers. Perhaps I should ask permission to join the Duke of York in France. I could regain some honour there."

I shook my head, "The war there is lost, my lord. All that we do is bleed away the lives of brave men so that the high and the mighty can feel powerful." I patted Isabelle's hand, "My wife is French and yet she and her sister left France for we could see that all was lost."

"None the less I will have to consider what I could do to atone." He gave a sad smile, "I was born at the wrong time. Two hundred years ago I could have gone on a crusade."

Father Bertrand said, "And that, too would have been a waste, my lord. It seems to me that nobility, chivalry, and knighthood are ideas from the past. Knights like Sir Michael are rare. If you want this old priest's advice then do as Sir Michael does and be a fair and just lord of the manor."

After they had gone, I thought about the priest's words. He was partly right but I had sworn an oath to the queen and while men like Günter of Brabant stalked the land then I would have to protect the queen's children.

Chapter 18

The departure of Sir Richard brought with it clear skies and spring sun. Mark the Mason and his men worked tirelessly once I had asked him to. He did not question my reasons but they finished the work in five days. The mortar would take longer to set but with a good roof, metal-studded door and sound walls we were more secure. I gave him a bonus for the work but he was loath to take it, "I quoted a fair price, my lord."

"Aye, and I am more than happy with it besides you may need this for the dowry."

The completion of the work coincided with the arrival of a messenger from Weedon. Eleanor was nearing her time and she had asked for her sister to be near her. Isabelle was torn. She did not wish to leave the hall when it needed work but she loved her sister. "Isabelle, take Sarah and the children. I will escort you thither and when the bairn is born then send to me and I will fetch you home."

"But the work that was done by Mark the Mason….!

"Marianne was caring for the hall whilst you were growing up. You trust her judgement do you not?"

"Of course."

"Then all will be well."

I left Thomas in charge of the hall and to keep watch for enemies while I went with my wife, Sarah and all the children. Four of my archers were my escort. Jack was in for a noisy time at his hall. We stayed overnight at Stony Stratford and it meant that we reached Weedon not long after the sun had reached its zenith the following day.

"My men and I will head back for you will have enough extra guests without me, Jack."

My former squire frowned, "It is not a problem, Sir Michael and it would be good to talk."

I would not tell Jack the real reason for my departure for he might inadvertently blurt something out and then Isabelle would be upset. "When I come for Isabelle and Sarah, I will stay longer for then I can see your new child."

We hurried back to Stony Stratford and made it just before darkness fell. While I was happy that my wife and children were safe, I did not want the responsibility of the defence of my hall to fall on Thomas. I prayed that the enemy had not yet come but I knew that it was only a matter of time. The killing of Iago and Rhodri had been upon the orders of the duke. My death would be for revenge. It mattered not if the duke wished me dead, Günter did and he would not rest until he saw the life

179

slipping from my dying body. I was relieved when I saw my hall still standing and men working on the new entranceway. Oil was being applied to the wood and the interior walls were having their second coat of plaster applied. Robbie Red Fletch waved from the top of the tower and I knew that all was well.

It was two days later that Nicholas, who had been out hunting, reported danger to Thomas and me while we were sparring on the north yard. "We have a pair of watchers in the woods, my lord." He shook his head, "They are not very good and I do not think that they are countrymen. They have two sorry horses and have made a hovel."

"They are watching the hall?"

In answer, he pointed to the woods that lay just half a mile north of the north wall. "I thought I spied something yesterday but I said nothing for it might have been just a villager collecting kindling. I confess the hunting was just an excuse to confirm what I saw. I found their tracks and I found their camp. If you wish it we could take them."

"I trust your judgement, Nicholas. It was good that you did not spook them for I want Günter to be complacent when he comes. If we took them then they might send better warriors the next time."

Thomas sheathed his sword, "He will be anything but complacent, my lord. You bested him twice and he will not underestimate you. The best that we can hope for is that he thinks we do not expect him."

"Nicholas, did you see any signs that others were nearby?"

"I checked the whole of the woods and all the camping places. The two are alone."

"Then when one leaves, we know how long we have."

He nodded having through all this through already, "Two days at the most."

One of the watchers left the next day. Nicholas was right, they were not very good. The archer in the tower saw him mount his horse and although he kept to the eaves of the wood his progress was easy to follow. He headed east.

I gathered my men and Ralph in the Great Hall. I told them of our fears. "Ralph, if you wish to send your wife and the women away, I will understand."

He shook his head, "Firstly, she would not go and secondly, the enemy might see them and you wish surprise. Besides, from what you have said, Sir Michael, they come for you. We can bar our doors at night. I will tell the women that bandits were seen. It is an easy lie."

"I hope that they will come through the front and have a surprise when there are double doors."

Thomas shook his head, "They saw the work, Sir Michael and they will find another way in."

"The back door." We all looked at Robbie who shrugged, "I am surprised you did not think of it yourself, my lord. There are more buildings at the rear where they could take shelter and hide. I have stood enough watches in the tower to know that. We have a good view outside the walls but there is a blind spot there. If they manage to get over the outer wall and then the inner wall unseen then they can easily make the back door."

Ralph said, "And that will be barred from the inside."

Nicholas rubbed his chin, a sure sign that he was thinking about something, "Whichever way you look at it they will have to make a noise when they enter. They must know that. How do they hope to succeed?"

I had listened to their words and it came to me like a flash of light. "Most of you sleep in the warrior hall. Apart from the four in the tower, and Thomas, who has a room here in the hall, the rest of you sleep in the some distance from the back door." I nodded to Robbie, "You are right Robbie, it is the eastern side of the inner wall where the danger lies. The warrior hall has but two entrances and they could be blocked or guarded. The watchers might not be very good, Nicholas, but they must have an idea of where we live. If they fired the warrior hall then they could make as much noise as they like breaking down the back door for they will assume there are just three of our warriors inside. We need to make our plans accordingly."

Cedric of Barnsley was keen to atone for the loss of Les Pérets and it was he who made the best suggestions, "Since your father-in-law and his wife were killed, I have thought long and hard how we might have done things to prevent their deaths. This is how I see their attack." He went on to detail how he saw the Swabians entering the grounds, climbing the walls, eliminating the threat of the warriors and then entering the hall to murder. "And make no mistake, Ralph, hiding behind a barred door will avail you little. The best hope would be that the noise would reach the village and they would come to our aid."

The village was more than half a mile away.

Doubting Thomas threw water on that idea, "And if they have eliminated us then the slaughter of villagers armed with the crudest of weapons will not stop them."

"Cedric, what would you have us do?"

He smiled at me, "Be more cunning than they are."

With the questions we all had it took more than an hour to finish but with refinements suggested we had a good plan and we put it into place immediately. We secreted weapons about the hall. While we would all sleep with weapons close to hand who knew when the attack would come. The men with families were excused from the night duty and they slept in their homes with their families behind doors that were barred while many of us prepared to sleep on floors. It was harder than I thought just to wait. We had to be vigilant all day and all night. It was wearing to stare into the dark looking for movement or smelling strange scent. I also found that I missed Isabelle and the children. This was not the same as being on campaign for here I was alone in my own bed and not sleeping in a hovel or a tent. The table where I ate was the one, I shared with my family. I had not expected it to be like this. The ones who were the most cheerful throughout all of this were my two billmen, Cedric and Robert for this was their chance to earn their place amongst my warriors. Not that the men at arms and archers thought any less of them for never having to have to fight for me; they respected what the two of them did. They guarded my hall. They had yet to draw a sword in its defence but if they had to while the rest of us were away then they might not survive. They understood that.

Sharp-eyed Robbie was the one who spotted the enemy. He had been watching the single man who had remained and knew where he was. When he saw the birds take flight, a mile or so to the east of the scout's position then he knew someone was in the woods. He was also clever enough to know that if it was not the enemy then their single sentry would move and he kept one eye on him. Elizabeth and this her son, Jack, who had lived with the bandits had stayed in the hall and Robbie had taken a shine to the young lad. He was teaching him to be an archer and the youth often shared a watch with him. He sent him for me while he and John the Fletcher kept their eyes on the men who were approaching the scout. Neither could see the men clearly but the movement in the trees and the birds above marked their progress. By the time I reached them Robbie and John had established that the enemy had come. The glint of metal from a careless warrior confirmed it.

We now had to go about our daily business as normally as possible. Of course, it was not normal for we all kept an eye on the woods, the walls and the road. The men practised with weapons, as we did every day when we were not working on the defences. That work was now complete and so we used our swords. The open gate to the north would afford the watchers an occasional view of us as we sparred. The archers set up their marks and loosed arrows. They were our best eyes as they used the field to the north of the outer wall. When they returned for the noon meal break, they confirmed that there were mailed and armed men moving in the woods. Numbers were impossible to ascertain. The enemy were trying to remain hidden but some were eager to spy out our home. I knew then just how disciplined my men were as they would not have done so had they been in the same position.

The days were longer now than they had been when we had dug the ditch but it was still close to the Spring equinox and the days and nights were of similar length. As the archers returned the outer gates were closed and barred. The enemy scouts would have reported that was normal. Passing through the orchards, formal garden, and herb garden they would then close and bar the inner gate. That too was normal although it was unobservable from the woods. We washed and then ate. That was where normality ended. Once we had eaten, we changed into war gear and my men took their places. Half of them waited by the gates of the inner wall. Four archers kept watch from the tower and the rest of us dotted ourselves around the hall.

We had a wasted, sleepless night. No one came. As my weary warriors entered, at dawn, once the sun was in the sky and a pale sunlight bathed the walls I wondered at the cunning of this Swabian. The cooks had been up early and the fresh bread was brought in, the smell wafting through the hall. We all dined in the Great Hall. The only watchers were the two who remained in the tower and they would be relieved once the first two archers had eaten.

I tore a piece of still warm bread and smeared it with the cold butter brought fresh from the chilled pantry. "They are clever. They rested last night and they may even rest again today. If they do then I intend to ride, on the morrow and take them in the woods."

Thomas suggested, "Perhaps we should do that today, my lord."

"I have thought of that but we know that they are mounted and that they would simply flee. Günter of Brabant knows the skill of my archers and that they have nothing to counter them. He lost men to your bodkins, Nicholas, the last time we met. No, if we are forced to ride after him then this goes on and we might have to do this with my family within these walls. We rest when we can this day. Half of us at a time will sleep. We will not get all the sleep we need but it will have to suffice."

I should have known that we would not be as alert as normal. Tired men make mistakes and I just hoped that the enemy would be as tired as we. Sleeping on hard ground never made for a good night of sleep. Thomas and I split the day between us. He slept in the morning while I made myself visible, visiting the archers at the mark and even riding to the village to speak to my people there. Thoroughly exhausted I ate sparingly and then slept in the huge bed in the bedchamber. I would like to say I slept like a baby but I did not. Something was nagging at me. I could not shake the thought that I had overlooked something but for the life of me I could not think what. Woken at dusk I washed and changed into clean clothes. I donned my mail; I had already decided not to wear plate. As we ate, I asked Thomas if he had seen anything.

"Just the normal, my lord and when I visited the archers, I caught sight of the occasional flash of metal from the woods. They are still there."

"Some are still there."

"My lord?"

"I am a fool, Thomas. We assumed or I assumed, that the enemy would all be together. We do not know how many men Günter brings with him. Suppose there are two groups and we only watch one of them?"

"That may be true, my lord, but we kept watch all around the hall. Cedric and his men watched, as they always do the main entrance and the south."

"But not with the same expectation of those looking to the north. Cedric, tonight I want more men watching the southern range."

"We will be spread out thinner."

"I know and that cannot be helped."

In many ways seeing the flaw in my own plan helped me. I felt pleased that I had seen the problem and while Cedric was right, we would have spread the butter even thinner we had the advantage that we would be closer together than the ones who were attacking. They have but two ways in. The new front doors and the kitchen entrance. They would still have as many guarding them even with the thinner defences.

As my men took their places and the brands were extinguished to give the darkened look an attacker would expect I did as I had the previous night. I ascended the stairs to the northwest tower to speak with the archers there. My eye was drawn, as it had been since Robbie had mentioned it, to the blind spots. It could not be helped and if we built any more towers then it would spoil tha appearance of the hall.

"Anything?"

"Just before dusk we thought we saw shadows moving from the woods but there was no signal from the north gate. If any moved then they are still hiding on the pasture where we set up our marks."

"They may have men as skilled as we, Mark. Keep a good watch."

I descended and went first to the kitchen where two of my men, David and Will were watching the door. As I passed the door that led to the cellar, I caught a strange smell. It struck me that in our tiredness some of the servants might have spilt something and failed to clean it properly. That would need to be remedied before my wife returned.

Cedric and Robert were behind the old front door. This was now the most secure part of the hall for the two doors, the outer and the original, were both barred.

"How goes the watch?"

Cedric shook his head, "Something makes my head itch, my lord. What have we overlooked?"

"I know not for my head itches too. What I know is that if they come this night, they have to get over two walls and through either this door or the back door."

"This one is secure, my lord. Even the back one is barred. They could not get in," I saw his eyes widen as the thought entered my head too.

"Unless they were already in!" I drew my sword, "The cellar door!" I now understood the smell. It was not the smell of something that had spilt, it was the smell of men who had not bathed for some days and ate differently to us.

The three of us ran through the hall which now seemed like a rabbit warren. Will and David lay dead in widening pools of blood. The kitchen door was unbarred.

"Alarm! We are undone! Alarm! You two stay here in case any have entered the hall."

"What of you, my lord?"

"The men on guard outside will not expect an attack on their backs. I have to help them."

Our thin defences would now come back to haunt us. Even as I stepped in the cold night, I heard the clash of steel and the cry as men fell. The north gate on the inner wall lay open and as I watched Günter the Swabian and half a dozen men race in. My archers were no match for them.

"Archers fall back to the hall. Men at arms to me!"

I saw bodies on the ground, at least one was moving. Two archers hurtled by as Thomas and Edward came to flank me. "How did…"

"They sneaked in during the day and at least two hid in the cellar." When I had seen the bodies of David and Will then I knew there had to have been at least two men. My men were too good to die at the hands of a single killer.

Cedric and Robert ran from the hall when the two archers entered. My bill men held their billhooks. The Swabians would not have it all their own way.

As the Swabians ran at us, I saw another six men flood through the gates. Two fell as arrows from the tower found them. I drew my dagger as I knew it would be needed.

"Keep tight!"

That was easier said than done for a two-handed sword swung at a man made him want to move away from its deadly arc. Our best defence was to present a solid wall of steel. I saw that Günter of Brabant has his eyes on me. Like me he wore a coif over an arming cap and that showed that not only was he fearless but clever for he wanted the advantage of good vision. A night attack somewhat negated our archers. Barely three of his men had been hit when they entered the gates for with the line of sight obscured and shadows making it hard, my archers had shown great skill to hit even three of them. The Swabians, dressed in plate, hurled themselves at us.

Cedric and Robert's billhooks saved us from immediate slaughter. Their weapons, swung across our front, made it harder for the mercenaries to use their long swords to the greatest effect. Even so Günter's sword came down at my head. One of the Swabians was hit in the side by Cedric's billhook. It struck where the breast plate met the faulds and Cedric was too skilled at his trade to miss the smallest of gaps. It sliced into flesh. Robert's was not such a good blow but the head smacked hard into the side of the breastplate and the two outside Swabians were both hurt. While that helped the five of us it did nothing to prevent the sword from smashing down at my coifed head. Had it connected then I would be dead. I held up my sword knowing that with two hands holding his sword my blade would be forced down and so I used that to my advantage. I angled my sword so that his long sword slid down to my hilt. The tip was within a handspan of my face but I was unharmed. I rammed my dagger up under his arm. He wore a besagew, a plate to protect the wearer from such a blow but a besagew is a small piece of metal and intended to stop a sword. My dagger's point insinuated itself through the plates and it found the mail beneath. The bodkin blade must have torn a link for I saw the pain in his eyes as the tip pricked his flesh. He knew the danger and he pulled away before I could sink the blade into flesh.

The five of us were now almost evenly matched. The one hacked by Cedric was too badly wounded to worry us and the other had been hurt and could not raise his sword as high as he might have liked. My bodkin blade had forced Günter back and so I stepped forward, bringing my sword down towards Günter's head while stabbing, almost blindly, sideways at the coifed Swabian next to me. My choice of bodkin dagger was fortuitous and it slid through the links, arming cap and into the side of the man's head. Edward Poleaxe needed no urging and his sword sliced through the man's neck. We were now even although when I heard a grunt of pain from Thomas, I knew that he was wounded. I had no idea how the battle was going elsewhere. This was the key encounter. My archers and other men at arms would have to deal with the other mercenaries. The ones we faced were the greatest threat.

Günter had regained his composure. Perhaps the death of one of his men made him wish to end the fight sooner rather than later. He was a strong man and he showed it by drawing his own dagger, a rondel blade. His guttural attempt at French was spat at me, "I too have a knife and now we shall end this. Only one of us will walk away and it shall be me."

This time when he swung his sword down, I easily blocked it but his choice of dagger, a rondel, was broader than my bodkin and when I blocked the stab the edge tore through a couple of the mail links of my hauberk. I saw his eyes widen at the thought of victory. I was unconcerned for the knife had just damaged the side and we were too close to other warriors to use a swinging blow that way. We were all forced to swing from above and go for the head with our swords. I heard a cry from my right and my eyes were drawn there, albeit briefly. Robert had used his hook to pull the metal plates of his Swabian and the man had tumbled to the ground. Even as I turned my head back, I glimpsed Robert take the man's head. Günter had not been distracted and he had swung again at my head. I barely had time to block the blow and I did not stop it from hitting my right shoulder. It sliced through the mail and the gambeson. The pain was excruciating. The blade came away bloody and that told us both that I was wounded but worse, I could not move my arm as well. Something had been broken. Rafe had always told me, when we had trained and sparred, that a fight was never over until one man lay dead on the ground and so I would never give in so long as I breathed. The look on Günter's face told me that he thought he had already won. My blows would now be weaker and I would not block his next strike. The man killed by Robert had allowed a wounded Thomas and he to face a single Swabian. The man was forced to move and I knew that I had the opportunity to swing. Timing would be all. As the two-handed sword was raised, I lunged at Günter's face with my bodkin. He easily blocked it with his rondel dagger but as his sword began to descend to strike my head, I swung my sword in a horizontal arc. It hurt me more than I had expected but I gritted my teeth and forced my arm to swing. His sword was just above my coif, I sensed it, when my sword struck the coif around his neck. The pain in my shoulder was so bad that I thought I might pass out but I continued to swing and the edge ripped through the mail and into his neck below the ear. As blood spurted, I sawed backwards with the edge and I watched the life leave his surprised eyes. The blow was almost the undoing of me but the death of their leader and the renewed attacks of my men who knew, as I sank to my knees, that I was hurt, swung the skirmish in our favour.

I had dropped my sword and was still on my knees when the last of the mercenaries tried to flee through the open gate. My archers had reformed and their dead comrades meant that there was no mercy shown. Arrows sprouted from the backs of the men who tried to flee.

Cedric knelt next to me, "Sir Michael!"

"It is my shoulder. I cannot raise my arm."

He turned and shouted, "Ralph, we need a healer!"

"How is Thomas?" Even as I asked my head was turning, slowly thanks to the pain, and I saw him lying in a widening pool of blood.

His eyes opened and he gave a weak smile, "My foes are dead but I am sorely hurt, Sir Michael." He passed out.

Ralph hurried out shouting, "I have sent to the priest."

"See to Thomas first. I am in pain but I will not die from this."

Cedric and Robert used their billhooks to improvise a stretcher and with Edward and Mark they carried my wounded man at arms indoors. Nicholas and John the Fletcher approached. John helped me to rise and Nicholas shook his head, "They almost caught us and we have paid a price. I have counted six men who will no longer follow your banner."

I nodded, "At least two must have entered the house during daylight and hidden."

"I wondered how we were attacked in the rear."

"Have our dead gathered and taken to the chapel. Collect the enemy, strip their bodies, and burn them where you set up your marks. Have their horses collected. They may have left men to guard them."

"I will do all that, my lord but John, take him inside. You may think the wound does not threaten your life but we do not know, do we?"

I did not even pick up my sword as John helped me into the house. David and Will's bodies had already been moved and so we had just an open doorway to negotiate. Even so when my arm caught the frame it sent such pain through my body that I thought I might pass out. Once in my Great Hall, which was now being used as an improvised infirmary, Elizabeth, Jack's mother, helped John to take my mail from me. I had never endured such pain in my life. I was able to bear it better when I saw Marianne and Ralph stemming the bleeding from Thomas's shoulder. The Swabian sword had managed to tear through the mail and almost severed his left arm. He would be lucky to live let alone be a warrior again. Once the mail was off John examined my shoulder.

"There is not as much blood as I thought, my lord. Something has broken. Sit here in the chair by the fire. You need its warmth."

The young priest arrived and headed to me, shaking my head I said, "See to him, father. I can wait."

Elizabeth said, "Jack, fetch some brandy." The youth looked confused, "It is in a leather flask in the kitchen. It is on a shelf, use a stool to climb." She smiled at me, "I must not be that bad of a mother if my son, who lived with bandits does not yet know what brandy is."

"You are a good mother, Elizabeth. You made the best of a life you did not choose."

"It is kind of you to say so, my lord, but now I have seen this life I pray it never changes for the worse."

"And it will not. You are here now and this is your home."

John said, "Aye, Mistress Elizabeth, Jack may not have one his own father but he has a band of fathers here for every archer views him as their foster son."

Jack arrived back and Elizabeth poured half a beaker of brandy into the flask. She handed it to me and I drank deeply. I felt the warmth and the pain became slightly easier. I handed it back and said, "This is not brandy, Elizabeth. It comes from Normandy and is made from apples. It is Calvados. I am glad we brought so much back with us now."

The priest was a young man who had come to the village from a monastery. I am sure that there was some story behind his arrival but, thanks to the threat of an attack, I had not time to investigate. Friar John seemed a diligent and pious young man. Father Baldwin had accepted him as a sort of assistant as with the enlarged household he had more work than hitherto. I saw, on that spring morning that he had been sent to us at just the right time. He looked at Thomas' wound and his authoritative commands made reassured me. He ordered Marianne and Elizabeth around as though he had been doing this for many years and yet he looked to have seen less than thirty summers.

As he began to stitch the wound he said, "Father Baldwin is saying words over those who did this, my lord. He said even evil men such as they deserved the chance to face God and ask for forgiveness."

I nodded, "Father Baldwin is a better man than these deserved."

When he had finished stitching Thomas, he washed his hands in water and then poured vinegar upon them. "Now let us look at this." He frowned. "The wound is not bleeding enough to warrant the pain you are obviously suffering." He nodded to John, "You look strong. Hold his arms by his side and do not let them move." John looked at me and I nodded. "This will probably hurt my lord but I need to test my theory out and I do not wish you to aggravate the wound."

He touched my shoulder and I felt such pain that had I not been held I would have thrown my arms into the air.

"Thank you, my lord. You may release him, archer. It is as I feared. You have had broken the bone that goes from here to here," he demonstrated using John the Fletcher. "It is called the clavicle. All that I can do for you is to make a sling and bind your arm so that you cannot raise your right arm. You will find sleep almost impossible at first." He nodded towards the flask, "If you have enough of that you might sleep."

"Can you not mend the bone as you would if it was my arm?"

"I am afraid not. War brings wounds and you are luckier than your man at arms. He will live but, I fear, he will not be able to fight as well as he once did and I would guess his fighting days are over."

Once the arm was tightly bound and with another beaker of Calvados inside me, I was able to endure the ache. His words, however, were prophetic and it would be a month before I slept well again. I sat in my chair until Thomas awoke. I smiled at him as he said, "I am still in this world then?"

"You are and Friar John has stitched you well but he fears you will longer be able to fight."

He nodded, "That will please Sarah then. Perhaps this was meant to be. How went the day?"

"The enemy were slain but we lost warriors and that angers me for Günter the Swabian would not have ended his days here if the Duke of Gloucester had not set him on this path. The duke may not have wished him to attack us but once he sent the killers after the queen's sons then he set in place events that were like an avalanche and could not be stopped. We will need to send for Mark the Mason again."

Ralph looked up, "You would have more work on the hall completed, my lord?"

I shook my head, "Those men sacrificed themselves for my family, me and for my men. We will remember them with carved stones."

I saw John and Thomas nod their approval. Our small graveyard was growing.

Epilogue

The messenger to say that Eleanor's baby, a boy, had arrived and I sent Edward and the unwounded men to escort our families home. I knew she would question Edward on the way back but I told him to tell the women that Thomas and I suffered slight injuries and could not ride. I wanted her to hear the tale from my lips. Whatever message I sent with Edward could be misconstrued and I did not want his version to be the one she heard. Edward was a plain-spoken man and I knew I would have to choose every word very carefully.

I saw the relief on both women's faces when they descended from the wagon. We were both standing and each having an arm in a sling did not seem so bad. Both women waited until the children were in bed before hearing the story. We told a version without the blood and the gore and hiding the pain of both the wounds and the pain that would never go away, the loss of oathsworn.

When we had finished the two women looked at each other and Isabelle said, "And now, is it over?"

"The truth is that I do not know. Sarah here will tell you, for she lived amongst them, that the people who rule our land do not care who is hurt so long as they cling to power. The Swabians are gone but I swore an oath to protect the queen's children. That is not only Margaret but Jasper, Edmund and," I paused, "King Henry himself."

"The Duke of Gloucester?"

I shrugged, "He has achieved what he wished. Owen Tudor is in gaol and the two boys are beyond his reach. He knows not about Margaret and he may well forget that his nose was put out of joint by me. The king has the reins of power in his hand and the duke is a bystander once more."

All might have been well but for one thing, Owen Tudor. We heard, in January of 1438, that Owen Tudor and Father Bertrand had fought their way out of Newgate prison and were hunted by the king as well as the Duke of Gloucester. I knew one thing, even though I was not part of the escape attempt, I would be scrutinised and, once more my family would be put in danger. I was the Queen's Knight and that single oath had tied my life irrevocably with the Tudor family. Would that be for good or ill? Only the future would determine that and I would have to see what fate had in store for me.

The End

Glossary

Alaunt- a hunting dog similar to a wolfhound
Aketon- padded garment worn beneath the armour also called a gambeson
Ballock dagger or knife- a blade with two swellings next to the blade
Barbican-a gatehouse which can be defended like a castle
Besagew- a circular metal plate to protect the armpit
Bodkin dagger- a long thin dagger like a stiletto used to penetrate mail links
Brigandine- padded jacket worn by archers, sometimes studded with metal
Chamfron- metal covering for the head and neck of a warhorse
Chevauchée- a raid by mounted men
Codger- the man who carries the cadge (a rack with hunting birds upon it.)
Cordwainers- shoemakers
Couvent- the French word for monasteries and nunneries
Cuisse- metal greave
Denizenship- rights that are given to a foreigner to live in a country
Esquire- a man of higher social rank, above a gentleman but below a knight
Familia – the bodyguard of a knight (in the case of a king these may well be knights themselves)
Fauld- hooped skirt which hung from a breastplate
Fowler-a nine-foot-long breech-loading cannon
Galoches- Clogs
Gardyvyan- An archer's haversack containing his war-gear
Glaive- a pole weapon with a curved head and short spike
Gules- a heraldic term for red
Houppelande -a lord's gown with long sleeves
Horsed archers-archers who rode to war on horses but did not fight from horseback
Hovel- a simple bivouac, used when no tents were available
Jupon- Short surcoat
Langet- a metal collar protecting the top part of a pole weapon
Livres tournois-French gold coins
Marchpane- marzipan
Mêlée- a medieval fight between knights
Mesne- the men who follow a knight
Pele or peel tower-a simple refuge tower with access to the first floor via an external ladder

Poleyn- a metal plate to protect the knee
Pursuivant- the rank below a herald
Pyx-a small, well decorated and often jewelled box used to take the host
to those too sick or infirm to visit a church
Rondel dagger- a narrow-bladed dagger with a disc at the end of the hilt
to protect the hand
Sallet basinet- medieval helmet of the simplest type: round with a neck
protector
Sack-generic name for wine from Spain, Portugal, and France
Sennight- Seven nights (a week)
The Pale- the lands around Dublin and Calais. The land belonged to the
King of England.
Yling- Ealing

Canonical hours

There were, of course, few clocks at this time but the services used by
the church were a means of measuring the progress of the day. Indeed
until the coming of the railways, there was no need for clocks. Folk rose
and slept with the rising and setting of the sun.
- Matins (nighttime)
- Lauds (early morning)
- Prime (first hour of daylight)
- Terce (third hour)
- Sext (noon)
- Nones (ninth hour)
- Vespers (sunset evening)
- Compline (end of the day)

Classes of hawk
This is the list of the hunting birds and the class of people who could fly
them. It is taken from the 15th century Book of St Albans.
Emperor: eagle, vulture, merlin
King: gyrfalcon
Prince: gentle falcon: a female peregrine falcon
Duke: falcon of the loch
Earl: peregrine falcon
Baron: buzzard
Knight: saker falcon
Squire: lanner falcon
Lady: merlin
Young man: hobby
Yeoman: goshawk

Poor man: male falcon
Priest: sparrowhawk
Holy water clerk: sparrowhawk

Maps

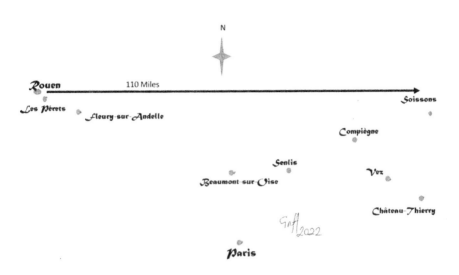

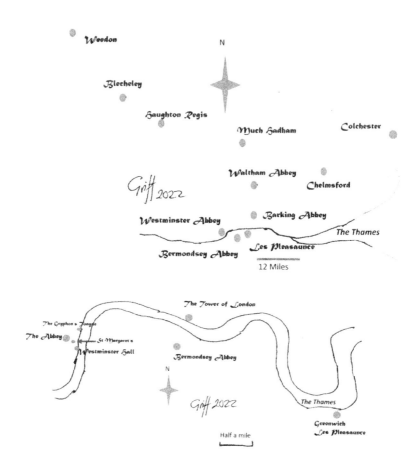

Weedon

Blecheley

Haughton Regis

Much Hadham

Colchester

N

Waltham Abbey

Chelmsford

Goff 2022

Westminster Abbey

Barking Abbey

The Thames

Bermondsey Abbey

Les Pleasaunce

12 Miles

The Tower of London

The Gryphon's Tongue

The Abbey

St Margaret's

Westminster Hall

Bermondsey Abbey

N

Goff 2022

The Thames

Greenwich

Les Pleasaunce

Half a mile

Historical Notes

For the English maps, I have used the original Ordnance Survey maps. Produced by the army in the 19th century they show England before modern developments and, in most cases, are pre-industrial revolution. Produced by Cassini they are a useful tool for a historian. I also discovered a good website http: orbis.stanford.edu. This allows a reader to plot any two places in the Roman world and if you input the mode of transport you wish to use and the time of year it will calculate how long it would take you to travel the route. I have used it for all of my books up to the eighteenth century as the transportation system was roughly the same. The Romans would have travelled more quickly!

Queen Catherine had four children by Owen Tudor although there was a rumour that when she wed Owen, she was pregnant with Edmund Beaufort's child. The children were Edmund, Jasper, Owen, and Margaret. Margaret was born and then disappears. There is no record of her death although one uncorroborated Tudor source claims she became a nun. On that flimsy evidence hangs a plot line from my story. Owen was entrusted to the monks of Westminster and he died in 1502, being the longest-lived of Catherine's sons. The dates I give for the illness and the queen's death are accurate. She died on the 3rd of January but was not buried for a month. The boys were taken to Barking Abbey but they did not enjoy the adventure I gave to them. Owen Tudor did seek sanctuary at Westminster Abbey although not immediately after the funeral. I have changed the timeline for a day to make a better story and to try to give an insight into the character of Owen Tudor. The Welshman did himself no favours by seeking sanctuary at Westminster. Although King Henry did give him an audience when he finally presented himself to the king and allowed the Welshman to return to Wales, it was the Duke of Gloucester who sent men after him to arrest him for breaking the rules of his parole. Perhaps Owen Tudor had reason to be paranoid.

Sir John Talbot was the great hero of the 100 Years War but he was doomed to failure. He held off the French for many years but after his death, in battle, England effectively lost France apart from Calais. The country then turned inwards and this book is the first of the Wars of the Roses section of Struggle for a Crown.

Books used in the research:
- The Tower of London -Lapper and Parnell (Osprey)
- English Medieval Knight 1300-1400-Gravett
- Norman Stone Castles- Gravett

- The Armies of Crécy and Poitiers- Rothero
- The Armies of Agincourt- Rothero
- The Scottish and Welsh Wars 1250-1400
- Henry V and the conquest of France- Knight and Turner
- Chronicles in the Age of Chivalry-Ed. Eliz Hallam
- English Longbowman 1330-1515- Bartlett
- Northumberland at War-Derek Dodds
- The Longbow- Mike Loades
- Teutonic Knight 1190-1561- Nicolle and Turner
- Warkworth Castle and Hermitage- John Goodall
- British Kings and Queens- Mike Ashley
- The Wars of the Roses – Dan Jones
- Tudor- the family story - Leanda de Lisle
- Ordnance Survey Original series map #81 1864-1869

For more information on all of the books then please visit the author's website at http://www.griffhosker.com where there is a link to contact him.

Griff Hosker
January 2022

Other books by Griff Hosker

If you enjoyed reading this book, then why not read another one by the author?

Ancient History

The Sword of Cartimandua Series
(Germania and Britannia 50 A.D. – 128 A.D.)
Ulpius Felix- Roman Warrior (prequel)
The Sword of Cartimandua
The Horse Warriors
Invasion Caledonia
Roman Retreat
Revolt of the Red Witch
Druid's Gold
Trajan's Hunters
The Last Frontier
Hero of Rome
Roman Hawk
Roman Treachery
Roman Wall
Roman Courage

The Wolf Warrior series
(Britain in the late 6th Century)
Saxon Dawn
Saxon Revenge
Saxon England
Saxon Blood
Saxon Slayer
Saxon Slaughter
Saxon Bane
Saxon Fall: Rise of the Warlord
Saxon Throne
Saxon Sword

Medieval History

The Dragon Heart Series
Viking Slave
Viking Warrior
Viking Jarl
Viking Kingdom
Viking Wolf
Viking War
Viking Sword
Viking Wrath
Viking Raid
Viking Legend
Viking Vengeance
Viking Dragon
Viking Treasure
Viking Enemy
Viking Witch
Viking Blood
Viking Weregeld
Viking Storm
Viking Warband
Viking Shadow
Viking Legacy
Viking Clan
Viking Bravery

The Norman Genesis Series
Hrolf the Viking
Horseman
The Battle for a Home
Revenge of the Franks
The Land of the Northmen
Ragnvald Hrolfsson
Brothers in Blood
Lord of Rouen
Drekar in the Seine
Duke of Normandy
The Duke and the King

Danelaw
Dragon Sword
Oathsword

New World Series
Blood on the Blade
Across the Seas
The Savage Wilderness
The Bear and the Wolf
Erik The Navigator

The Vengeance Trail

The Reconquista Chronicles
Castilian Knight
El Campeador
The Lord of Valencia

The Aelfraed Series
(Britain and Byzantium 1050 A.D. - 1085 A.D.)
Housecarl
Outlaw
Varangian

The Anarchy Series England
1120-1180
English Knight
Knight of the Empress
Northern Knight
Baron of the North
Earl
King Henry's Champion
The King is Dead
Warlord of the North
Enemy at the Gate
The Fallen Crown
Warlord's War
Kingmaker
Henry II
Crusader
The Welsh Marches
Irish War
Poisonous Plots
The Princes' Revolt
Earl Marshal
The Perfect Knight

**Border Knight
1182-1300**
Sword for Hire
Return of the Knight
Baron's War
Magna Carta
Welsh Wars
Henry III
The Bloody Border
Baron's Crusade
Sentinel of the North
War in the West
Debt of Honour
Blood of the Warlord

**Sir John Hawkwood Series
France and Italy 1339- 1387**
Crécy: The Age of the Archer
Man At Arms
The White Company
Leader of Men

Lord Edward's Archer
Lord Edward's Archer
King in Waiting
An Archer's Crusade
Targets of Treachery
Thew Great Cause (April 2022)

**Struggle for a Crown
1360- 1485**
Blood on the Crown
To Murder A King
The Throne
King Henry IV
The Road to Agincourt
St Crispin's Day
The Battle for France
The Last Knight
Queen's Knight

Tales from the Sword

Conquistador
England and America in the 16th Century
Conquistador

Tudor Warrior
England and Scotland in the 15th and 16th Centuries

Tudor Warrior

Modern History

The Napoleonic Horseman Series
Chasseur à Cheval
Napoleon's Guard
British Light Dragoon
Soldier Spy
1808: The Road to Coruña
Talavera
The Lines of Torres Vedras
Bloody Badajoz
The Road to France
Waterloo

The Lucky Jack American Civil War series
Rebel Raiders
Confederate Rangers
The Road to Gettysburg

The British Ace Series
1914
1915 Fokker Scourge
1916 Angels over the Somme
1917 Eagles Fall
1918 We will remember them
From Arctic Snow to Desert Sand
Wings over Persia

Combined Operations series
1940-1945

Commando
Raider
Behind Enemy Lines
Dieppe
Toehold in Europe
Sword Beach
Breakout
The Battle for Antwerp
King Tiger
Beyond the Rhine
Korea
Korean Winter

Other Books
Great Granny's Ghost (Aimed at 9-14-year-old young people)

For more information on all of the books then please visit the author's website at www.griffhosker.com where there is a link to contact him or visit his Facebook page: GriffHosker at Sword Books

Printed in Great Britain
by Amazon

78917596R10119